*Fur*tive Investigation

A Psycho Cat and the Landlady Mystery

Joyce Ann Brown

This story is a work of fiction. Some Kansas City place names are real, but the names, characters, incidents and places of action in the story are the product of the author's imagination. Any resemblance to real events or persons, living or dead, is entirely coincidental.

ISBN-13:978-1508636151

ISBN-10:150863615X

DEDICATION

For Carl and Betty Stocker

CONTENTS

Joyce Ann Brown

ACKNOWLEDGMENTS

I want to thank the many people in my writing groups, mystery groups, and book groups who listened to my ideas with open minds and good advice. Thank you Larry Schaffer for arranging a visit to the Johnson County Sheriff's Office CSI laboratory and to Crime Laboratory Director Gary R. Howell and Crime Scene Supervisor Ryan M. Rezzelle for giving me a tour and ideas for my story. Thank you, Sandy Schaffer, Joyce Greer and Vicki Gaughan for giving encouragement. Thank you, Rich Brown, for your patience—sorry about the late dinners. I am grateful for the expertise of my editor, Debby McDonald and to Jean Slentz for her copy editing skills.

Joyce Ann Brown

Chapter 1

Arizona RV Resort

The cell phone vibrated on the picnic table next to Beth's elbow. She twitched, and her paintbrush slipped. "Oh, geez..."

The phone's caller ID read "Clay Stockwell." It was her son. "Hey, Clay," Beth said.

"Mom, you sitting down?"

"I am." She dropped the paintbrush on the table. Where was the cheerful *'Lo, Mom* Clay always, always used? He had used that greeting since childhood, even during his years in the Marine Corps."

"What's up?" Beth set the glaze aside, ignoring the slip-up on her handiwork.

"Psycho Cat found a skeleton in the attic!" Clay said.

Her eyes popped open. "You mean, in the attic of the duplex?" That cat would find something bizarre. But a dead body in the attic? "Psycho Cat found a skeleton in the attic of the duplex where you live?" she repeated. Maybe it was in one of the other rental units Clay was managing while she was away.

"Yeah, Mom, where we live. In a trunk right above our bed."

What had she done?! She'd let her son and his wife, Janae, take care of the trouble-seeking Psycho Cat, just so she and Arnie could spend the winter in an Arizona RV resort? And now...

"How...?"

"I know it's hard to believe, but listen. Since he's been here, Psycho Cat has jumped onto the top storage shelf in the back of the master bedroom closet every time we opened the closet door. We thought he was being curious and exploring. Then Janae saw him

1

pawing at the door in the ceiling. I saw him one day, too. The cat walked around on the shelf, reared up on his haunches, and pawed at different places, like he was trying to push the cover open."

"So you...?"

"I thought maybe he smelled mice or a squirrel. So this morning I opened the cover, and Psycho Cat jumped into the attic. I had to crawl up there to get him."

The word picture appeared to her like one of those satellite map images that pops up on a GPS and grows more and more detailed as one presses the + sign. How often had she cleaned and painted that closet after tenants moved out? Beth could visualize the two wide wooden shelves. She was never even curious to see what might be in the attic—just cobwebs and dust, she always thought. However, the duplex was built in nineteen fifty-two, long before she and her husband, Arnie, owned it. Not surprising that someone stored something up there at one time. Then it hit her— this was one of Clay's little jokes. What they found was a Halloween skeleton. Beth snorted an involuntary chuckling splutter at the thought.

"What?" Clay said.

"Oh, I can just see that crazy curious cat escaping into the attic and then you pulling the door open and fitting your big shoulders into a cramped space."

She relaxed enough to hold her phone to her ear with her shoulder, pick up the paint brush, and eye the goof-up on the clay pot. When she turned her head slightly to better see the far side, the phone fell with a bounce and slid across the table. Beth clambered to grab it and shove it against her ear.

"Oops. Sorry, Clay. That was me dropping the phone on the table, not your skeleton rattling around in the attic."

"Mom! Seriously. I'm trying to tell you this before the detective gets here."

"Detective?"

"Yes, an investigator is coming. There is a dead person in the attic!"

Beth opened her mouth, but no words came out. She stood up as if to drive right over there, until her logical mind reminded her she was a thousand miles from Kansas City. She paced back and forth with the phone to her ear.

Clay continued. "So, this morning, I got a flashlight and a whisk broom for the cobwebs and crawled in there to find the cat. Psycho Cat was up there pawing at a wooden trunk—a carved, sea chest kind of trunk. It was dark, but the flashlight beam caught the metal latch. I kneeled on the floor under the sloped roof. Then, I scooped up the cat, lifted the lid with my free hand, and shone the light inside. I thought there might be a nest of rodents inside and that Psycho Cat had heard or smelled them.

"Mom, there are human remains in that trunk! It took me a few minutes to figure out what it was, because it had some plastic sheeting around it. When I pulled the sheeting off the top, I practically gagged. The gruesome thing is bent at the knees, and the dried-out skin looks like leather, like it's partially mummified. There were some rotted-looking pieces of clothing and some kind of white powder. I shut that lid, and got out of there with the cat as fast as I could."

"Oh, Clay, that's horrible." All kinds of questions raced through Beth's mind. Who, when, how, why? "So you called the police?"

"That's what I'm telling you. The police came, and now we're waiting for a…"

"…detective….. I'm sorry. This is just hard to take in. How's Janae dealing with this? How are you doing…?"

"Janae was out doing some Saturday errands when I went up there. The police were here when she got home, and she's a little rattled. She wants the thing out of there and away from the house, but detectives and CSI people have to come out and gather evidence before they can move anything. This isn't the most pressing case on their agenda, since a missing person report about it would be old. Janae is real spooked, and we may be staying in a hotel room tonight, even though, I keep telling her, we've been sleeping with the skeleton above us for more than four months now."

"Oh, I'm so sorry this happened."

Beth thought again about how problems seemed to follow that Psycho Cat around, but she didn't say so. She and Arnie had adopted the cat from their niece, Adrianna, after the unpredictable feline jumped a murderer to save her life. The young lady was devastated to have to leave her heroic kitty behind when she

3

married and moved away, but she seemed happy her aunt and uncle would care for him. Now it appeared as if Psycho Cat had discovered another nasty situation.

"Could you tell if the—the dead person is a male or a female? Or a child?" Beth shuddered.

"Not really. I had a little experience with cadavers in pre-med, but this one has some powdery stuff on it and some decayed clothing. There's hair, but I didn't examine it enough to be able to tell you the length or style. It's too large to be a young child, but it could be male or female. I didn't stand there and look at it for long."

Clay and Beth talked for a while, speculating about how authorities would determine the age of the skeleton and how it got there. Beth assured Clay that Psycho Cat would do fine alone in the duplex if he and Janae left and spent the night elsewhere.

"Mom, someone's here," Clay said. "I need to go."

"Call me the minute you know anything more." Beth said before he could hang up. Then she stood still, holding her phone at arm's length, regarding it as though it could give an explanation for all this.

Chapter 2

Ten years earlier—Frog Springs, Arkansas

Ten years before the big tom, nicknamed Psycho Cat, located a skeleton in the attic, fourteen-year-old Caitlin Turley slumped forward toward her mother's bed from a hard, straight-backed chair.

"Mom, I'm so stupid. I should have realized you were sick a year ago. If I'd known, I could have done more. Maybe I could have talked Dad into taking you to a doctor in Little Rock or somewhere. Debbie's mom was cured of breast cancer. Remember? We can still do it—if you can hang on. Please, Mom."

Caitlin's mother half opened her eyes and tried to raise her hand from the bed. She opened her mouth to speak, but her voice came out as a croak, and she lapsed into a weak cough. For a few moments, she fought to control the cough. Then she closed her eyes, and it looked to Caitlin as if she had fallen asleep.

Caitlin rested her head on her mother's arm. Earlier she had opened a bedroom window a smidgen in case fresh air, even the hot, humid Arkansas summer air, might help her mom breath. She sprang up at the smacking sound of her older brother's baseball hitting a backboard outside. She'd go tell him to quit. How could he make all that noise while their mother was trying to sleep?

She turned back to the bed when her mom stirred and spoke in a coarse whisper, her eyes still closed, "Katie, my good girl."

Caitlin slipped back into the merciless chair and leaned close. "What is it, Mama? Can I get you something?"

"Rob."

"Dad is out—uh—at a sales meeting with one of his prospects, I—think."

"Quinn." Her mother paused to take a quivering breath. "Where's Quinlin?"

"He's in the back yard, getting ready for a baseball game. Dad told him to practice for the ballgame instead of practicing his violin today."

Her mom nodded the slightest bit and attempted a smile. "Call him for me, will you Caitlin?"

When Quinn joined his sister by their mother's bed, the fragile woman, frowning with the exertion, raised her head an inch from the pillow and focused on each face, one after the other.

"Promise me… Promise you'll look after each other." She took a long, shallow breath. "And take care of your father the best you can. He's having a hard time… Help each other, for me, please…"

Caitlin and Quinn whispered their promise to their beloved mother while they watched her close her eyes and lay still. She gasped for an instant, and then her breath became more and more shallow and finally ceased.

Quinn sobbed with his face in his hands, but it took Caitlin a few minutes to understand. Not until her mother's face relaxed from its scrunched-up look of pain did Caitlin grab her limp hand and then touch the still face.

"Mom! Mom! No! Quinn, call 911. They can bring her back. We've got to save her." She shook her weeping brother's shoulder. "Quinlin!"

Quinn shook his head and then reached for the telephone. He dialed his dad's cell phone number. After five rings, there was a fumbling scratchy sound before his father answered with a slurred shout so loud Caitlin could hear from the bedside, "Ya'llo."

~~~

Rob Turley stayed sober during the funeral and the graveside service. Later, at home, where all the relatives and a few long-time friends gathered with dishes of food and memories, Rob and his male relatives retreated to the back porch and opened up a cooler full of beer.

Caitlin spied the exit from the dining room where she was helping arrange the food and make sure there were clean plates. She grabbed Quinn after one of his aunts released the visibly discomfited seventeen-year-old from a firm hug.

"Dad and the uncles are out there drinking," she whispered. "What'll we do? You know Dad isn't going to listen to me if I tell him he needs to be in here to greet the guests."

"Well, he won't listen to me either. He'll get sore as hell if his sissy musician son says anything. Maybe Grandma will say something to him."

When they asked her, their father's plump, graying mother looked at the floor. "Your dad hasn't listened to me since he was a little child. Your grandpa showed all those boys that women are just here to be ordered around." She looked at them with sad eyes. "Rob was different to Martha for a time. That pretty college teacher was his goddess, 'til she had you'uns and he started to lose the business. I'm sorry, kids. I'm not the one to get that dad of yours straightened out. He loves you. He'll be better after this funeral business is all over. I know he will."

Caitlin and Quinlin coped with their father's conspicuous absence and the loud guffaws audible from the porch in different ways. Caitlin stayed busy greeting visitors and taking charge of the dishes of food each of them brought. Whenever she saw someone staring out the sliding glass doors, she rushed to explain.

"Sorry. My uncles and cousins get louder at funerals than they do at weddings. Just their way of dealing, I guess."

Carrying a covered dish she'd heated in the oven, Caitlin stopped short inside the kitchen door when she overheard two of the aunts discussing her dad.

"Martha was so good for him. He stayed sober and treated her with respect. That blue-eyed rogue even quit his philandering ways for a time."

"She deserved respect after switching from an English teacher to a—whadya call it?—English-as-a-Second-Language teacher for those immigrant farm workers' kids at the Community College."

"Yeah, but after they had their own kids and Rob started losing hardware customers to that big box store out on the highway…"

"I know. Rob started acting like his dad."

"I feel for the kids."

The aunts moved on, and Caitlin walked into the dining room with a fake smile plastered on her face. She managed to set the hot dish onto a trivet with only a slight quiver. The doorbell rang, and she raced to the door. She greeted some long-time neighbors.

~~~

Quinn, meanwhile, retreated to a corner where he stood with his arms crossed. He kept an eye on Caitlin and an ear cocked to

7

pick up any obvious swearing from the gang in the back while he worked on a plan to stop any brawling that might disrupt his mother's funeral reception. What could he do? Call the cops? He was not likely to do that.

Maybe he'd run out there and tell them he'd seen a stranger skulking around one of the cars parked out front. They'd have to refocus their bullying behavior to another cause. Yeah. It might work.

Three of his mother's colleagues from the college stopped in front of him. Quinn grasped the proffered hands, but he didn't know whether a smile was expected. He tightened his lips.

A rotund, balding man, head of the Language Department, Quinn remembered, tucked his hands behind his back and looked almost as uncomfortable as Quinn felt. "I just want you to know how much we miss your mother. She was an excellent teacher."

"An excellent person," said an English teacher who had known Quinn since he was born. She looked as if she'd been crying.

"You know," a soft-spoken young woman said, "I took over some of her classes. She left a thick portfolio of notes detailing the goals for each of her students so I could continue the work with no disruption. The young folks miss her. She helped some of them for years while they took college classes as they could between working minimum wage jobs and helping at home."

"You can be proud," the man said.

"Thank you." Quinn studied the floor. Were these people trying to make him cry again? He'd been able to let the tears loose only in private for the last few days.

The teachers moved on toward Caitlin, and Quinn ducked into the half bath off the hallway. He needed time to regain control. It took a while. He sat on the toilet remembering his sick mom's upbeat encouragement word for word.

Quinn, my dear son, don't give up your dreams. You have more musical talent than anyone in this town, and I know you'll find a way to use it in a spectacular career.

Was that still possible? He thought about what she said to Caitlin.

Katie, you are smart and so serious. Please have fun in high school. Then go knock 'em dead in college. You can be anything you want to be.

Quinn had smarts, athletic ability, and popularity—despite what his father thought. He'd make it through his senior year, no problem. But Caitlin had three more years. Was he strong enough to help his shy little sister get through this?

When Quinn re-entered the dining room, everyone stood with wide eyes and open mouths, facing toward the sliding glass doors. The only sound was his dad's bawling voice. Quinn stepped back into the hallway, his mouth dry.

"It's just another boulder thrown in my path." Rob Turley bellowed loud enough for the whole countryside to hear. "That damn Home Décor Station took my business, but Martha took my best years and left me. She left me! With what? A bunch of medical bills, a house with a mortgage, and a couple of namby-pamby kids to provide for."

A few grunts from his relatives.

"Well, you aren't the only one who got kicked in the butt when you couldn't make a go of the store. I lost my share of the hardware business, too, ya know," his older brother, Charlie, said in a gruff voice.

"Yeah?" Rob yelled. "You had money and refused to help keep it going. You weren't there when it needed just a boost. I gave it my life, and you couldn't fork over a dime?"

"It was a lost cause."

Rob grabbed his brother's shirt with his left hand and balled his right fist, but one of the cousins took hold of him in time. Quinn stepped toward the porch, ready to put his fight break-up plan into action when his Aunt Sharon took his arm and corralled him toward the kitchen. Aunt Sharon, his mother's sister from California, was the only relative on her side to make it to the funeral. They found Caitlin standing with her hands in a sink full of dirty dishes, tears running down her face.

Aunt Sharon put an arm around each of them. "You two can come live with me, if you need to."

Chapter 3

Arizona RV Resort

Beth remained by the picnic table, staring into space, wild images frolicking in her head. Arnie played golf on Saturdays, or any other day he could find a willing golf buddy, which turned out to be several times a week, at a course several miles from the RV Resort. They had been here for only a short time, but her friendly, peppy husband had jumped right in. To call him right away would serve no purpose other than to ruin his game. Beth sat back down at the picnic table. Some folks walked past and gave her a friendly wave, but she only raised her arm, smiled absently, and forgot to say hello.

She dabbed at the mistake on the clay pot where she had slipped with the brush. It was already dry. The problem was correctable with more glazing, but she was too distracted to work on it right then. Instead, she put away all of her materials and went inside the RV to pace from the living area, through the kitchenette, up the two steps to the bedroom and bath, and back again, until she plopped down on the couch to think bad thoughts about slow-poke police investigators. It was two o'clock on Saturday afternoon, three o'clock back home in Kansas City. How long would the investigation take?

This skeleton, or uh, mummy, may have been in that attic for decades, a clue in a very old case. At any rate, Beth envisioned detectives and special inspectors and yellow tape and photographs—all at the pace of the slowest specialist involved—all needed before they could move the skeleton. That's how it worked on television shows. It might be Monday before the kids would know anything.

How could a body be in that attic? Arnie and she had owned the two-unit building for almost thirty years, and they never had any inkling that there was even a trunk up there. Clay and Janae lived in the A side of the duplex and had been there for almost five months, but some previous tenants had lived there for as many as five years. No one found those remains before? It was hard to imagine any of their tenants putting a body up there, but even if they did, the tenants in the attached side would have smelled the rotting body and complained to them about the stink.

The two-story brick and stucco duplexes on that street were built as beginner homes for families in the early nineteen-fifties. This skeleton could be forty, fifty, or even sixty years old. It could have been in the trunk before the house was built and stored in the attic by the first residents. That reasoning made Beth feel better, and she decided to call Janae and try to calm her jitters.

"Janae," Beth said, without preamble, "I've just decided that the skeleton Clay found could be more than sixty years old and must be at least thirty years old. Otherwise, our tenants would have smelled the decomposition and reported it to us."

"If only!" Janae replied, "I could live with that. It would be like an old mystery. But we heard the investigators say that the corpse—they called it a *corpse*—didn't look that old. They asked us all kinds of questions and told us to stay in town. Well, of course we're going to stay here. I have a job, for Pete's sake, and Clay has school."

A shiver ran through Beth's body. "Don't worry," she said. "They'll have the thing out of there and give you the all clear in no time."

"Maybe, but that trunk's in the attic right above our bed. We've been sleeping beneath a dead body! It gives me the creeps."

Beth thought of attempting some humor, suggesting they could put a stake through the rib cage into the heart, in case it was a zombie, or call the ghost squad to rid the house of its ghost. But she sensed Janae was much too upset for levity.

"The police don't have the proper equipment, dear. I'm sure the relic is a museum piece. An expert examiner will find out how old it really is. Please call me or have Clay call as soon as you know more. I can hardly stand being so far away and unable to do anything for you."

~~~

Arnie was incredulous when Beth told him the attic skeleton story. Her trim, only slightly graying husband was soft-hearted and easy going, but he wanted everything categorized and logical. A career in the insurance industry had taught him to believe everything must be explainable. He had retired from his full-time position, but now he worked, usually from home or from wherever they went, as a consultant, helping underwriters and claims adjusters decide the logistics of their cases. "There are no coincidences" was one of his favorite phrases.

"Psycho Cat would have to have some kind of ESP to have been so obsessed with the attic door that he got Clay to investigate," Arnie said. "You are absolutely sure the kids aren't just playing a joke? Maybe this is some kind of school exercise Clay has to undertake. He didn't join a fraternity that hazes its members by making them pull a hoax on someone in order to be admitted, did he?"

"I don't think it's a joke," Beth said. "I heard the distress in Clay's voice, and Janae sounded nearly panicked. It isn't possible that a body could have decomposed in that attic since we've owned the duplex, is it? I mean, think of the smell. Think of the blood! It must have already been in the trunk when we bought the place, or it was placed there after it was already a skeleton, right?"

"Hmm, I remember seeing a trunk near the entry when I was in the attic with the building inspector before we bought the rental property. I opened it, because it was decorated with oriental carvings and looked as if it held treasures, but it was empty." He frowned and scratched his head. "I would have removed the trunk then and tried to find out if the previous owners wanted it, but it was too heavy and clumsy to bring down through the door in the ceiling and through the closet. Instead, I left it there, thinking someone might use it for storage. Then I forgot about it."

"Well," Beth said," No one has ever asked to have it removed or even mentioned it in almost thirty years, as far as I can remember."

Arnie grimaced. "If this is all true, I guess someone did use that trunk for storage, after all."

"Yuk! Oh, wait. I just thought of something." She closed her eyes for a minute. "Remember the time when we thought squirrels were getting into the attic and dying? A bad smell permeated the duplex for a few weeks when I was repainting one of the sides."

"Was it that duplex?"

"Yes, but I think I was fixing up Side B, not Side A where the kids are living. I couldn't tell if the odor came from the fireplace or the attic or even from inside the walls, but I knew we'd had some little animals get into the chimney before. Finally, you came over to help me check, and you found that the old roof had some gnawed places where the squirrels must have chewed their way into the attic."

"I remember. Didn't you decide the building needed a new roof?"

"Yeah. You know me. I'm always reluctant to spend the money. But after we had the roof replaced and the tree trimmed, the stink was gone. The roofers put new shingles over the old ones, if I remember correctly, and probably never looked into the attic, or if they did, they just saw the old trunk."

"You're right," Arnie said. "That's been what, seven or eight years ago, at least? But I'd think a dead human body would smell much worse than a dead squirrel."

Chapter 4

Kansas City, Missouri

Janae Stockwell paced from the kitchen back to the living room, sat down on the sofa, stood and peered up the stairway, and then crossed her arms and addressed her husband. "I wonder what they could be doing up there for so long."

"Probably just standing around shooting the bull," Clay said. He was sitting in an easy chair with a textbook in his lap, but so far he had not turned a page. "They already put orange tape everywhere. My guess is they have to stick around to keep us from messing up anything before the CSI investigators arrive."

"Like I'd even go close to that closet until they get rid of the skeleton."

"Maybe we'll get some answers soon." Clay pointed toward the front window. "That unmarked black Ford is definitely a police car."

They watched a man approach on the front walk, a fiftyish man with a stocky build, a round face with heavy eyebrows, and unruly hair. He was wearing what the fashion catalogs would term "cross season" khakis and an unzipped brown leather jacket.

Janae shivered and said, "The wind is shaking the huge branches of the oak trees. It must be bitter cold. That guy has to be chilled through with his cotton shirt exposed like that." She opened the door before he rang the bell.

Detective Carl Rinquire, unaffected by his arctic walk in any noticeable way, introduced himself and started asking Clay and Janae some of the same questions asked by the police. While he was quizzing the couple, two more people arrived. They carried satchels and were dressed in boots, police pants, and white uniform shirts. Detective Rinquire introduced them as Crime Scene Investigator Angela Topping and Crime Scene Supervisor Marcus Overos.

Although the inspectors headed for the attic carrying such tools as cameras, gloves, and what looked like special lighting equipment, Detective Rinquire appeared to need only his notebook. He interrogated Clay and then Janae for endless background information until he seemed convinced they had lived in the dwelling for only about five months and Clay had merely done his civic duty by reporting the body.

Then the Detective Rinquire started asking questions about the proprietors of the duplex. He raised his shaggy eyebrows slightly on learning that the duplex owners were Arnie and Beth Stockwell, living in Arizona for the winter, and that they were Clay's parents. "Did your mother once get involved with a case involving her missing niece, embezzlement, and a murder? Oh, yeah, and a big orange cat?"

Clay nodded. Janae's eyes strayed toward the inscrutable Sylvester, aka Psycho Cat, sitting on the back of the sofa, watching them with his wide green eyes. Detective Rinquire's eyes followed.

"That cat." The detective rubbed his arm across his forehead and closed his eyes briefly. "What a coincidence," he said in a monotone.

After being questioned at the kitchen table, watching a black van appear and two more investigators head into the attic, and being asked to stay put while Rinquire made some calls, Clay and Janae were the ones full of questions.

"When will we know the age of the body? Will the CSI be able to figure out how the person died? Was the body placed into the trunk before it was stored in the attic? Will police be able to get fingerprints or DNA off the trunk to help discover who put the body into it?"

"Hold on." Rinquire lowered his phone. "These investigators are good, but they can work only so fast. Your house is a crime scene now, and you'll need to make arrangements to spend the night elsewhere. I think we can get you a stipend to pay for a hotel room if you don't have somewhere else to stay. "

"What'll we tell my mom and dad?" Clay asked. "My mother owns and manages this property. She'll be frantic until she knows the details."

The detective raised one side of his mouth and nodded. "I'll contact your parents at the numbers you gave me. Their cell numbers, right?"

Clay nodded.

Janae raised a weak arm toward the stairway. "Can we get our...?"

"Find a place to stay, and I'll let the CSI people know you'll be packing what you need for tonight and tomorrow. They'll supervise if you need to get into the closet."

Janae wasted no time packing a bag. She told Clay that, after having heard his description of the trunk's contents, she wasn't the least bit curious to peek into the attic. By the time Clay completed his own packing and a phone call for a hotel room reservation, they were in the kitchen looking for Psycho Cat.

"Sylvester, drop that thing immediately!" Janae shouted out the back door. Through the kitchen window they had seen the kitty prancing proudly toward the back of the duplex carrying a dead bird. He dropped the limp pile of feathers on the porch and rubbed against Janae's leg on his way into the house. When Janae closed the door against the winter cold and looked around, the big cat was on his back, paws akimbo, on the kitchen floor, undoubtedly presuming he deserved the reward of a tummy rub for being a great hunter. Janae shook her finger at him instead.

"Naughty Sylvester." Janae was the only person in the family who called the orange and white striped cat by his original name. His past behavior, a tendency to jump on people and onto high places at unpredictable times and to get into any food or project left unattended, had earned him the nickname Psycho Cat during his first year on Earth. Not even his fairly recent status as a family hero had caused anyone to change the moniker. Janae, however, told everyone the name Psycho Cat was politically incorrect and disrespectful, and she refused to use it.

"I might have to reconsider calling you Psycho Cat," She said now. She stepped over the contented cat and asked Clay to please remove the dead bird from the porch.

Clay set his phone and his overnight bag on a chair. Neither of them felt comfortable spending money at a hotel, and they didn't know for sure if they would receive money from the police department to help pay. But they'd decided, under the circumstances, to go ahead and make it a memorable Saturday night by lodging in a fancy hotel on the Country Club Plaza, a shopping and dining district close by. There, they could enjoy a panoramic view of the splendid Plaza Christmas lights, on display until the end of January, and spend a romantic evening not only away from the daily grind, but also away from reminders of the human remains. They would designate the hotel stay an early Valentine's Day celebration.

Clay patted Psycho Cat on his way to the back stoop where he scooped up the limp gray bird with a paper towel, dropped it under the bushes behind the garage, and then covered it loosely with stones and sticks to discourage Psycho Cat's further investigation of his prey. On the way back through the kitchen he bent down to rub the kitty's ears.

"You are a terrific predator. We'll count on you to get rid of mice and bugs, too."

"Don't encourage him," Janae said. "He's caused us enough grief today with his hunting."

"If not for him, you'd still be sleeping below a skeleton tonight." Clay sat on his haunches to pet the cat. He affected a soothing tone. "We should call you Hunter Cat, shouldn't we ol' feller, or maybe Stalker Cat?"

"Geesh," Janae scoffed, "just what Sylvester needs, another nickname. Let me fill his bowls with enough food and water to last until tomorrow, at least, and then I'll be ready to go. I just hope the investigation gets finished fast and this night away from home will clear the feeling of revulsion out of my head. I'd like to have time to work on my art project tomorrow afternoon, and I want to get ready for work on Monday in my own bedroom."

"I've got tons of studying to get done, too, but let's live it up tonight and worry about all that tomorrow, okay, Hon?" Clay said. He hugged his tense wife and stroked her back while she sagged against him for a few moments before she pulled away and straightened her shoulders.

"I agree." She shook her soft mane of shiny reddish-brown hair behind her back. Replacing her worried look with a coy smile and skimming her hand down one curvaceous hip, she gazed up at Clay with big, brown, bedroom eyes. "I'm ready for a romantic get-away, Lover Boy."

Chapter 5

July, Seven Years Earlier—Frog Springs, Arkansas

"Bring me a beer, Katie, zat's a goo' girl." Rob Turley emanated the sour-sweet smell of too many beers, and he burped.

The man could be a happy drunk, and he did love his daughter, in his own muddled way. These days, Rob was drunk, period, and in that condition, he had mastered his dad's chauvinism. After his wife died almost four years before, Rob did try to be a genuine father to his children once in a while, but he was too far into bars and booze and babes to give up the saloons where he could malinger, rail against providence, and anesthetize his consciousness. Close to a year ago, his only son left, and Rob was now often tanked-up at home as well as at the bars.

Using the pet name, Katie, when he told her to get him a beer was the nicest her dad had been to Caitlin in several weeks. Of course, he was *very* drunk, and he had told her he might have made a big sale. Caitlin rushed off to get the beer, hoping to prolong his good mood until she could make it out the door and to her evening fast-food job. On the way to the refrigerator, she thought of her brother, Quinn, and the letters he'd been sending, telling her again and again how he wanted her to join him in Kansas City if she couldn't hack it at home with Dad.

~~~

After his mother died, Quinn lived at home for his senior year and then a year after graduation. He took a job at the same big box home improvement store that had caused the decline of his father's business, but he spent most of his hours practicing with his band, *Glory Days*. Quinn's musical interests were diverse, from classical, to Celtic, to jazz, to R&B, and more. He'd learned to play a wide variety of instruments—the violin, bass, and saxophone in orchestra and band classes, the piano and guitar from private instruction arranged for by his mother. The study of music at a university or conservatory became Quinn's dream, one that grew dimmer each day he stayed in Frog Springs. There was no money, and there was the incessant insinuation by his dad that he should be doing something *masculine* with his life.

Quinn's former high school band had broken up after graduation when one member went off to college and another, still in high school, was forbidden by his parents to play with a band until his grades improved. Bernie Landoff and Quinn Turley had been the only band members left. Bernie, a big stocky kid with long straight blond hair, a mustache, and deep set eyes, looked older than his eighteen years. He hooked up with the elder members of their new band, *Glory Days,* at a bar where he had been drinking with a fake I.D. *Glory Days* was the opening act for a popular local country band.

When Bernie learned *Glory Days'* members were seeking new talent in order to expand their repertoire, he told Quinn, "We should audition with this group. We're just what they need, and it'll be better than our old band. They play gigs all over the county."

Impressed by Bernie's proficiency on percussion and by Quinn's multiple musical talents, the *Glory Days* trio incorporated them and became a quintet. Its members included Quinn and Bernie, Tony and Chip, two men in their late twenties, and Tony's girlfriend, Nicole. They were usually booked three out of four weekends a month. However, the pay was minimal, the tips were meager, and the take was split six ways—among the five band members and their equipment fund. Quinn and Bernie weren't making a whole lot more than they had during high school when their amateur band was hired to play at private parties and events around town.

"I'm doin' alright," Quinn told Bernie. "I'm good at helping people who shop in the home improvement store. I grew up working at my dad's hardware store, remember. It's easy to save money by living at home, and maybe I can put back enough for college. And—I promised Mom I'd look after Caitlin until she graduates from high school.

"I get it, man." Bernie said. "But I gotta get out of here. No future for musicians in this Podunk town. Think about it."

"Just another year and we'll discuss it."

Quinn knew Bernie had no responsibilities at home, plenty of money from his parents, and no job other than the band. His interests included bar hopping every night, even though he was underage, and hanging out with musicians, who would let him buy their drinks after their gigs. He hung on every word of the guys when they talked about their aspirations of becoming recording artists, playing venues in the big cities, and ultimately hitting the big time.

Quinn detected when it became Bernie's objective to instill those ambitions into the members of his own band. Tony, Chip, and Nicole weren't even a little bit interested. They had jobs, families, and futures in Frog Springs. Music was only part of their lives. When Bernie wasn't able to convince the others, he began working on his buddy.

"Look at this," he'd say when he brought music magazines to Quinn at work, "These guys from a pinprick town in Iowa went to New York and made it big."

Bernie persisted when they met to play computer games at McDonalds. "Here's a great website. It lists tons of opportunities for musicians in Little Rock, St. Louis, Louisville, even L.A. and New York."

Quinn participated in the Web survey of music groups and venues as if it were a diversion, a daydream about an improbable future, while Bernie became more and more pushy.

"You owe it to yourself to show your dad you can make it in the music world. You owe it to your sister to get away from here and make enough to help *her* break away from your dad."

This remark made Quinn consider, even if only in theory.

"You've got talent, voice, soul, and—I gotta admit—looks girls scream over. We could make it big. You owe it to me, as your best friend who stuck with your music groups all these years, to help get me away from my suffocating parents. You owe it to your dad to fly the coop. He'll give you credit for getting out on your own. Most important, how are you going to help your sister if you can't get your own career started?" On and on, Bernie didn't ease up, and Quinn slowly broke down and began to consider the possibility.

A year and a half after they joined *Glory Days*, Bernie finally pressed the button that put Quinn in motion. A former high school band member they called Rocky, who'd gone off to college in Kansas City, came back for a visit that summer. The kid had chosen Kansas City because he had relatives living there, and, when pressed and handed plenty of free beer by Bernie, agreed he could help them find a place to live and introduce them to local music groups.

"Kansas City has a decent Music Conservatory," Bernie told Quinn, "and there are tons of music venues in the city and in Lawrence, Kansas, which is real close. There are audiences for all types of music. It's the home of Kansas City Jazz. And, it's within a day's drive of Frog Springs. You can come see your sister any time."

He didn't mention that Rocky lived with his relatives, had a part time-job at a gas station, played music only on the radio, and was too young to get into the over-21 bars where the R&B, Rock, and Blues groups played. Quinn heard only the promise of assistance at a time when his father was giving him nothing but grief. The slim hope of help from Rocky did it.

Quinn said, "It sounds good. We could probably figure out how to make it work."

"We're a team," Bernie said. And his face said, "Yes! Quinn's in."

But then there was Caitlin. Not that she urged Quinn to stay. No, Caitlin encouraged him to go to Kansas City, display his talents, and save to get into a good school. To help him get started, she offered him some of the money she'd saved. She implored him to quit fretting about her and take this opportunity for himself. Quinn was reluctant to leave his sister. Their father verbally abused both of them, but it was easier to take when they had each other. He reminded Caitlin of the promise he'd made to their mother, the promise to take care of Caitlin. She countered that she had made the promise, too, to take care of him.

"Besides," Caitlin said, "as soon as I finish my senior year of high school, I'm going to move out. This is your time. My time is coming."

Quinn shifted back and forth between convincing himself he should take the opportunity to go and scolding himself for thinking about leaving his sister alone. Then one evening, as if providence was sending a sign, Rob Turley, in one of his brutal moods, sneered at his son in Caitlin's presence.

"You sissy good-for-nothing. When I was your age, I practically ran my dad's business. What're you doing? Playing worthless music and doing grunt work for some big corporation? That's rubbish. I oughta kick your butt out of here."

It wasn't anything Quinn and Caitlin hadn't heard before, in various ways, but this time they'd looked at each other and left the room together.

"Get back here, you losers. I'm talking to you." Rob Turley had shouted.

But by some unspoken understanding, they both climbed into Quinn's car where Caitlin picked up Quinn's cell phone and called Bernie. They met him at a local café and made their plans. At one point, Bernie grabbed Caitlin's hand with both of his and thanked her for being a good sister. Quinn winced. He knew Caitlin was not a fan of Bernie Landoff and wished Quinn had someone else with whom he could stay in Kansas City.

She pulled her hand away. "Listen, Bernie. You're going to the city to play serious music, not to drink and do drugs."

Bernie ignored Caitlin's counsel and turned rapt attention to Quinn's list of arrangements needing to be made before they could move.

~~~

A year later, Quinn made the trip home for Caitlin's graduation ceremony. They had written to each other and sent e-mail, from public library computers, whenever they could during Caitlin's senior year of school. Quinn had asked how his sister was getting along but had never asked about their father's escapades that year, and Caitlin hadn't volunteered any stories. Likewise, Quinn hadn't let on how hard it had been for Bernie and him to get started in a city where they knew only one person, one young college student, who was no help at all after his relatives located a duplex for them to rent.

It barely seemed to register with Rob when Quinn tried like crazy while he was home to help his dad get sober and civilized. A long pattern of ranting on about Quinn's "girlish" choice of music as a passion and a career and his undisguised disappointment with Quinn's minimal interest in succeeding in sports was an ingrained habit of Rob's woozy consciousness, practiced all through Quinn's high school years and after. For the few days Caitlin's brother was there, it was as if he'd never left. Rob blamed his drinking during that time on the celebration of Caitlin's graduation, as good a reason as any to imbibe, as he resumed his pattern of haranguing his son.

"Dad," Quinn said, more than once, "I know where you can go to get some help with your drinking problem. You need to do it for Caitlin's sake—and for your own."

"Quinlin," Rob mimicked, "I don't know where you can go to get over your limp-wristed music penchant, but maybe it would help to come down to Jake's Bar with me, have a few beers, and prove yourself at the pool table. Maybe end up in some gal's bed, eh? Whadya say?"

Caitlin could only stand and listen, and then close her eyes and pretend she was a little kid, her dad throwing a baseball to Quinn and yelling at him with enthusiastic encouragement to watch the ball. In her daydream, she tried cartwheels and jumps like a cheerleader rooting for her favorite team, and both her father and her big brother stopped practicing every once in a while to clap. Her mother, young and vibrant, came to the back door and called them for dinner. If only she were still alive….

~~~

When Quinn had gone to Kansas City, the stipulation had been for Caitlin to finish high school and then move in with him until she could start college. Failure hadn't occurred to either of them when Quinn had planned for success in the big city. It hadn't been complete failure—Quinn was playing with a band. But his earnings from the nights' revenues plus the little he made at his part-time job had barely paid his share of the rent, utilities, gas, and food. Bernie spent the money from his parents as fast as he got it. Quinn then lost his job and had not yet found another that fit with the band's schedule. Also, Bernie was completely against having Caitlin as a third roommate. Quinn was still committed to honoring his promise to Caitlin, but he knew he couldn't be her sole support if he took her in.

~~~

The night after graduation, Quinn took Caitlin out to celebrate at the same little café where they'd made plans for Quinn's move.

He didn't bring up the subject of her moving to Kansas City and looked at the table more than he looked her in the eye.

Caitlin sensed Quinn's unease. Hints of his poverty were apparent—the car that needed servicing, his lame excuse for no graduation gift, complaints about Bernie's spendthrift habits. Caitlin, although disappointed, was determined to save her brother the embarrassment of admitting how difficult it would be for him to fulfill his promise to take her in. While they ate their sandwiches, Caitlin sat straight, took a deep breath, and made an announcement.

"Quinn," she said, "I've decided to stay in town, look for a job, care for dad, and then take a class or two at Frog Springs Community College starting in the fall. I know we decided I'd go to Kansas City with you after graduation so we could look after each other, but remember, Mom told us to look after Dad, too. He needs me here, and I can start my education at Community College. I was granted a small scholarship from the school if I decide to use it."

Quinn looked visibly relieved, but Caitlin saw him catch himself and frown. "Are you sure? We planned for you to move out as soon as you graduated. There are community colleges in Kansas City you could go to part time until we can save enough money. Dad can look after himself."

"Yes, I'm sure. There's no guarantee I can find work in Kansas City. I think it's best if I start school here where I already have a job. You need to save for your own education. I can move up there after I have more money saved and some college hours under my belt."

"Okay," he said, "but I'm going to call and write every week. If it gets to be too much, if Dad treats you so badly that you can't stand it any longer, you are to come to Kansas City immediately. We'll manage up there together. Will you agree to that?"

Caitlin had been willing to agree to the stipulation. She had barely known if she could stick with her new plan at all. It was a plan she'd devised on the spur of the moment. Now, it was July, and Quinn had been back in Kansas City for two months. Caitlin still didn't know if she could honor her plan to stay with her father. The use of her pet name, Katie, and one half-way pleasant request for a beer hardly made up for the name-calling, man-handling, and general bullying Caitlin had been putting up with all summer. She needed to get away, but she hadn't quite made up her mind to do it.

Chapter 6

Arizona RV Resort

As if Clay and Janae were ten-year-olds, Beth worried Arnie about them all Saturday afternoon and early evening. She talked his ear off telling him about the skeleton in the attic, speculating about how it got there, and wondering what was happening in Kansas City. Arnie didn't seem as concerned. Maybe it was just that she had nurtured those duplexes for the past twenty years as if they were…what? Like her own children? She needed to let Arnie know how important this was.

"You know how sensitive Clay is to other people and their problems. He'll be worrying about the family of the person whose body is stuffed into that trunk. And poor Janae—from what Clay said she seems to have become unglued by the whole thing."

"Relax," Arnie said. "They're adults. They'll be okay. We'll find out more when they call, but we can count on Clay to handle it."

Part of what Beth felt was guilt, she knew, because such a large part of her concern was about the rental units. What would happen to their agreement with Clay that he was to manage the properties while they were gone? What would happen to the rental value of the property? And—come to think of it—what was the probability they'd have to cut short their first attempt to winter away from Kansas City to go home and deal with an investigation?

She shook off those selfish thoughts. She was getting confused. Her concern needed to be with her family. The police would want to talk to her and Arnie about the body, skeleton, uh…mummy, or whatever remains remained in that attic. They could tell the police about the new roof and the smell of something dead seven years ago. Beth had little idea what all might be involved in the investigation of a so-called "cold case," apart from what she saw on TV.

"Arnie, don't you think maybe the police will need no more than a short statement from us? We will tell them how shocked and concerned we are and tell them to let us know what they find out. I mean, what could we do to help?"

"I don't know how much they'll need from us. Meanwhile, I wonder how long the kids might have to stay away from the duplex while the police investigate. Do they have a key to our house?

"Yes." Good grief. She hadn't considered suggesting their house, but Arnie didn't have to think twice. She hugged him.

"What was that for?"

"Just felt like it."

Arnie and Beth tried to concentrate on reading, gave up, cooked their dinner on the grill, rescued some of the potatoes Beth accidentally spilled into the coals (she wasn't hungry, anyway, was her rationalization) and then tried to watch a video. They kept their phones in their pockets the whole time, and Beth kept checking hers to make sure she hadn't somehow missed a call. No other time passes as slowly, and sometimes painfully, as that spent waiting for news, good or bad, she thought.

"Beth," Arnie said later when she looked at her phone for the fifth time during the ignored movie, "those kids have enough to think about without you pestering them. Clay will call as soon as he knows anything."

She knew he was right. She set her phone on the table with a resigned look. Thoughts whirled around under her curls like sand swirling in a dust storm on the Arizona desert. She pictured the duplex, a square building with doors to each unit, a cement porch, brick front, black shingles, and fireplace chimneys on each side. Two huge oak trees dominated the front yard. In the back yard thick bushes grew alongside the unattached garage. Beth knew the duplexes inside and out, having painted, mowed, raked, torn out, replaced, and even learned how to install tile herself in order to save money to pay off the mortgage and let the rents help provide retirement income—Income for snowbird trips to the South, for instance. It was hard to reconcile that a dead body was in one of the attics all that time.

This winter trip was their first foray into semi-retirement, a deserved break, they thought, after years of hard work. Arnie enjoyed his golf games with folks from the RV Resort. He could schedule his part-time work, insurance consultation conference calls, around tee times without a problem. Winter golf in a warm climate was an incredible gift for Beth's sports-minded husband. He found sports bars with satellite hook-ups where he could watch the Kansas City Chiefs play, too.

Soon after they'd arrived, Beth had joined a hiking group, and she participated in water aerobics and morning exercise sessions, because she had always been an exercise nut. She also found great pleasure in the art classes at the resort. Artistic endeavors in her life so far had been limited to making Halloween costumes for her children and helping to create a papier-mâché animal or two with her daughter's Girl Scout group. Since they'd been at the resort, she'd enjoyed drawing classes and pottery making and was, to her astonishment, delighted with her crude beginner accomplishments. Beth felt like a young child who draws something that looks like a tree and then feels her heart beat with pride when she shows it to people.

Art was her favorite class in high school, but she hadn't even considered it as a college major. Better late than never. It's been said that boys often marry girls who are like their mothers. Clay married an artist. Maybe Beth had been an artist all along and didn't know it.

In her head, she started designing her next pottery project—crazy how far from the crisis at hand she'd let her mind drift—when she was jerked back into reality by a sudden apprehension. She might have to leave her newly discovered art groups if she and Arnie had to go deal with a nasty skeleton found in a duplex attic!

Finally, Beth could stand the suspense no longer. She screwed up her face. "It's getting late. Let's just call Clay to find out what's happened." She picked up her phone with a questioning look at Arnie.

Beth turned off their unwatched video and called Clay.

"Lo Mom," Clay answered.

"Hey, Clay. You're sounding more like your old self. I was getting so worried."

Arnie reached for the phone and pressed the speaker button. "Clay, we've been waiting to hear what's happening there with the skeleton you found. Your mother has been fidgeting over this until she's driving me crazy. What's going on?"

"Sorry, Mom, Dad, I haven't had time to call. Janae and I escaped the house and are treating ourselves to a nice hotel on the Plaza tonight. The police will be working at the duplex tomorrow, at least, and maybe longer."

Beth cut her eyes at her husband and spoke in a high pitched voice toward the phone. "What did the detectives find out?"

"They haven't found out much about the body yet," Clay said. "A detective named Carl Rinquire asked Janae and me tons of questions about how long we've lived there, how I happened to find the trunk, and what we know about the body…which is zero. The detective was skeptical about Psycho Cat…"

"Sylvester!" sounded Janae's voice from a distance."

"…about *Sylvester* somehow knowing there was a body. He thought the cat probably just heard mice up in the attic and wanted to get to them. Otherwise, he wrote down our story in his notebook and told us we might be 'interviewed' again at a later time. Oh, and he asked for information about you and said he would contact you. Has he called yet?"

"No," Arnie said, "This is the first we've heard since you called your mom earlier today."

Beth again raised eyebrow at Arnie's grumpy statement. "We've been on pins and needles." she said.

"Sorry. First chance I've had to call. Janae and I are in a hotel. The police, some investigators, and Detective Rinquire were at the duplex from the time I talked to you until we left. They finally let us go. We're staying at this hotel, like I told you we might. In fact, we may have to spend another night somewhere. The investigators will take the trunk and the body, and we're hoping they finish at the duplex by tomorrow so we can go back to normal."

Arnie said, "Don't worry, Clay. You don't have anything to do with this. It's really our problem, and we'll pull out of here and be home to take care of answering questions and finding records, or whatever the police need. Would it help for you to stay at our house while you have to be away from the duplex? You'd have to de-winterize it."

"Thanks, that's a thought, but we're already here for tonight, and we think we might be reimbursed for our hotel stay. Like I said, we're hoping the investigation will be over fast."

"Please don't worry, Clay." Beth echoed Arnie. "You and Janae are busy enough with work and school without a police investigation to deal with. We'll be home as soon as we can."

"Another call's coming in," Clay said. "It might be from the detective. Gotta go."

The good parents, Beth thought while she set down the phone. Arnie was right to say they'd go home. Even so, her insides sank an inch or so at the thought of leaving her new-found artistic endeavors to go back to managing the rental properties, dealing with a dusty mummy skeleton, and (yikes) being interrogated by Detective Rinquire. She remembered Rinquire, a nice enough man but a staid investigator, from the time she had, quite by happenstance, helped solve one of his cases, the one involving her niece. She had no doubt his first words to her would be to the effect that she should stay out of this investigation.

Arnie got a call from Detective Rinquire about fifteen minutes after they talked to Clay. "We've owned that duplex for over twenty-five years," Arnie said. "We've never had any indication that a person died, or was possibly murdered, in it." He listened some, then looked at Beth with an apologetic expression.

"Murdered," she said.

"Beth is the one who runs the business and keeps the records. You'll need to ask her about locating the tenant accounts."

Arnie handed her the phone, and she took it with a huff. "Hello, Detective Rinquire, can you tell us..." He didn't let her finish.

"Sorry, Mrs. Stockwell. I'm the one asking the questions right now. The duplex will be considered a crime scene for a few days, at least, while our investigators comb every inch of it for evidence. Only after they finish will I know what information about the case I can share with you."

For the next half hour, which felt like several hours, the detective conducted his interrogation. "Does the trunk belong to you? How long has it been in the attic? Why have you never looked inside it when a tenant moved out?" Detective Rinquire asked each question in various ways several times.

Some of the queries were about Clay and Janae, but many of them inferred Arnie's and her involvement with that body in the attic. She realized they had access to that duplex whenever anyone moved out, and it would have been a perfect place to hide a body if both sides were empty at the same time. Just wait until the smell was gone, rent the unit to someone new, and blame it on a renter if the trunk was ever opened. But the implied accusation was hard to take.

"Wait a minute," Beth said, "If we killed someone and put the body in the attic, why wouldn't we sell the duplex and make it someone else's problem?"

Detective Rinquire reminded her again who was asking the questions and continued his questioning. She racked her brain to remember the various renters of Clay's and Janae's duplex over the past decade or so. She admitted not being able to pair names and dates very well. They owned, and she managed, seven rental properties.

The renters tended to run together in her mind after a while, especially if they rented for only a year, as some did. Beth remembered one couple with kids and a dog—they left the duplex and lawn a disastrous mess. Oh, wait, that was Side B, not Side A.

There was one young man who'd filled the garage and basement with junk and scraps of wood and metal she'd had to have removed after he moved out. She'd sent an eviction notice to that guy and his wife—they'd paid their rent late every month, skipped a month here and there, and from the look of the place when they went in to clean up, the couple must've been smoking something not found at the convenience store counter.

Beth remembered a nice divorced lady with two daughters who'd lived there for several years. Was that Side A or Side B? Finally, with a sigh of acceptance, she told the detective the same thing Arnie had told Clay.

"We're pulling out of here tomorrow and will be home in a couple of days. Then I'll be able to go through my records for names, dates, forwarding addresses, and phone numbers."

Rinquire gave Beth some leeway after she told him about her rental records being in several different file drawers in a bedroom used as office space in their home, maybe hard for anyone but her to readily access. He said the Crime Scene Investigation team would continue gathering evidence at the duplex, and his detectives would be questioning neighbors. Beth rather doubted any neighbors knew about the dead body if she didn't, but some things just wouldn't have occurred to her—like the possibility there would be skeletal remains in a trunk in the attic of one of her duplexes!

Chapter 7

Kansas City, Missouri

Gray drizzly dusk arrived around Four-thirty on this January Saturday afternoon in Kansas City, and it was as dark and gloomy as a winter street in Dickens's London by the time Clay and Janae stuffed their bags into the back seat of Janae's little car and set off for their Plaza hotel. Tiny wet snowflakes glistened in the streetlights and in the glow of their headlights. Bare, black-silhouetted tree branches, shivering slightly in the chilly wind, and ghostly mansions, surrounded by their expansive obscured lawns, lined each side of Ward Parkway. Clay kept his eyes on the road and both hands on the wheel as he maneuvered the slick streets, and Janae sat stiff and unmoving. They rode along in silence until they drove under the brightly-lighted overhang at the entrance to the hotel.

"Whew. A port in a storm," Clay said.

"Like landing in Oz after escaping a tornado," Janae said.

The hotel looked like a palace from another century where footmen rushed to open their carriage doors, as if they were royal visitors, and carried their small bags into a vast reception room filled with glittering chandeliers and colossal crystal-like vases filled with flowers. While Clay checked in, Janae stayed with the luggage, gazing at the elegant surroundings. She looked a tad underdressed in her jeans with other guests sauntering past in evening clothes and fashionable couture outfits. This place hosted many Saturday evening events. Clay couldn't have cared less.

He turned toward Janae with a wink, one elbow resting on the counter. "Just waiting for the keys, Babe." She rewarded him with a warm smile.

It seemed uncanny to Clay that all this was happening during a snowstorm. He'd met Janae in Minneapolis where he was a pre-med student using the G.I. Bill. He, having developed an interest in chemistry, decided to study to be a pharmacist. They married after her graduation with a Fine Arts degree and moved to Kansas City, Clay's hometown, anticipating a good university pharmacy program, a notable art environment, an offer to trade duplex management for rent, and a warmer climate. Now, here they were, in a snowstorm as blustery as any they had experienced in Minnesota.

But the unusually cold, wet weather wasn't the first deviation from their expectations. After the first couple of weeks in Kansas City, Janae had applied for a job at a public relations firm.

"I'll be doing some graphic art work and some copy work. It's something I can do to keep us solvent until you graduate," she'd said.

"Honey, no. I promised you we'd move here and you could work on your sculptures and paintings. We can make it. I'll get a part-time job and just take a smaller load each semester."

"No, Sweetie, I don't want you to get another job while you're in that intense pharmacy program. You're already going to manage the duplexes this winter. Besides, I'm not even sure I'll be able to sell my art. We've got car payments, insurance, utilities, your mega-expensive books, clothing, and…food. I'll work on my art in the evenings and on the weekends while you study.

It made sense. "Well, okay, it'll only be three years. I'll have a good career then, and you can concentrate entirely on your art."

Clay realized, as the weeks passed, that to Janae, while she was working as an underappreciated beginning graphic artist in an ad agency, the three years were already beginning to feel like forever. Her job entailed some creativity, of course, but Janae wanted to paint and sculpt. Those were the media for which she had talent and education, the works she created in her sleep and tried to find time to create in reality on the weekends. Evenings were too short after the commute from downtown.

The duplex was a fine home for them. The neighborhood was peaceful and in a convenient location. Their side of the duplex was roomy. Clay had forfeited the use of the one-car detached garage out back, which provided space for Janae's car so she wouldn't have to scrape ice off the windshield in the winter.

"My car's an old beater," he'd said. "After living in Minnesota, I'm used to scraping snow while the car warms up."

Janae used the extra bedroom as an art studio. The room didn't have much natural lighting—just two narrow windows with trees outside blocking the sunlight.

Janae's initial response to the potential art studio had been, "Yikes! Oh, Clay, I'm not sure this will work."

Clay, with his dad's help, had built a table from one side of the room to the other along one wall, and they'd installed track lighting above it. Janae's eyes had lit up when she'd seen the finished project. "The first pieces of art I create here will be dedicated to you two super craftsmen," she told them.

As much as he admired her artwork, Clay marveled more at the intensity of spirit she exhibited in creating them. For several weeks, Janae had been working on a sculpture that she seemed excited about. Clay had not yet been allowed to see it. He had only glimpsed some of her planning sketches, but he was relieved to see her contented and glad she could use part of her earnings each month to pay for materials.

Now, this bizarre attic thing. They'd been told that every marriage has troubles from time to time, but not one family member ever mentioned a skeleton in the closet, let alone a skeleton in the attic. The police had taken all of their identification and contact information and told them to stay close—as if they had something to do with the dead body! No one had suggested they were free to go about their business. The discovery seemed exciting, in a way, but they were so busy. Clay couldn't imagine what was going to happen next.

In their hotel room, Janae checked out the minibar. "Can you believe these prices? Look at this, three dollars for a candy bar. Four dollars for a bottle of water. Where's the Quik Trip when you need one?"

"Not on the Country Club Plaza, for sure, but take a look at this view." Clay motioned Janae toward the large window that looked out over the Plaza's Spanish architecture decorated with colored lights and reflected in the water of Brush Creek. The formerly wild stream had been carefully widened and landscaped through the district after it'd flooded the businesses there several times.

"Lovely," Janae said. "I know I should be in a better mood and enjoy tonight, Clay, but I can't help thinking about that body. I heard you tell the detective it had leather-like skin and white powder around it. A horrible image keeps popping into my head, and I want to go grab my art away from there. Not only our bed, but also my studio is underneath that attic. It's silly, I know, but it feels like bad karma for my work, and I was excited about that sculpture. How can you be so calm about it? You saw the thing, for heaven's sake."

"Remember, I'm a pharmaceutical student, and chemistry is my foundation. The more I think about it, the more this whole thing intrigues me. The white powder I noticed inside the plastic sheeting around the body could be lime. Quick lime has been used for centuries to help dissolve dead animals and people in mass graves. Whoever put that body up there knew what they were doing."

"Well, *that's* comforting. Really, Clay, I don't know if I'll ever feel at ease in that duplex again."

Clay shoved his hands in his pockets. "We could move. I know you've wanted to live closer to the Crossroads Art District downtown, anyway, haven't you?"

"True. There'd probably be lots more opportunity for collaborating with other artists. I need that kind of inspiration and encouragement." She stood up from her crouched position in front of the minibar. "But we need the extra money we're saving on rent. The utilities, the insurance, gasoline…. Good grief, even groceries are sky high. We should stay…"

Clay's phone rang. His parents. He tried to reassure them and tell them what he knew, but then a call from Detective Carl Rinquire interrupted. Janae stopped puttering with her personal belongings, sat silently on the big bed, and listened to Clay's end of the conversation with the detective—mostly "Yes," "I see," "I understand," "Okay, we will," and "Thank you."

"Well?" Janae demanded when Clay finished his conversation, "are they going to be out of there tomorrow?"

"Detective Rinquire said…" Clay looked serious and held Janae by the shoulders as if to help her bear up under bad news, "…that his team will get all of the evidence they can from the attic tonight and tomorrow, and then…." Janae began to look worried. Clay continued with a grin, "They will have to take the skeleton and evidence back to their lab to continue the investigation. Everything should be normal at the duplex in a couple of days, but meanwhile they'll pay for our hotel bills."

"Good!" Janae raised her arms and flung herself backward onto the bed. She smiled up at Clay. "I don't think I could return there as soon as tomorrow, anyway. Now we can enjoy this evening and not worry about the expense."

All thoughts of braving the winter winds to walk to a Plaza restaurant were forgotten as Clay sat down beside his contented wife and took her hand. She kissed him softly and nuzzled. He kissed her neck. She pulled him close, and the comfortable sensuousness of their lovemaking became new and exciting in the unfamiliar, luxurious surroundings.

Later, they ordered dinner from room service. "I wonder if the police department will pay for our dinner," Janae said as she took her last bite. "This is too decadent."

"You deserve it," Clay said pouring seconds from a bottle of Merlot, a rare treat for a couple used to Coors. "Even if they don't pay for the food, the shrimp cocktail, prime rib, and an evening with no cooking or cleanup is worth the splurge."

"This room is cushy, too. Let's pull these chairs over by the window. We can turn out the lights and enjoy the Plaza scenery while we finish the wine."

"I'll move the chairs. The view *is* spectacular from here. Great spot to drink a fine wine. And…" He cut his eyes sideway at Janae and smiled. "We can look forward to getting back in that comfy bed."

Chapter 8

July, Seven years earlier—Kansas City, Missouri

"**D**on't be a friggin' coward!" Bernie Landoff said. "What's going to happen? All you have to do is ask some questions, send people my way. I'll do the rest. You just be your own self and get paid."

Bernie paced across the living room of the duplex he and Quinn Turley shared in Kansas City, Side B of the two-story white structure, with a fireplace they had never used and a detached garage that sat gathering dust and mouse droppings because they never took the time to open the garage door and drive one of their ancient vehicles inside. Quinn sat slumped on the well-worn sofa they had purchased at a thrift store. The small TV, which sat on a red plastic crate across from the sofa, emitted a fuzzy signal. There was no other furniture. The hard-wood floor was littered with piles of shoes, dirty clothes, and entertainment news fliers. Sometimes the pungent odor of the litter and leftover fast-food containers permeated the living room, but Quinn couldn't stand that kind of mess and ended up cleaning up after both of them.

"It's not a matter of being afraid," Quinn said. "I just...I've seen what drugs and alcohol can do to a person. It drags them down. My dad... I don't want to... Well, for me to help get drugs to people—it'd be like dredging up nightmares of watching my own dad get sucked farther and farther into the sewer."

"Listen man, those druggies'll get their shit from somewhere else if not from us. It's not like we're dragging kids off the street and getting them hooked. You know these punks who hang out after hours. They idolize you. All you have to do is put in a word about the stuff I'm selling when they're hanging all over you, and we're in business." Bernie stopped pacing and held his thumb and forefinger close together in front of Quinn's face. "We'll grab a tiny amount—I'm talking a microscopic amount—of the dough that's being tossed around. We'll put it into our music, be able to pay for lessons from the best musicians. You'll make enough to send money to your sister for her education."

Bernie and Quinn had been friends since grade school, and, as usual, Bernie tap, tap, tapped away in a search for his talented friend's motivation key. Ever since Quinn returned from Caitlin's graduation in Frog Springs, he'd been miserable and depressed. He wasn't quite up to par even during his performances with the band, which was unprecedented. Spending his days looking for a new job, unsuccessfully, made the depression spiral worse. When Bernie had tried to get him to lighten up, Quinn had snapped at him.

"I told you from the start I was going to bring Caitlin up here after graduation. But since I lost my job, I can barely afford to stay here myself, let alone take care of my sister."

"She'll be fine," Bernie'd reasoned. "You said yourself she has a job and a scholarship waiting for her."

"She puts up a front," Quinn had said. Then he refused to talk about his sister anymore.

Quinn knew Bernie wasn't in favor of having Caitlin Turley around the duplex. However, Bernie kept trying to get Quinn to bounce back from his slump. Quinn had the talent and looks that drew the crowds. And Quinn was loyal. He made sure Bernie was part of every deal.

"Hey, I'm doing my part," Bernie said, "but I can't support us both forever."

"Got it, man. Look, I've been out every spare minute. It's not easy in this economy, but I'll find something."

"A bird in the hand, Baby. You won't find nothing like my offer. Easy money."

They eyed each other. Bernie sneered. Quinn looked stubborn, and a bit scornful. He made it a point to never shoot off his mouth about Bernie's lifestyle, but he had to bite his tongue. Bernie lived on a nice stipend that came from his parents each month. He'd spent the past year sleeping until noon and hanging out at clubs the rest of the day.

Bernie broke the eye-hold first and slumped onto the sofa beside Quinn. "Awright, here's the deal. No more money from my folks. My dad gave me an ultimatum. I have to get a job to support myself here or go back to Frog Springs and go to school. Crap! Can you imagine me at junior college, carrying a backpack?"

"Oh, man. Why didn't you tell me?"

"That's the thing. Tucking my tail and hightailing it home isn't an option for me. This set-up with Essie Wild can solve the problem for us both. I mean, it's a no-brainer. She lives next door. Who's going to question a visit between duplex neighbors? You help me by working your normal charm, and I'll do the rest."

"Humph."

"No, I'm serious. Then, when we've got our clientele, you can go find a day job if that's your thing, and I'll be able to keep hanging out at the clubs to find out which bands need subs and when agents will be looking for talent."

"We can read that online."

"Hey, it takes finagling. Haven't I been the one who found out about open mic nights and jams? Didn't I get us the gig with *Novel Invasion* after their guitar player left? Those happened face-to-face, man."

Quinn clenched his jaw. Bernie loved to take credit. True, one night Bernie had found out about the guitar player leaving *Novel Invasion*. But Quinn had accomplished all the follow-through. First, he'd attended two of the local rock band's shows and had decided the members were talented and that he could fit in. Then, he arranged an audition for Bernie and himself. The band members offered Quinn the position of lead guitar and singer, but he hadn't accepted until Bernie was included. After some haggling, instrumental parts were redistributed, Bernie became the new percussionist, and Quinn agreed to play acoustic guitar, sing, fiddle, and play some keyboard.

Novel Invasion had opened with its new format three months ago. One month later, Quinn had lost his day job at a Kansas City Home Décor Station.

Quinn ignored Bernie's bragging. "You know, I only lost my job because I got that promotion and had a schedule change. I was supposed to work the night *Novel Invasion* had its first big opening with us on board. I was so up for the opening that I forgot about the change. Since the recession hit, there are a hundred workers out there looking for jobs. With my experience, though, and workers who will vouch for me, I should find a job soon. I have some savings left, and the band's doing well. I'm sorry, but I won't consider working with you and Essie to sell drugs—not unless I become destitute and have to take care of my sister."

~~~

Unless he became destitute— Bernie would have to make do with that, for now. Quinn was sorry to make even that concession, Bernie could tell. The world of drug dealing, he decided, was a lot like a pyramid scheme. The more people under you, the more valuable you became in the organization and the more perks you earned from the guy at the top. Essie acquired drugs for him, at first just marijuana, later K2, crack cocaine, and even heroin. Bernie used some himself and sold the rest to certain people he met at the bars and clubs, not the guys in his new band, *Novel Invasion*—they were clean—but mostly to hangers-on who had no talent themselves but loved the scene. If Bernie could get Quinn involved, it would increase his importance.

Essie Wild didn't have a middle man. She went straight to the top and received her drugs for performing various services for the top guy, Double M—Bernie supposed that stood for two names beginning with M, but he was smart enough not to ask. Supplying users and convincing sellers were valuable services, and Essie had a sexy, winsome way about her with people, especially if she thought she could get something from them. It was a different area of expertise that made her special to Double M, though. Bernie saw the guy pull into her garage sometimes, only when Essie's husband, the big, cheery grease monkey, Devin Wild, was at work.

From a distance, Double M didn't look like the notorious chief of a Kansas City drug ring with a reputation that rivaled *The Godfather*'s—short, thin, light brown hair, an ordinary-looking face, slacks, and expensive loafers. Only when Bernie happened to accidentally glimpse his face close up through the kitchen window one day when the man put his key into the lock of Essie's door, did he perceive the reason for the reputation. It was the cold look in his hazel eyes and the hard set of his mouth. Bernie ducked away from the window that day before being seen, but he considered himself lucky to be working with Essie and not with her boss, at least not until he had proven himself extremely indispensable.

This Double M character stayed too long each time for the visits to be merely drug handoffs. Bernie wished he could get a piece of that action from Essie, too, but he figured it would be suicidal to compete with the notorious drug lord.

In fact, Bernie didn't want to do anything, even by accident, which forced him to be noticed negatively by Double M. Getting Quinn to help him out would be a little insurance policy. They could pull in more revenue together, making themselves more valuable, and there would be two of them to take the heat in case there was ever a dispute. Bernie couldn't help formulating a plan about how he might conveniently shift the blame to Quinn if sometime Double M noticed a small amount of money missing from their take. He wasn't planning to make it happen, but just in case he had trouble with one of the drops.... Bernie had many good reasons to convince Quinn to work with him.

He had to be sure Quinn knew the drug money should be sent to help Caitlin at home, not to bring her to Kansas City. He'd tell Quinn his sister shouldn't be around the drug scene. That would be one of his ploys as Quinn's situation became more *destitute*.

Chapter 9

End of January—Kansas City, Missouri

"We can't drive this thirty-eight foot Fifth Wheel RV thirteen hundred miles in the middle of winter in two days' time," Arnie said. He craned his neck to peer through the truck's side mirrors as he eased out of the truck stop.

Beth checked the GPS and picked up her phone to check the weather forecast again. "Partly cloudy until we reach Kansas. Then there's only a fifty percent chance of scattered snow showers the rest of the way home."

"Scattered right across our path, no doubt."

"Don't be a pessimist. If we stay the night at that Kickback RV Park in Raton, New Mexico, we'll be half way and can make the rest by tomorrow night. The weather gets too bad, we can just stop at a roadside park. If it takes three days, so be it, but this RV camp, just south of the Colorado border, is open all year. Is that okay for a goal today?"

"We'll try for it," Arnie said with a grim look on his face.

Luckily, the weather didn't hinder them too much. Ice on the roads in New Mexico and some snowflakes across Kansas made driving hazardous for only a couple of hours. Arnie drove with both hands clenched on the wheel through those patches. Beth sometimes took over, but only on dry pavement. Two long days of driving, with stops for fuel and bathroom breaks only, and they spent a short night parked in Kickback RV Park. They didn't unhitch the truck or slide out the slides. They ate cold cereal for breakfast and prepared sandwiches and fruit to eat while they drove.

By the afternoon of the second day, Arnie rolled his head for five minutes at a time to relieve a stiff neck, and Beth forced herself to keep her eyes open and talk to Arnie. But they were compelled to get back home and see for themselves what was happening with Psycho Cat's grisly attic discovery.

Arnie parked on the narrow street in front of their house in Brookside. This neighborhood sat in a comfortable part of mid-town Kansas City, where the century-old, brick and stucco houses were well-maintained, and residents could walk, bicycle, or drive to several stylish shopping areas close by. The residential streets were just wide enough for two cars. It was definitely not a place where people kept their campers in their driveways or on the street, even if enough space had existed. They needed to move their RV first thing the next morning, as soon as they could transfer their clothes, food, and belongings into the house and crawl back into the huge home on wheels to haul it back to its storage area.

"It's freezing in here," Beth yelled as she entered the front door of their dark house.

"Nah, fifty-two degrees isn't freezing. Just warm enough to keep the pipes from freezing. All the gadgets are unplugged, though. It'll take a while to get everything going."

The thought of de-winterizing the house and re-winterizing the RV, along with the other difficulties they were facing, caused Beth to puff out a long dejected sigh. One thing at a time, she told herself as she switched on lights and looked around.

"I'll run upstairs to turn up the heat if you'll turn on the water line in the basement," she said when Arnie brought in the cooler and picnic supplies. "We might as well get comfortable, because we have a long day ahead of us tomorrow. As soon as we can store the RV away we have to call Detective Rinquire, answer more questions, I'm sure, and give him copies of all the rental records for the duplex."

"I wonder how the kids are doing. They didn't say what hotel they found, did they?"

"I don't remember them saying the name. But Clay sounded as if Janae isn't going to be anxious to go back to that duplex."

Beth thought about poor Psycho Cat, all alone at the duplex for the past couple of days. Another worry. She envisioned a bedraggled orange kitty, a haunted look in his green eyes, huddled in a corner of the basement, while a gruff group of CSI investigators used fact-finding instruments. (Those tools she could not visualize exactly, but they were surely high tech and emitted loud beeps and screeches, which would be terribly scary for a cat.) Beth wondered how many people had been tromping in and out of Clay and Janae's home and how much longer it would take them to thoroughly search the residence so those kids could return.

~~~

The next morning, they unpacked the fifth wheel, dumped all of their gear in a corner of the living room, and were in the truck headed south toward their RV storage space before eight o'clock. Beth felt bad about appropriating half the street with the big rig. She would much rather have taken an early morning walk, lazed through a hot breakfast with the daily paper to read, and eased into unloading the RV.

Since Arnie was driving, Beth took the opportunity to call Detective Rinquire. Talking to him wasn't at the top of her list of preferred activities, but she had promised they'd call as soon as they got to town. Rather than the message machine she expected, Carl Rinquire answered the phone.

In a voice as calm as she could muster, she said. "Detective Rinquire, this is Beth Stockwell. My husband and I are home from Arizona and can meet with you any time today after we take our camper to its storage space."

The detective was interrupted twice while they made an appointment to meet at the duplex at eleven o'clock. That would give Beth time to go home and copy the rental records. He wanted all the information she had about the tenants of Side A of 829 Sycamore for as long as they had owned it—twenty-eight years' worth of records.

"About how many tenants have lived there in that time?" the detective asked.

"I can't remember exactly. Quite a few. I'll bring all the folders with me to the duplex."

Pulling a fifth wheel through rush hour traffic on a major street on Wednesday morning turned out to be about as much fun as running twenty-eight years' worth of rental records through the copy machine. But with a minimum number of expletives, they finished everything and arrived at the duplex at 10:35. Beth's mouth fell open. There were two big equipment vans parked out front, one white and one black, both with Jackson County Sheriff's Department emblems on the sides.

"Geez, Arnie," she said, it looks as if it won't be a slam dunk to get this over with and have everything back to normal."

Arnie shrugged. "We're a little early. Let's go in and see what we can find out."

When Beth had copied the paperwork, she'd discovered how long she'd owned and managed the building. This was the first time she had felt her heart race while walking up to the front door. All of the blinds were raised. Arnie tried the door but found it locked. He rang the bell while Beth stood to the side and peeked through the window. A tall, nice-looking man, about her age, a little gray around the edges, and frowning slightly beneath his horn-rimmed glasses as if he'd seen enough gawkers, came to the door and opened it half way. He wore what looked like army pants tucked inside leather boots and a long-sleeved, light-blue uniform shirt with an official-looking insignia above the pocket. Inside, she saw a young woman, dressed in similar apparel, using a light of some kind, like a huge flashlight on a flexible tube connected to a black box sitting on the floor, to examine every square inch of the brick fireplace. Their greeter stepped through the door onto the small porch outside, causing them to back down onto the top step.

"Excuse me," he said, "this is a crime scene, and I can't allow visitors inside. I'm Mark Overos, the Crime Scene Supervisor. How can I help you?"

"I'm Arnold Stockwell, and this is my wife...."

"I'm Elizabeth Stockwell. We're the owners of the property, and I've operated this rental for twenty-eight years. We're meeting Detective Carl Rinquire here at eleven o'clock. Wow. The investigation is taking a long time. Hasn't the CSI been here since Saturday?"

"Good to meet you both." Mark Overos took off his latex glove to shake hands. "Angela Topping, one of our Crime Scene Investigators, is working inside." When he nodded toward her, she waved then returned to her job. "To answer your question, yes, I agree it takes a while, but we have to be thorough. We've been here off and on since Saturday evening scouring first the attic and second story, now the first floor and basement, for evidence. We check the floors, walls, furniture, and even ceilings."

"What kind of evidence would be here after so many years?" Arnie asked.

Mr. Overos gave Arnie a piercing look. "How many years has the body been here, Mr. Stockwell?"

Beth realized Arnie must have been thinking the skeleton was as old as the roof, but her eyes opened wide when the CSI supervisor asked him that question in such a blunt manner. In no way was she prepared for how it felt for either one of them to be treated as suspects. Before she could get her mouth working and attempt an explanation of her husband's thinking, Arnie piped up. He knew how to subdue his indignation and answer in a businesslike manner.

"I don't know exactly. I mean, it wouldn't be a skeleton unless it was old, would it? I thought the CSI could determine how old a body is and who the body belongs to with dental records."

"A crime scene is like a big puzzle. We're looking for blood, hairs, fabric, and even latent prints on the premises. The trunk with the body is now at the crime lab being examined. We're attempting to come up with an approximate age and the identity of the body. Dental records are another thing... But any information you have will help. Will we find your and your wife's prints and hairs in this duplex?"

"Of course you will," Beth said. "Mine are here, for sure. Probably you can find some of my blood here, too, because I'm notorious for cutting myself with sharp tools while scraping paint or knocking out old tile or removing pieces of glass from a broken window."

"Exactly!" Overos said. "We'll find samples from you, your husband, your son and daughter-in-law, and any of the people who have lived here since the duplex was built. Some of it has been covered up by all the painting and renovating, but our equipment can help us locate more than you think. Solving the puzzle means sifting through all these pieces, eliminating the misleading ones, and finding the pieces that fit.

"So anything you can tell us, even observations or hunches, will help eliminate your samples from the mix and will help narrow the search." He looked at Arnie. "How many years are you assuming the body must have been here?"

Arnie and Beth looked at each other. Then Arnie shook his head with a smudge of a frown and said, "I'm not sure. It's just the picture I have in my mind of a skeleton in that chest. At first, after hearing about Clay's discovery, we imagined the skeleton being here before we bought the place, since we couldn't figure out how it could get here without us finding out. Then I remembered opening that trunk when I went into the attic with the home inspector before buying. The chest was empty and close to the attic entrance. I guess, to me, the idea of a skeleton found inside a sea chest is like a pirate story, something from the past."

"Well, if you think of anything at all that could give us a clue as to when this happened and who to suspect, a character trait of one of your tenants, an unusual incident, a tenant with enemies, or a smell that couldn't be explained, please tell Detective Rinquire or me. It could help us solve our puzzle. I'm sorry I can't let you wait inside, but Carl Rinquire should be here any minute."

As soon as Arnie and Beth were in the car, she confronted him, "Why didn't you tell him about our 'dead squirrels in the attic' theory? That could have been when the body was put in there."

"*Could* have been," Arnie said. "And we *could* cause some innocent people to be suspects. I need to find out more about dead bodies and how long it takes for them to decompose. There were people living in that duplex, at least in Side A, when you smelled the dead animal smell in Side B. I don't think they would have been able to stand the stink if it was a dead person."

"Arnie, Mr. Overos said to tell him about any unusual happenstance. I've got to go back and tell him about the dead animal smell. If the tenants who lived in A at that time are innocent, they will be able to explain what they did about the smell."

Beth felt she needed Arnie's approval in order to do this. She didn't want this negative ordeal to cause a rift. He ruminated over it a bit, but he finally gave his okay. Beth checked her records before she went back to the duplex door. The CSI Supervisor looked surprised but was cordial when he answered the door again.

"Mr. Overos," Beth said.

"Please call me Mark," he said.

"Mark, Arnie and I remembered something unusual. We don't want to cause an innocent person or people to be suspects, but we thought this might be important."

"Please continue, Mrs. Stockwell."

"Beth."

Mark Overos smiled, and Beth told him about the time she was renovating Side B, thought she smelled dead squirrels in the attic, had a new roof put on, and never smelled the stench again. Mark had taken a pen and notebook out and wrote while Beth talked.

"All this happened seven years ago. According to my records, the tenants in this side of the duplex were Devon and Essie Wild. Bernard Landoff and Quinlin Turley moved out of Side B before I started the renovation—before the roof was replaced. The Wilds stayed in Side A for almost another year after the new roof."

"Did you talk to any of them about the dead animal smell?"

"I didn't talk to the two young men who had already moved. They hadn't mentioned it before they left, and I figured the animal died in the attic after that. I vaguely remember asking Devon Wild about it, but I don't remember what he said. I guess I wasn't too concerned because, by then, the smell had dissipated."

Chapter 10

July, Seven Years Earlier—Frog Springs, Arkansas

Rob Turley grabbed the can of beer from Caitlin's hand with a vacant, unfocused look on his haggard face and zigzagged toward the front door. The pop top landed on the dingy carpet, not even close to the wastebasket toward which he flung it. Rob dug around in his pants pocket for his car keys. "Gonna get a big commission for the deal I make tonight, Martha. You'll be proud of me," he slurred over his shoulder. "Don't wait up. I'll be celebratin' after."

Caitlin had observed, more and more lately, her dad getting loaded even before he went off to the bar. But this was the first time he'd called her by her dead mother's name. Caitlin, despite her usual inaction for fear of the consequences of contradicting him, reacted on impulse to the shock of having him call her Martha.

"Dad!" she shouted after him as her father wobbled like an unsure bowling pin down the sidewalk, "You shouldn't be driving." When he looked around with a confused look on his face, she said in a quieter manner, "You're a little unsteady on your feet. Why don't you come back inside and rest a little? I can drive you to your meeting on my way to work."

By this time, Caitlin had reached her dad, ready to give him a guiding hand back to the house, expecting a vehement argument, but driven on by her dread of what would happen on the road if he drove anywhere. Her promise to her mother that she'd look after her father stared her in the face. It was as much a guiding force in her life as if she were three years old and her mother was telling her to play nice with the kids on the playground, especially those little slow ones who might get hurt if she wasn't careful.

The change in Rob's attitude was immediate, and his response vicious. "Who do you think you are, telling me what to do?" Rob said, as, all of a sudden steady on his feet, glassy eyes turned to stone, he grabbed Caitlin's arm in a steely grip. "You plannin' to go to that bar and sell your body, like those other sluts down there? I'm the man of this here house, ya hear me? I'm goin' there to do business, and you're goin' to stay here and keep house. That's what a woman is supposed to do."

His beer splashed out and onto his shirt when he shook Caitlin. The wet shirt seemed to infuriate him beyond measure. He backed away as if she had thrown acid on him. "Now see what you did? Go get me another beer. A clean shirt, too."

Caitlin stood there for a moment, stunned, feeling the ringing in her ears caused by the brutal shaking she had just received, and rubbing her bruised arm. She saw her father coming toward her and started to take a step backward. "Now!" he growled, and with all his 185 pounds behind him, he gave her a powerful shove in the middle of her chest with his open palm, sending her sprawling backward onto her bottom in the middle of the sidewalk. In one fluid motion, Rob raised his right arm and propelled the almost full can of beer with all his might, his daughter the target, as if finishing her off might eradicate his feelings of pain and guilt. He darted to his old green sedan, which was parked in the cracked and weedy asphalt driveway, backed so far out that he spun into the curved driveway on the other side of the street, plowed across that yard to the road, and screeched around the bend, without looking back.

When Caitlin came to, Mrs. White, the seventy-five-year-old lady from across the street, whose hair matched the color of her name, was holding a wet towel to the side of her young neighbor's throbbing head. The smell and taste of beer and blood assaulted Caitlin's senses as she cautiously rose to her elbows. She pushed herself to a sitting position while fighting a nauseous feeling caused by the brutal pain in her head. Her immediate and overpowering emotional reaction was embarrassment.

"Thank you, Mrs. White. I—I guess I fell down and hit my head." Even as she said it, it sounded silly to her. How did a fall explain the beer can she spied on the grass a few feet away and the beer that soaked her hair and shirt?

"You fell, alright, dear," said Mrs. White, with a wry look. "You're just lucky the rock that bounced off your head is made of aluminum."

~~~

The plucky little lady had not witnessed the actual attack. She had looked out her front screen door when she heard Rob's tires rocket into her driveway, back out, and squeal away down the street. Seeing her young neighbor bleeding on the sidewalk, she quickly soaked a towel in cold water and ran over to help. Calling 911 was somewhat foreign to Mrs. White's rural roots, but now, looking at the mass of blood and hair on Caitlin's scalp, she thought of getting medical help and looked to see if anyone else was around to make the call while she continued to monitor the hurt girl.

The Turley's ranch style house stood in a desirable area on the outskirts of Frog Springs, where the private and secluded lots consisted of an acre or more and were separated by shrubs and trees. The houses were set back from a curvy road running up and down hills. When Caitlin and Quinlin were young and their mother worked at the Community College in town, the family would often have backyard cook-outs and parties.

Since Martha's death, the back yard and the driveway had gone to weeds, the house needed painting, and Rob wouldn't spend money on water and fertilizer to care for the old flower beds. Mr. and Mrs. White, living directly across the road, were the only neighbors who could see the shabby condition of the Turley residence on a regular basis, but they hadn't complained.

~~~

"Caitlin, dear," Mrs. White said, looking around. "Are you able to hold this towel to your head while I go in and call for help?"

"No, I mean, you've been help enough, Mrs. White. I'm okay, truly. You don't need to call anyone else," Caitlin took the towel from her neighbor and slowly got to her feet. Her head hurt like crazy, but it felt like a surface wound. "This looks worse than it feels. I'll go wash it off and it'll be fine." Caitlin forced a smile. "Please don't worry any more about me. I'll wash your towel out and bring it back tomorrow."

Her neighbor wasn't easily talked into leaving. Caitlin ended up letting Mrs. White walk her inside, get her a drink of water, put some antiseptic on her wound, examine her pupils to see if they were dilated, and help her remove her bloody shirt and put on a clean one. Finally, after promising she would call immediately if she felt dizzy or needed any kind of help, Caitlin stood in the doorway faking a smile while she watched Mrs. White cross the road at a snail's pace and make her way up the rise to her house.

Half way up, the little lady turned around and shouted, "Please call me, Caitlin, if you need help, help for *any* reason. Mr. White and I will be here for you!"

Caitlin raised her hand and strained to sound upbeat as she shouted back, "Thank you so much for your help today, Mrs. White. I'll call if I need you."

She waited until her neighbor disappeared into her house before she sagged to the floor of the living room. No tears came. Instead, Caitlin's mind started racing. In every e-mail he sent, Quinn stressed his willingness to have her live in Kansas City with him. She might have to work at a low-end job for a time, he warned, until his band started making good money and she could go to school. If Dad became impossible to live with, if he made it unbearable for her to fulfill her promise to her mother to take care of him, they could still honor their promise to take care of each other.

No matter how many times, in her e-mail replies, Caitlin had assured Quinn that she was doing fine, Quinn remained skeptical. He knew his father's abusive nature too well. Until now, however, neither had feared that Caitlin's physical well-being might be threatened.

From the time Caitlin was able to earn money from babysitting, she had always saved part of her earnings. She kept her money in a shoe box under her bed until she was fourteen, when her ailing mother helped her and her brother obtain savings accounts of their own. Their father's name was not on the accounts, and Caitlin had regularly added to her savings during her years of working after school, on weekends, and summers while in high school. Over the years, the money had grown to several thousand dollars, interest adding to the amount until rates dropped to near zero percent when the recession hit. At least it would help her get started.

First, she needed to withdraw her money in some form she could carry with her. The people at the bank would know, and they stayed open until five o'clock. Next, make the difficult, last minute call to Taco Bell to say she they needed to find someone to fill in for her. There was time. Caitlin grabbed her purse and keys to the old jalopy she drove, tied a clean strip of cotton cloth around her injured head, covered it with a ball cap, and headed to town.

No panic, no regrets, no second thoughts. This wasn't the first time Caitlin had rehearsed this departure in her mind. She had the route to Kansas City memorized. A printed map and directions from Frog Springs to Quinn's address on Sycamore Street in Kansas City had been hidden in the back of her closet for a year. The preparation list rolled through her mind as easily as the car's tires rolled into the tiny burg—withdraw her money, fill up with gasoline, drop in to the library and send an e-mail to Quinn to let him know she'd be coming, pack the trunk and back seat of the old car with clothing and a few personal items, grab a sandwich to eat on the way, leave a note for Dad… No, she'd call or write to him later, after she was safely with Quinn and had time to think about what to say. Her father probably wouldn't even realize she was missing until tomorrow sometime, maybe not even then. And he most likely would never remember what he did this afternoon.

Chapter 11

End of January—Kansas City, Missouri

While Beth watched CSI Supervisor Mark Overos write down the information she gave him about what had happened seven years ago, a whiskered orange head appeared. Beth saw her kitty rear up on his hind legs against the door and peer through the screen. It was just like that cat to want to be in the middle of the action.

"Psycho Cat, I've missed you!" Beth said, bending toward the screen with a guilty twinge. With everything else to think about she had forgotten to ask about the cat.

She noticed Psycho Cat was not huddled in a corner of the basement as she had assumed and seemed quite comfortable with the CSI folks. These investigators defied her imaginings of tough, grim, Dracula's Monster-type scientists. They seemed nice. Psycho Cat meowed a greeting, and Beth looked at Mark Overos for permission to open the door and pick up the furry fellow. The cat put one paw on each of her shoulders, rubbed his head against her chin, and purred loudly. Mark smiled and stroked the kitty's back.

"The cat seems to know you well."

"This is my cat. Or maybe I'm his person. My son and his wife have been cat-sitting while we've been traveling, but now I can take him home. Has he given you trouble while you've been working here? He has the nickname Psycho Cat for good reason."

"I don't think he quite trusted the agents who were working upstairs yesterday, and I'm not sure if he's made friends with

Angela today. But he's been following me all over the house like a little dog. I think Psycho Cat may be a harsh moniker for this guy."

When Mark stuck out a finger to gently scratch the kitty's head, Psycho Cat turned abruptly from Beth's shoulder and nipped at the quickly retracted hand. Then the cat meowed loudly and pulled himself farther up onto her shoulder with his back toward the investigator.

"Naughty boy," Beth said, without much conviction, and held her cat tighter.

"Well," Mark said with a grin, "maybe Psycho Cat is an appropriate name, after all." He handed Beth his card and told her to be certain to call him or Detective Rinquire if she thought of anything else that might help with the case.

With an apology and a quick decision to wait until later to go back for the cat's food, bowls, and litter box, Beth retreated to the car, lowered Psycho Cat to her lap, and gave him a gentle massage while she told Arnie how appreciative the Crime Scene Supervisor seemed to be for the information about the dead animal smell. Arnie gave the cat's head an absent-minded rub and nodded toward the closed duplex door.

"You seem a bit taken by this scientist guy," he said.

Beth gave Arnie a sharp look. He didn't usually display jealousy, and she hadn't given him any reason. Maybe she did think Mark Overos was rather tall, and, uh, handsome, and strikingly, intelligently, scientist-in-charge looking. That didn't mean she was taken by him. If she was a little flushed, it was because she was happy to have Psycho Cat give her such an affectionate welcome home.

"It's not that," she said. "I'm just inclined to believe him when he says they need all of the information we can give them, all our observations and hunches included. He's in law enforcement, after all, and is trying to help solve this case. I think we need to cooperate fully."

Hum, that sounded a little pompous. Arnie had good reason to be skeptical. Beth wasn't known for following good advice about keeping her nose out of solving enigmas, especially when they involved her family and property. She opened her mouth to tell Arnie she could never be *taken* by anyone but him, but a plain dark Ford pulled in behind them, and they both turned around to see Detective Carl Rinquire behind the wheel. The sight of the detective made Beth's stomach sink a little. What would he think of another of her rental properties showing up in a homicide case? Well, he couldn't blame her or her properties, could he? She was less happy to see him than he was to see her, she was sure.

Gently pealing the cat off her shoulder, Beth plopped him onto the back seat. Then Arnie and she stepped out onto the sidewalk to meet the detective, who greeted them in his serious, businesslike manner, with no indication Beth's properties or relatives had given him a tad bit of trouble in the past. Her queasiness subsided, and she handed over the packet of rental records for the duplex.

"Thank you, Mrs. Stockwell," Detective Rinquire said. "If you'll come inside with me, we can be more comfortable while we talk. I like to discuss cases at the scene. It helps to jog memories."

He stepped ahead of Beth and Arnie, found Mark in the basement, informed him and agent Angela Topping that he'd be conducting an interrogation in the front room, and then suggested they all sit while they talked.

"Of course," Arnie said. He and Beth sat on Clay and Janae's sofa, and the stout detective pulled a straight-backed chair into a position in front of them.

"Now, what do you know about this duplex and how that body got into the attic?"

Beth took a deep breath and repeated the information she gave the CSI supervisor about her concerns with dead animal smells seven years ago and about Devon and Essie Wild, the young couple who lived there at the time. Arnie seemed more eager to share his thoughts now Detective Rinquire was asking the questions—he didn't seem to appreciate the way Mr. Overos had questioned his innocence. He told Rinquire about the old cars, auto parts, and the van Devon Wild had kept in the driveway and garage. Beth remembered Arnie's reluctance to throw suspicion on people, but she wanted to tell everything that might be helpful.

"I kind of wondered if the Wilds, the young people who lived here at that time, weren't into drugs or something," she said. "They were usually late with their rent. Sometimes when I was here working on the lawn or another duplex, I'd see spacy-looking people show up to visit this duplex, and the place was messy when they finally moved out. Yellowed ceilings, some broken fixtures— I don't know if those things point to drug use. I mean, cigarette smoking yellows ceilings. But Mark Overos told us even hunches could be important."

She glanced at Arnie.

"We're not making judgments—just telling you what we noticed." Arnie gave Beth a sideways look she interpreted as—you need to keep your nose out of this and let the detective come to his own conclusions.

"Our investigators have been questioning people in the neighborhood," Detective Rinquire said, "but so far no one has given us anything helpful.

Mark Overos walked into the room. Beth turned to him.

"Has the CSI forensics lab been able to determine the age of the body yet?" she asked. "Wouldn't that information tell you exactly which tenants to question?"

"Bodies decompose at different rates and in different manners depending on environmental factors," Overos said. "That's one reason your anecdotal testimony is important. Do you remember having an unexplained leak in the master bedroom ceiling that had to be painted over with a stain killer?"

"Well, we have plumbing leaks sometimes. That kind of stain happens so often, and I repainted this entire duplex, top to bottom, after the Wilds moved out. I don't remember. Oh." She paused with a distressed look. "Are you talking about blood and stuff from the dead body leaking through the ceiling?"

"We need your knowledge of the conditions here during the time the body may have been putrefying," Mark said. "Have you heard of quick lime?"

"I've heard of lime."

"Is quick lime the substance people used in mass graves after plagues or genocides?" Arnie asked. "It makes bodies decay faster, I think, and doesn't it reduce the stench?"

"Interesting you know about quick lime," Mark Overos said.

"I've just read about it."

"He's a history buff," Beth hurried to say.

One side of Mark's mouth turned up as if he was half amused, either by Arnie's response or by Beth's. Beth guessed these questions and insinuations were merely part of an agent's repertoire. Arnie didn't look too happy about the new veiled accusation, though.

After a few more questions and a look through the rental records with her, Detective Rinquire tucked her copied papers under his arm and escorted Beth and Arnie to the door. He reminded Beth to call or e-mail with the names and contact information for the tenants in the adjoining duplex and the two other rental properties they owned in the neighborhood for the past several years.

At home, while Beth gathered the rental records for Side B of Clay and Janae's duplex building, Arnie went straight to the computer to look up quick lime. He summarized for Beth as he read about it.

"This rocky material, or true lime, was used in mass graves. When slaked, or combined with liquid, it became a powder. Therefore, it helped reduce the body liquids and made the bodies decompose more quickly. The skin shrank and mummified, or became like leather.

Reduction of the fluids helped cut down on the bloating and gases, also, thus lessening the smell.

"That could explain why it didn't smell as bad as a rotting corpse and went away so fast. And listen to this.

The hot, dry conditions in an attic and the lack of soil and foliage for insects to complete a life cycle are other conditions conducive to the probability of mummification.

"Remember, Clay said it had skin that looked like leather."

"Oh, wonderful," Beth said as she located the final records for Side B of the duplex and tamped the papers into an even stack on the desk, "now we know why the body looks mummified. Clay understood what he was seeing."

Chapter 12

July, Seven Years Earlier—Kansas City, Missouri

Filtering through oak leaves, screen, and window pane, beams of sunlight seeped into the room, creating warm splotches on Caitlin's sleeping figure and on the crumpled sheets surrounding her. She awoke feeling sluggish, not wanting to open her eyes and face this day far away from the only life she'd ever known. Dried blood made her hair stiff on one side of her face. Over the edge of the mattress on which she lay, Caitlin stretched a hand, palm down, and felt a hardwood floor. She took a deep breath, which ended in a sigh, and detected the distinct odor of dirty socks. Her brother's room, her brother's dirty socks, no doubt.

Their mother had never expected Quinn to help with the laundry. Caitlin spent several minutes imagining her brother taking his clothes to a laundromat, figuring out how to use laundry detergent, and dumping clean clothes from the drier into a bag without folding them. Or, maybe this duplex included a washer and drier. She'd soon find out.

It took her another minute or so to turn over and open her green eyes. Did the laziness in her limbs and the queasiness in her stomach reflect her uncertainty about the future? She turned her face toward the sunny window. Maybe she was nervous about making a new and exciting start.

Still garbed in the rumpled and soiled shorts and T-shirt she wore yesterday, Caitlin pushed herself to a sitting position, her head wound throbbing with a dull thump. She looked around.

Besides the small suitcase she brought in last night, she saw dirty clothes wadded into three paper grocery sacks near a closet door, musical instrument cases, a music stand with sheet music, a comb on a cardboard box that served as a table, and the double mattress with its frayed bedding. Quinn had insisted his sister sleep in his bedroom last night, and she had resisted, insisting she could sleep on the sofa. But she had been comfortable here. The room had the aura of her brother—quiet and filled with evidence of Quinn's musical aspirations.

"Ten o'clock," Caitlin whispered as she looked at her watch. Silence filled the house. She opened the bedroom door and peeked out before padding quietly to the bathroom in her bare feet. In the upstairs hallway, she noticed the door to the larger master bedroom was closed. Bernie got the big bedroom from the start, Quinn had informed her, because he had the more certain income from his parents.

Caitlin tiptoed halfway down the staircase to peek into the living room. Quinn was asleep on the sofa, dressed in the clothes he wore when she arrived. She knew she'd looked pitiful then, her hair still matted with blood, her eyes swollen from crying, her sweaty clothes clinging to her skinny body because her old car didn't have air conditioning. Quinn had expected her because, besides her e-mail, she'd also called and left a message while he was at a performance, but she doubted he expected to see her looking as bedraggled as she did.

Quinn had sat on the sofa with his arm around her for an hour after she arrived, listening to her story and reassuring her. It was after 3:00 in the morning before he'd talked her into taking his room. She'd fallen asleep immediately.

During her drive, Caitlin had rehearsed what she planned to tell Quinn about her reason for choosing to come to Kansas City a few weeks before she should have been starting community college. She'd known she looked awful, and it'd hurt too much to think about shampooing her hair before she left, but she could explain the wound as resulting from a bumping into a sign post in the dark at a rest stop on the trip. She concocted another story to explain changing her mind about school and wanting to experience the big city, nothing in there to elicit pity. But the story fell apart almost immediately as she fell into the safety of her big brother's empathetic understanding. She told him exactly what happened.

This morning, standing on the steps watching Quinn sleep, a sneaky, recurring shadow of a doubt crept into Caitlin's mind—maybe her loyal brother was in no position to welcome her here. She'd been so self-absorbed last night. She'd told Quinn all about her own plight, but she hadn't questioned him about his circumstances.

His only hint at a possible problem was a statement he made when she went on about being an imposition. He said he'd make it work, even if he had to…an unfinished thought that only now started to worry her. Even if he had to—to what? It would be the first thing she'd ask him when he woke up.

Caitlin wondered what time Quinn needed to get up for work. She worried because he didn't have an alarm clock downstairs and she'd kept him up so late he wouldn't wake up in time. "No," she said under her breath, "he's responsible. He would have thought of that." She tiptoed back upstairs to take a shower and change into the clean outfit she'd remembered to put into her overnight bag. The rest of her stuff was still outside in the car.

It's amazing what clean hair, teeth, and body can do for one's outlook. The partly formed scab on Caitlin's head wound was barely noticeable after her clean hair was pulled over it into a pony tail, and with fresh shorts, shirt, and sneakers she felt almost presentable again. She found Quinn in the kitchen drinking instant coffee and was so glad to see him that she pushed her questions about his money issues to the back of her head.

"Oh, I hope I didn't wake you," she said.

"Nope. It's almost eleven o'clock. Time to be up and about. You look much better this morning. Did you sleep all right? Do you want some coffee, Miss Up-and-At-'em?"

"I slept like a log, and yes, I'll have a cup of coffee, since you probably don't have a tea bag."

"Right you are, but I do have toast and jelly, believe it or not. I'm going to clean up while you help yourself—only one bathroom, you know—and when I come back down, we'll bring your things in."

Quinn reappeared a short time later, while Caitlin was washing up their few dishes, and told her his plan to buy a mattress at a thrift store, build a base for it out of some wood he'd seen in the garage, and fix up a space in the basement for his bedroom. "It's dry," he explained, "and there's even a sink in the space designated for laundry. We don't have a washer or dryer. We only use the basement to practice with the band sometimes and to store a few things. I can hang some rope and build some shelves for my clothes. It'll be perfect."

Despite all her planning, Caitlin had never thought through the problem of sleeping arrangements. "Sounds perfect," she said, "for a guest. I'll take the basement for my bedroom, and you won't have to change rooms."

Her determination lasted until she flipped on the basement lights, consisting of two bare bulbs attached to the unfinished floor-joist ceiling. She paused for several minutes at the bottom of the chipped, open wood steps to peer at the space—a stained bare concrete floor featuring a rusty drain near the furnace and water heater, cracked concrete walls with two small dirty windows near the top, and an old-fashioned, self-standing metal sink between the washer and dryer hook-ups. She turned to look up at Quinn, two steps above her and looking at it himself in a speculative way, as if seeing it from his sister's point of view.

"I can fix it up," Caitlin said. "It'll be fun designing my own room from scratch."

"You can help clean it up for me. I don't want my little sister sleeping in the basement. Besides, there are spiders down here."

They argued about it as they returned to the first floor, but the mention of spiders made Caitlin's argument much less vehement. All talk stopped when they spied Bernie Landoff lounging on the sofa, wearing only briefs, his tongue between his teeth, brandishing the television remote like an intense symphonic orchestra conductor wielding his baton. It was Caitlin's instinct to back up and look away from her brother's half naked roommate, but Bernie glanced at her with an insolent grin.

"Well, well, Kate, my girl, Quinn didn't tell me you were coming," he said. "A nice short visit before school starts, right?"

The way he emphasized "short" made Caitlin's stomach lurch. Bernie's attitude was another roadblock she had considered, but only briefly, relying on Quinn's reassurances that she would be welcome in Kansas City. Now she had no reply for her brother's scruffy friend's question. She remained mute and glanced at Quinn.

"Don't mind him, Katie. Bernie and I have talked about this many times." He turned to his roommate. "I didn't have a chance to tell you about Caitlin's call last night during our performance. She's staying. We were just talking about how we can transform the basement into a bedroom for me so she can use my room."

Bernie set his lips in a hard straight line, and his eyes took on a calculating squint. "Is she going to pay her share of the rent and utilities and yours too?"

Quinn put his hand on his sister's thin shoulder when she started to say something. He said, "If I help you with that job you told me about, we shouldn't have a problem."

Bernie nodded with a smirk on his face and turned his attention back to flicking the TV remote from channel to channel. Quinn guided Caitlin past him and out the front door toward her car before she could ask all the questions she wanted to ask. On the way, Caitlin rounded on him.

"Quinn, I can help pay utilities and rent with the money I brought from home. It won't last long, but I intend to hunt for a job, too. What did Bernie mean about me paying your share, too? And…what job did Bernie tell you about? I thought you already had a job. With your band, you can't take on a third job. I don't want to be that kind of burden."

"It won't be a third job," Quinn told her. "I didn't want to worry you, but I lost my hardware job a few weeks ago. The retail business schedule and playing with the band weren't compatible. I've had a little trouble making ends meet since then. It's okay. I can do work with Bernie at the clubs until I find something else."

Caitlin would've asked what kind of work Quinn and Bernie would be doing at the clubs. Would they be doing janitorial work? Kitchen work? Clean-up work? It would be up to the proprietor to hire those kinds of workers, not Bernie. Caitlin gathered a pile of her clothes on hangers from the back seat of her car and pondered how to ask her questions without sounding suspicious of Bernie. She knew Quinn was sensitive about her disapproval of his roommate. A deep, smooth woman's voice interrupted her thoughts before she could voice them.

"Quinn, sugar, how could you not tell me you were having a little girlfriend move in with you? You're breaking my heart."

It sounded like a tease, but there was a hint of something more, maybe accusation, as if the speaker was in charge here and entitled to know everything. Caitlin stood up with her bundle to see approaching, from the adjoining side of the duplex, a curvaceous blond, dressed in the tightest mini-dress she'd seen outside of the bars where she'd had to go find her dad on occasion. The gal sported tattoos on shoulders and ankles, piercings in various places, and a lit cigarette between two fingers. She swayed her hips down the sidewalk toward them. Her young made-up face framed by the loose bleached-blond hair attracted attention, in a flashy way, and Caitlin found herself staring.

"Caitlin," Quinn said in a cold voice, "this is my neighbor Essie Wild. Essie, Caitlin is my sister. She just arrived from Arkansas."

"Your sister?" Essie sounded not just surprised, but almost shocked. Then she turned to Caitlin with a big red smile. "Well, a pretty little southern belle, you are, Caitlin. Welcome to the neighborhood. We'll have to get to know each other better, and I can show you around. I know some guys who'd love to meet you." She looked Caitlin up and down and raised her eyebrows.

"Oh, uh, thanks, I-I need to get settled first." Caitlin felt her face turn red. "It's nice to meet you."

"Later," Essie said and dropped into a VW bug convertible.

Caitlin stood watching as she drove away, and Quinn, in a flat tone, described Essie as the neighborhood flirt. He advised Caitlin to ignore her suggestive remarks and to stay away from her as much as possible. If she needed to be in contact with anyone next door, he explained, Essie's husband, Devon, was a good guy, ready to help anyone any time. The big guy worked long hours at a small, independently owned auto repair shop. When he was home, he spent his time working on old cars in the duplex garage or driveway, listening to music, and drinking a can of beer. He'd gladly stop what he was doing, though, to answer a question or give someone a helping hand.

In a serious tone, which she found disconcerting, Quinn told Caitlin, "Ask Devon, not Essie."

She saw Essie again a couple of hours later. Caitlin was dumping a bucket of dirty water off the back porch, water she'd used to clean the basement walls and ceiling by tying a rag to a broom, dipping it in the soapy water, and scrubbing. Essie had parked her car in front of Caitlin's by the curb out front and then walked down the driveway to the back of the house to meet a man who drove in and parked his BMW in front of the Wild's garage door. Caitlin self-consciously rinsed her bucket in water from the spigot off the side of the porch and prepared to go inside to refill it with hot soapy water. Essie rounded the side of the house and saw her. She waved her fingers, with the long red tips, in Caitlin's direction.

"Caitlin, honey, have those boys got you cleaning house for them already?" Essie asked. "There are more enjoyable things you could be doing, you know. I want to introduce you to my friend, Double M. I told him about you." She crossed her arms and looked at Double M with a shrewd look, letting him take charge.

Double M's eyes appraised the seventeen-year-old girl as if she was a piece of furniture he might consider purchasing or a nice dinner that had just been served to him. He nodded and greeted her in a smooth, radio-announcer voice. Caitlin was at once impressed and repulsed by this well-dressed, self-confident, yet somehow disconcerting man. She mumbled, "Nice to meet you," excused herself, and scampered back into the house.

Chapter 13

End of January—Kansas City, Missouri

"Listen, Mom, I'm sorry. Janae just can't bring herself to come back here to live. She keeps thinking about what happened to the grisly mummy in the trunk, and she'll have nightmares every night if we stay here." Clay stood by the kitchen counter at the duplex.

"I understand Janae's squeamishness, but she should reconsider for the sake of your finances. After all, the trunk is gone. This place comes rent free, close to the university, has tons more space than a loft, and includes a garage and a laundry room."

"We discussed all that, but Janae found a loft near the Crossroads Arts District. You know that's where artists have established galleries, showings, and classes. She wants to be in the middle of that scene."

"Okay. I don't blame her. Sometimes the financial considerations aren't the most important."

"Don't worry. I'll still maintain the rental properties when you're out of town, or all of the time, if you'd like," Clay promised, "and you can pocket the rent from this duplex rather than letting us stay free."

"Thanks, Clay. We'd rather pay you than someone else to help with the yard work and to do handy man repairs, but are you sure you can afford to pay rent on a loft while you're still in school?"

"Janae expects another raise soon, and she's working on some artwork she hopes to sell. She's excited to be moving to the area where she can be inspired and supported by other artists, and there's a space with a whole wall of windows in the loft, which she can use as a studio. Also, I saw an opening for part-time work in the lab at school, and I still have one semester left on my GI Bill. We'll do fine."

The day after Arnie and Beth met Detective Rinquire at the duplex, Clay had informed Beth, the CSI team finished its examination of the premises, and the detective had called to tell Clay and Janae they could have access to their home again. Since there were only a few days left in January, they'd asked if they could stay at Beth and Arnie's house until they moved into the loft the first day of February.

Clay had time between classes, and Beth met him at the duplex to help pack dishes and other kitchen supplies into boxes. Whenever she noticed a mark or an old fixture while she worked, she jotted down maintenance and restoration that should be completed before the unit could be rented again. Beth had a compulsion for upgrading her rentals whenever possible. It kept up the neighborhood. This kitchen could use some renovating, for sure. Maybe she'd install ceramic tile above the sink and counter tops as she'd done in a couple of her units. It brightened and modernized the kitchens.

Clay and Janae would do fine, but she wasn't so sure she'd do a dandy job of renting the duplex. Caroline, the lady renting Side B, was leaving. Her contract called for thirty days' notice, but Beth had waived that stipulation for Clay and Janae—so how could she refuse to allow another renter on the attached side of the same building to end her contract early? The tenant told her she couldn't stay in a place where police were investigating a body found in the attic attached to hers.

Beth understood why Caroline wanted to move, but now she would have two duplex units for rent in February, not a good time of year to find renters in the Kansas City area when everyone was settled in for the winter. Also, if that neighbor knew about the body, then more people in the neighborhood also knew the story. People wouldn't be recommending this duplex to their friends, and recommendations from neighbors were her number one method of finding new tenants. It might be a long, cold season. She hoped the case could be solved quickly, and life could return to normal.

All these thoughts swirled through her head, and, at the same time she reached for a drinking glass to pack, she spied a nick in the cabinet door. Smash—the glass slipped out of her hand and broke on the counter top.

"Ah! Dang. Clay, I'm sorry."

"Don't worry about it, Mom. We bought that set of glasses at a garage sale." He found a broom and dust pan.

"Well, I'm always klutzy when I think too hard. You probably expected me to do some damage when you let me help pack dishes."

Clay smiled and winked at his mother. "These need to last only until we start making enough money to buy some decent glasses and dishes. Or—receive some as birthday and Christmas gifts."

"Oh, good hint. I've been thinking about scouting out the garage sales this spring."

"Yeah, thanks, Mom."

"Seriously, Clay, it seems strange to me, but we haven't heard a thing from the police detective unit or from the CSI since your dad and I talked to investigators here a few days ago. I haven't seen any evidence of detectives canvassing the area residents for clues, either. I half expected a follow-up call with more questions after Detective Rinquire had a chance to look over the rental records and after the CSI had a chance to get DNA from the body and examine their clues. I could call one of them, but what's the point? They probably won't be able to share their findings with me unless it will help with their investigation."

"True."

"On the other hand, it won't hurt to try."

"Go for it, Mom." Clay continued to wrap dishes in newspaper and stick them into cardboard boxes. "I'd like to know where this thing stands, too. Janae will be uncomfortable until the case is solved, no matter where we live."

Beth set down a casserole dish, pulled out her cell phone, and called the office number she had for Detective Rinquire. She looked up at Clay and pointed to the phone. "An answer machine. He told me to always leave a message, because the office messages are forwarded to his cell phone."

"Hello. Detective Rinquire, this is Beth Stockwell. Were the rental records for our duplexes helpful? Have you been able to locate Devon and Essie Wild or any of their neighbors from seven years ago when we replaced the roof? Do you need any more information from me?"

It's all she could think to ask. She would have liked to ask if they knew the identity of the victim and how he or she died, but it hit her they would be keeping that information confidential until they could question suspects. She started packing again but then froze for a moment when a thought occurred to her—Arnie and she might be suspects.

Beth decided she'd have to wait for a call back to find out if Rinquire would tell her anything about progress on the case. Clay stood up from a carton he finished filling and taping. He stretched like a cotton picker recovering from hours in the field and observed his mother's troubled face.

"Try to be patient, Mom. It takes time to solve a case like this. Give the detectives time to do their job."

Patience wasn't one of her virtues, but Beth hugged her son because she knew him to be right and because he sounded so much like Arnie. In the middle of the hug, her phone rang.

Rinquire wasn't at all forthcoming or encouraging about the case being solved soon. No missing person report had been matched to the case, and the DNA of the victim fit no one in the CODIS, or Combined DNA-ID System, file. The residents of the duplex during the probable date of death hadn't been found. In fact, he admitted his team members were told to put this case on the back burner and had been assigned to current, more pressing cases. He didn't sound apologetic, but he didn't sound happy about it, either.

"So who decided this?" Beth asked with a lump in her throat. "Who assigns cases?"

"The Police Chief decides the priority of cases and gives assignments, but the Chief can be influenced by heads of all departments involved, including CSI, the Missing Persons unit, and even the Mayor and City Council."

Detective Rinquire had never shown any emotion to Beth, not in his voice or attitude, but the way his normally flat, even tone became flatter at the end of his statement, she sensed he disapproved of political involvement in police matters. She hung up feeling frustrated and foolhardy enough to think about figuring this case out herself. How could the police drop a case that was affecting her livelihood and her daughter-in-law's peace of mind? And what about the family of the person in the trunk?

When she returned home, Beth immediately went to her office and scanned her records from seven years earlier. As she looked through the names of tenants from that era, one stood out—Talia Johnson. She'd lived for five years in another of her duplex rentals, the one right behind the one in question. Therefore, Talia had been a back-yard neighbor of Devon and Essie Wild for two years before the Wilds left. Talia knew of the Wilds. Not long after she first moved in, Beth had asked her how she felt about the old cars and car parts in their driveway. Talia had said she didn't mind because she'd met Devon, a talkative guy, and respected his ability to rebuild cars.

Talia had been a friendly young gal, and since she'd officed at home—some kind of computer work—and went to school evenings, she often talked to Beth and offered her cold drinks when she was doing yard or maintenance work. Talia hadn't had anything nice to say about Devon's wife, Beth recalled. In fact, she'd mentioned to Beth the men she saw from her office window who visited Essie while Devon was at work.

There was a forwarding address and phone number in Beth's records for Talia. About three years before, the young lady had moved to a condo in a pricy neighborhood on the Country Club Plaza. When she gave her notice, she said she would miss the duplex but had received a promotion at work after she received her degree, and she wanted to be closer to the office where she'd be working. Beth was sure her condo would be lovingly cared for, if her upkeep of the duplex property was any indication.

Detectives had probably already talked to her, but maybe she could tell Beth something that would help her put together some of the circumstances or come up with a good clue. Then, maybe the police chief would make this case a top priority again.

"This is Talia Johnson." Her former tenant answered in a professional manner after the second ring.

It sounded as if she'd disturbed Talia at work, and Beth almost hung up, but instead she surged ahead and announced herself. Talia sounded most pleased to hear from Beth and not in a hurry. They reminisced for a short time before Beth delved into the reason for her call.

"Last week a skeleton, that is, a decomposed body was found in a trunk in the attic of one of my duplexes."

"I heard about it. I originally learned about the body being found in my old neighborhood from a coworker who saw something about it on an inside page of the *Kansas City Star*, but I didn't think about it being in one of *your* duplexes. It wasn't until a police investigator called me to ask questions that I realized it was the duplex right behind my old one. I've been thinking about you since then and wondering how you've been dealing with the investigation. But I haven't seen anything else about it on the news or in the paper."

"I'm glad it isn't being played up big in the news, at least. I've lost both my tenants in that duplex because of what happened there, and I'm afraid it will be hard to rent a place connected with death and probably murder."

"Oh, you're right," Talia said—an affirmation Beth would rather not have heard.

"Were you able to give the police anything helpful?" Beth asked.

"I doubt it. I told them I barely knew the people they asked about, the ones who lived in the duplex where the body was found. There was Devon, who worked on cars, and his sleazy wife, and then a single man and his cats lived there for maybe just a year. I met the cats but rarely saw their owner and never met him. I have no idea where any of them are now."

"Oh, I was thinking you knew Devon and Essie Wild better. They were the folks who lived there at the time we suspect the body was put into the attic. That was seven years ago, after you had lived behind them for about a year. There were two young men, Bernard Landoff and Quinlin Turley, living in the attached unit. They moved out, and while I was cleaning and painting there, I noticed what I thought was a dead animal stench. We never found anything in that side, but it could have been the body decomposing in the attached attic. We had a new roof installed to keep rodents out, and the smell went away."

"I did slightly know Bernie and Quinn. I met them through Quinn's little sister. She lived there for only a couple of months, just before they relocated, and she was the sweetest girl. She asked me all sorts of questions about how I managed to work full time and go for my degree at the same time. I thought she would stay in town to do the same. Maybe she did. She seemed bright and capable, although unsure of herself, or maybe of her situation. After they moved away I didn't keep up with her. I mean, I knew her for only a month or so. She told me about the great band her brother and his friend played in, and I followed it for several years.

When I said hi to them during their breaks, I should have asked about Quinn's sister, named, uh, Charlotte—no, no, Caitlin—but they were usually preoccupied. So I never did ask about her."

"Talia, did you tell the detectives about Caitlin? I didn't know about her—tenants don't always tell me when they bring in another roommate—but if she lived there just before they moved out, she might have a clue about the smell, or the body."

"No, I didn't. I told them I slightly knew the men, and they asked me about the tenants who lived there after them. Remember the couple who had the sweet baby named Pete? I watched baby Pete grow into a mischievous toddler while I lived there. I just didn't think to tell them about Caitlin. She was there for such a short time."

"You said you followed Bernie and Quinn's band. Do you know how to get in touch with either of them? I don't have a forwarding number, and it's been so long ago, any number I had would be out of date."

"Well, I don't have a number. I was never that close to them. I only knew them because of their sister. Their band is called *Novel Invasion*. Bernie left the group, but Quinn was still with them the last time I went to a performance. I can look it up and let you know where they're playing, if you'd like."

"Sure."

"I'll have it in a minute. It's listed on the Kansas City Events page." After only a short pause, Talia said, "Okay, *Novel Invasion* is scheduled for a concert Friday night at 8:00. Quinn is listed as the lead singer, and it's designated an R&B band. I remember it playing mainly rock. I guess the format has changed a bit."

Talia told Beth where the band was playing, at a club in Kansas City, and then, with obvious delight, suggested they go to the show together with the purpose of saying hi to Quinn and asking about his sister.

Beth was grateful to take her up on the proposal. She wasn't at all sure she could talk Arnie into such an adventure, and she wouldn't feel comfortable going alone. It would be fun to go with Talia to hear the band of one of her former tenants. Best part, Talia might help her find an opportunity to talk to Quinlin Turley. She arranged to meet Talia at her condo on Friday evening.

"Thanks so much for your help with this," Beth said. "I'm looking forward to seeing you again."

"I haven't been to one of their performances for a long time, and I love to hear Quinn sing and play. He's so...so...so talented. And of course I'd like to catch up with you."

If they had been Skyping, Beth was sure she would have seen Talia blush. Maybe she was a groupie. But if she hadn't heard the band for a long time... It didn't sound like groupie behavior. She was probably just star-struck. Beth remembered having a doozy of a crush on Jon Bon Jovi when she was younger. She went to his concerts whenever he came to town. Wow. What if she'd actually talked to him? She would probably have been tongue-tied.

"See you Friday at 7:30," Beth said.

Chapter 14

Beginning of February—Kansas City, Missouri

The concert remained a whole week away. Meanwhile, Clay and Janae moved into their new loft apartment. Arnie and Beth lifted and carried boxes and smaller items from the duplex to their cars and from their cars to the loft multiple times on Saturday and Sunday. Arnie accepted the backbreaking honor of helping to carry furniture from the rented U-Haul, into the freight elevator, down the hallway, and into the loft. Beth helped Janae clean and line her new cabinets with shelf paper. She forgave the two the job of cleaning their duplex because she would be working there, anyway.

For helping with the move, Beth and Arnie and a few of Clay's friends were rewarded with a pizza party on Sunday evening, and both Janae and Clay appeared proud to have a hip downtown dwelling. Beth and Arnie excused themselves early from the party of young people still going strong to go home and flop on the sofa in front of the TV. A big blow-out after two full days of physical labor was great for the twenty-somethings, but not for their parents.

Psycho Cat sat in front of them and yowled until Beth refilled his food and water bowls. Then the furry critter sat directly in front of the TV, switched his tail, and stared at them with squinty eyes instead of jumping up to the back of the couch, his normal resting place.

"Psycho Cat seems to be angry with us," Beth said. "Maybe it's because we haven't been home to cater to his needs all weekend."

"You think? Seems he's lucky to have you back home to spoil him."

"You do a good job of that yourself. Maybe we can take him with us the next time we take off in the RV."

The cat's sulky behavior reminded Beth of when their daughter was a teenager. She would cross her arms, press her lips together, and stare at them with a hurt and angry frown whenever she couldn't have her way. Beth thought they were done with that, but now they were to be punished the same way by this crazy feline. Arnie must have had the same thought. They both started giggling at Psycho Cat until he jumped up onto a chair to lick his wounds.

Beth took Monday off to get her own house in order and spent an hour with a friend on the Trolley Track Trail, which was close by and dry enough for a good hike. It wasn't quite shirt-sleeve warm as were the invigorating hikes she experienced in the high dry desert of Arizona, but she'd always liked the convenience of the mid-town trail built on the city's old trolley run. Not even in this time of trouble could Beth give up her daily workout. She counted the lifting and carrying over the weekend as exercise. The ride in a truck pulling an RV across country—not so much.

Tuesday, she arrived at the duplex at eight-thirty in the morning to start her clean-up, fix-up work. She decided to work on the skeleton side first. Mainly, it was because the tenant in Side B cleaned well before she left, and Beth had already inspected. That side could be shown to prospective renters in its present condition. If it didn't rent by the time she finished the redo on Side A, she would do some upgrading on B, also.

Psycho Cat went with Beth to the duplex, and he acted right at home. He fell back into his litter box routine in the basement, just as if he'd never left, and he started following her from room to room as she removed picture hanger nails from the walls and cleaned the window blinds. When they got to the second floor, however, Beth noticed the cat hovering near the sink in the bathroom.

"Are you thirsty?" Beth asked, as if he could answer her question.

He gave her a knowing green-eyed look before he leaped onto the edge of the pedestal sink and pawed at the drain, much as he pawed at her leg when he wanted food or water or a good rubbing. Beth plugged the drain and ran a little water into the sink for him. She acknowledged spoiling the old fellow, but she rationalized it to herself—this little exception at the duplex wouldn't translate to home. For sure, she didn't want him drinking from the sink where she brushed her teeth.

To her surprise, the cat started slapping at the water and meowing. Instead of drinking, he pussyfooted all the way around the bowl, jumped down, and batted at the pedestal with a paw.

"You just want attention, Mr. Psycho Kitty," Beth said with disgust while unplugging the drain. "I need to get my work done."

However, the sink drew her attention. The water drained in a sluggish circular pattern. In retrospect, Beth remembered Clay telling her about the slow-running drain after they moved in. She told him to try a commercial drain cleaner, the same kind she had used over the years for this sink. It must have worked for a while, but this looked like an ongoing problem she needed to have fixed.

She would have to ask Arnie, her first line of defense for plumbing problems, to see if he could manage to get the drain to run freely. He was home working in his office on a big consulting job, but she called him anyway, just to let him know about the problem. Working around a plugged drain wasn't something she wanted to do while trying to clean tiling tools and paint brushes. Psycho Cat was sitting in the doorway staring at her, with self-congratulation, she thought, when she finished her phone call.

It took a day and a half of using the kitchen sink for cleaning tools, but late afternoon Arnie found a slice of time to work on the bathroom sink. Beth stayed busy with her kitchen backsplash tiling job, her paint-spattered old-fashioned transistor radio's volume turned up, while he worked in the bathroom. She wanted to avoid hearing the grunts, groans, exclamations, and self-talk that came with all of Arnie's do-it-yourself jobs.

The truth was she hadn't wanted to work upstairs much while she'd been here. A sad feeling—no, more than that, a nagging feeling she had an unfinished duty— affected her when she got close to the master bedroom closet with its sinister attic opening. In a quick run-through, she filled the nail holes, touched up the wall paint, and mopped in the master bedroom the first day but otherwise kept the door closed. Beth feared she might end up as part of the problem in finding new renters if she felt queasy about showing the upstairs. Arnie came down after a short time and interrupted Beth's mulling.

He gave her his frustrated amateur-drainage-fixer frown. "I tried super-strength drain cleaner twice. It hasn't worked. Do you have a bucket or a wide-mouth container of some kind? I'm going to have to take the drain pipes apart and clean the trap manually. I can't believe the kids lived with this. It's taking ten minutes for a bowl of water to drain out. They must have opened it up just enough with the drain cleaner once or twice a week to be able to wash their hands and brush their teeth. I'm going to have a talk with Clay about plumbing care before we let him take over the inside maintenance."

"It's been slow for several years. I should have had it fixed long ago, but I didn't know it was that bad." Beth said.

She produced a plastic cleaning bucket for Arnie to catch the water and debris when the pipes were disconnected, and he disappeared upstairs, mumbling something about plumbers being worth their weight in gold. Beth could hear the clanks of the pipe wrench and the grunts of the stubborn plumber-wannabe over the news announcer on the radio. Then quiet from upstairs—all she heard was a gloomy stock market analysis and the scrape of her notched trowel making grooves in the adhesive on the back of a tile.

"Beth, come look at this," Arnie shouted from the top of the stairway. "And bring your latex gloves."

He sounded urgent. Beth hurried upstairs still wearing the gloves she used to protect her hands while tiling. Arnie pointed toward the bucket. Inside, there was a slim, clear container almost covered with slimy soap scum and hair.

"That was stuck crosswise in the drain. No wonder the drain was constantly clogging, with this thing catching material against it," Arnie said.

It became Beth's job, since she wore the gloves, to pull the container out of the mess. She used as few latex-covered fingertips as possible to accomplish the task and then pulled the remaining goo off the vial. Inside, they saw a hypodermic needle, the kind of needle doctors and nurses used to give shots, or, Beth recognized, the kind a person might use to self-inject drugs.

"How long do you think this has been in there?" she asked.

"Probably for several years by the looks of all the mess trapped around it. We've had to use drain cleaner in this sink to keep it open every year for…"

"Maybe for seven years?" She looked Arnie in the face and raised her eyebrows.

"Could be," he said. "It just darn well could be seven years we've been having trouble with this drain. I should have cleaned out the J trap the first time the drain clogged. If I had, though, we would probably have thrown the needle into the trash and forgotten about it. Now, I think we'd better call Detective Rinquire and give it to him."

Beth thought about it for a minute, eyeing the container she still held between her thumb and forefinger above the sink.

"My phone is downstairs," she said. "After I find a container for this thing, I'll take these mucky gloves off and call right now. But I'm going to call the CSI."

Beth ran downstairs, not looking back at Arnie's face. She remembered his remark about her going back to tell Mark Overos about their dead squirrel theory, and she didn't want to deal with Arnie's dislike of the guy. Beth stored the vial containing the needle inside a paper cup cushioned with paper towel shreds, shucked the gloves, grabbed her purse, and pulled out her phone. For good reason, she would not call Detective Carl Rinquire who said he was no longer investigating this case. She found the card given to her by Mark Overos, the CSI Supervisor. He had told her to call with anything new pertaining to the case, and testing a hypodermic needle for DNA or fingerprints or drugs would be the CSI's job, wouldn't it?

Mark answered right away. However, he had the same story and apology as Detective Rinquire about this cold case being put on hold by his director. Beth hurried to tell him about finding the hypodermic needle in the drain sealed inside a container, and about the drain running slowly for the same number of years it had been since the dead body smell. He agreed it could be important.

"I don't understand why this case has been set aside," Beth said. "It's important to me and my family to have it solved, and it must be important to the family of whoever was jammed into that trunk. *I'm* not dismissing the investigation, even if the police are."

Something in her voice rankled Mark's scruples, because he made an appointment to meet her at the duplex the next morning on his way to the investigation of another case. He would take the needle and test it on his own time, he told her, but it could be someone's insulin needle, someone unrelated to the residents who were here at the time the victim died.

Ah, ha, he had said victim. The mummified body must have been a murder victim, as they all had suspected.

His words confirmed her suspicions but didn't address her confusion about why the police put the investigation on hold. The murderer might be still out there killing people and stuffing them into trunks or barrels or refrigerators or.... Beth shoved those thoughts aside and concentrated on centering the tile design in the backsplash. When Arnie came down with his tool box all packed up and good news about the now fast-draining sink, she told him she arranged to give the needle sealed in the glass container to the CSI.

"I think Detective Rinquire is in charge of the investigation," he said. "I hope the CSI will relay their findings to him if they will help the case."

"It's hard telling what will convince the police to continue the investigation, but if we come up with enough evidence, they'll have to, won't they?"

~~~

Mark Overos arrived at 8:00 the next morning. With a firm grip on her prize, Beth opened the duplex door.

"Thanks for coming," she said. She held the cylinder containing the needle out for Mark to see. "I wondered about drug use here all those years ago. Maybe you can find DNA on this needle or—or find out what kind of drug they were using. It should be useful, right?"

Mark took the needle. "Like I told you on the phone, there's no guarantee the testing of this needle will produce any helpful evidence at all. It's good you found it, though. We never know when something will crack a case."

"So if it does, will they open the case back up?"

"I'm sorry, Mrs. Stockwell…"

"Beth, please."

"Beth. I'm going to test this on my own time and keep the results on file. But this is a cold case, and there's a huge backlog of fingerprint and DNA testing at the lab for all of the criminal investigations in Kansas City. So much that we have to send some of our work to the CSI lab in Johnson County, Kansas. Unless we run across evidence that solves this case, it's not likely to be put on the front burner soon."

He paused for a minute, seeming to consider whether to say any more.

"The decision to drop this case came from someone with influence," Mark said with a furrowed brow. "Our director told me to store the evidence away and work on other cases for the foreseeable future. He said the word came from the top. It worries me when we are directed to kill an investigation in progress with no explanation. That's one reason I'd like to help you, if I can. There's someone in a position of authority we suspect of having a deep connection to drug trafficking, but the police department has never had enough evidence to charge him. If he's the one whose influence with the department or with the CSI caused the case to be dropped, then this needle may be important."

All of the internal intrigue amazed Beth. She thanked Mark profusely for deciding to continue investigating on his own, and since he was definitely an ally, she told him about her call to Talia Johnson and Talia's memory of a teenager living in Side B of the duplex for about a month before it was vacated. It was after the tenants of Side B moved out, she reminded him, that she'd noticed what she thought was the bad smell in the building. The smell could have come from Side A where the skeleton was found.

"Talia is helping me locate one of the young men who lived in Side B at the time. The teenager was his sister. Detectives may have questioned him already, but maybe they didn't get that far before the case was dropped," Beth said.

Mark reminded her that this was a police matter and she shouldn't pursue any dangerous investigating.

"I'll let you do the investigating," she said. "Believe me, I don't want to get involved in anything unsafe. I'm no hero."

His advice sounded a lot like that of her husband and her son. However, if she didn't look for clues that might lead to the murderer, who would? She had to admit to herself, though, that her underlying motive for hoping to bring the case to a satisfactory conclusion was that it might remove the stigma against the property for potential renters.

There it was. Despite all of her noble thoughts, part of her motivation was still a basic scramble to preserve her own best interests. Still, the main considerations remained—to get this whole thing cleared up for the sake of the family of the unfortunate victim and for the peace of mind of everyone involved.

Chapter 15

July, Seven Years Earlier—Kansas City, Missouri

It took only a few days for Quinn and Caitlin to transform the basement of the duplex into Quinn's new bedroom. Quinn found a used mattress and begrudgingly allowed his sister to pay for it. Caitlin searched the thrift store and added bed clothes, a rag rug, and some curtains she could hem up for the windows. After Quinn put together a wood base for his mattress and the two finished cleaning and decorating, the siblings stood on the steps and admired their work. It was a bright self-congratulatory moment, and, for the first time since she came, Caitlin felt everything was going to work out.

Bernie had made himself scarce while his roommates were cleaning and building. When he appeared the afternoon they finished, Quinn stopped him on his way upstairs to ask if he wanted to share a pizza with them to celebrate the new third bedroom they had just created in the basement.

Bernie sneered. "Are you kidding me? Playing house with your fu..."

Quinn's face turned to stone, and he fisted his hands until his knuckles turned white.

"Just kidding," Bernie said, as if that would excuse his snarky remark. "Couldn't turn down free food, now could I? You guys look proud as sows with new piglets. Let's party. There's probably some beer in the fridge, and Essie's getting a fresh delivery of some good stuff this afternoon." He narrowed his eyes at Quinn. "Course most of that's for a big party later tonight after the show, right man?"

Quinn gave Bernie a warning look. "Whatever."

~~~

Caitlin, in the kitchen getting plates for the pizza, overheard only part of the exchange and missed the looks the guys gave each other. Hearing Bernie cut someone to the quick and then turn on the charm was nothing new, but Caitlin wasn't naïve, and she cringed at the way he referred to party stuff, even though she didn't hear exactly what he said about it. She peeked through the doorway to try to get an idea of what Bernie was up to this time, but he saw her and, with an innocent look, asked to see the results of their big project before they ate the pizza. On the way through the kitchen to the basement door, following behind Caitlin, Bernie grabbed a beer out of the refrigerator and popped it open. Caitlin jumped, and her heart raced.

"You show him the room, Quinn," she said with a slight shake in her voice. "I'll be right back."

Upstairs in the bathroom, Caitlin felt as if she wanted to vomit. The feeling passed. Instead, she sat on the toilet and shed a few tears. Her dad, Bernie, drugs, beer cans, mental and physical abuse—all were swarming through her mind in nightmarish images. It was several minutes before she could compose herself. She splashed her face with water. Caitlin often missed her mother, but now the need for her mom's comfortable presence and guidance felt like a weight pressing against her insides. She forced herself to return to the kitchen and nibble on a slice of pizza. Quinn found a lone Coke in the fridge and shared it with her. The food restored some of Caitlin's resilience.

Bernie, after a brief sneer at the frozen pizza, unexpectedly remained in high spirits while he downed close to half the pizza and two beers. He shot frequent looks toward the back door. Of course he was oblivious to Caitlin's depression. Quinn, on the other hand, intermittently scrutinized his sister with concern.

"Tonight's our big chance," Bernie said, raising his eyebrows at Quinn, "in more ways than one."

Caitlin shot a questioning look at Quinn.

"Yeah," he said, "this might be our most important gig yet. I guess our founder thinks we're ready. I know he's had some scouts looking us over the past two months."

The performance, arranged for by the founder of *Novel Invasion*, would be the opening act for one of Kansas City's most popular groups on a Friday night at one of the most popular music venues in town—a dream gig for a relatively unknown group. Quinn acted excited, and listening to the two musicians talk timing, chords, and vibes finally brought Caitlin out of her doldrums. She ended up giggling with them when Quinn described one of the antics of their band clown, the bass player, at a performance two weeks ago, standing and dancing with the instrument while the vocalists' backs were turned, leaving the audience laughing instead of listening. Bernie and Quinn agreed to warn the bass player during their warm-up this afternoon to keep it professional at this important performance.

~~~

As yet, Quinn had not had an opportunity to follow through with his agreement to help Bernie sell his drugs during breaks and after their performances. He knew Bernie was looking forward to the big sales he might make at the gig as much as to the band's performance. It seemed unreal to Quinn, as if he would magically get a call to start at one of the jobs for which he'd filled out applications and would be able to tell Bernie he had a better offer.

This was more than just taking a job, though. Quinn knew it was the price Bernie demanded to leave Caitlin alone. Otherwise, Bernie would make Caitlin's life hell, and he knew that would make Quinn suffer. Or, Bernie would move out and leave jobless Quinn and Caitlin with no way to pay their rent and nowhere to go.

All he had to do was point toward Bernie if anyone brought up the subject of a drug source. Quinn told himself it was only temporary. As soon as he could find a regular job, he'd be able to make ends meet without Bernie.

~~~

A sharp rapping on the back door found Caitlin daydreaming again, her hands in sudsy water at the kitchen sink. This time her reverie involved creative wording for the résumé Quinn told her she must write to accompany job applications. Caitlin looked over her shoulder to see if either of the guys was nearby to answer the door, but they had both drifted off to their rooms. She dried her hands on her jeans while taking a cautious peek through the blinds. For a moment, she hesitated. It was Essie from next door. Caitlin remembered the warning from her brother to stay clear of the woman. Essie, however, looked innocent enough standing on the stoop, looking around, holding a package.

"What could she do to me?" Caitlin thought.

Before she could open the storm door, Bernie charged into the kitchen, grabbed her arm, and shoved her aside. Caitlin was a statuesque girl, five foot eight, but she weighed almost seventy pounds less than tall, burly Bernie, and his thrust knocked her full force into the wall.

"I've got this," he declared, with a somewhat wild look in his eyes and no recognition of the results of his brutish behavior.

With that, the bully went out to greet Essie, banging the door closed behind him. Caitlin pulled herself away from the wall, ran to the window over the sink, and spied on them through the translucent curtain. She could see Essie point toward the back door and then, with a pout and an indignant toss of her head, hand her package over to Bernie. The two appeared to glance around, making Caitlin back away from the window for a second, before something else was passed between them. Caitlin caught only the end of the motion, but she saw Essie slip a fat envelope into her purse before she entered her own back door. Bernie burst back into the kitchen, and Caitlin eyed the package he held.

"Is this the party stuff Essie brought you?" she asked. "What kind of job do you and Quinn have tonight?"

Bernie altered his headlong dash toward the stairs and strode toward her, his eyes squinted, a lascivious look on his face. "Come on up to my room with me, Katie girl, and I'll show you what big boys and girls do for fun."

Caitlin refused to back away. In the hallway by Bernie's room she had tried to ignore the aroma of marijuana, but this package, the money exchange, and Bernie's obnoxious behavior suggested more potent drugs, something she couldn't abide, not after seeing how addiction had affected her father. Drug use could explain the moody behavior Bernie had been exhibiting since she arrived, red-eyed exhaustion one minute and aggressiveness the next, abusive insults followed by charming persuasiveness, and a curious amount of time spent alone in his room. Now, it occurred to Caitlin, he intended to lead her brother into that deep quagmire of obsession. Caitlin's ire grew, and her normal restraint dissolved like that of a moose cow charging to protect her calves from approaching danger. Her lip curling, her eyes flashing, Caitlin stepped toward her nemesis.

"I'm not interested in your kind of fun," she snapped, "and I'm certainly not interested in you. I'm telling you, you will *not* pull Quinn into your druggie world if I can help it."

"What're you planning to do about it?"

Caitlin raised her voice and leaned into Bernie's face. "I'll kill you if I have to."

"No one is killing anyone," Quinn said, appearing from the basement door. "What's this all about? I thought we were all friends now."

"Quinn," Caitlin said, "promise me you're not going to help him with his drug business, and *please* tell me you're not ever going to use!"

"What've you been telling my sister?" Quinn asked Bernie.

"Nothing! I didn't tell her nothin'. Your sister is crazy." He shouldered past them and hoofed it up the stairs with his bundle.

Caitlin turned her anxiety toward her brother. "Please Quinn, I just ran away from the results of addiction, and so did you. You can't get into it yourself. I'll leave so you won't have to work with Bernie and his drugs. I'll go to California. After Mom died, Aunt Sharon invited us to come any time, remember? She said we could live with her. I have enough money left to get out there. You can take a fast food job or something to tide you over until your band starts making enough money to live on. You won't have to worry about me."

"Wait! Wha...? How'd you figure all this out?"

Quinn stood for a moment, but when Caitlin didn't reply, he looked her in the eyes. "Okay, now calm down. You don't have to leave. I won't have anything to do with drugs. Just stay. We'll start again looking for work tomorrow—both of us. We probably won't be able to live here, but we can find a little place for the two of us, and Bernie will have to be on his own. It's the end of July. I'll give notice to Mrs. Stockwell, the duplex owner, tomorrow, and we'll start looking for a small apartment. Caitlin, don't go off trying to cross the country alone, looking for a relative we don't even know. Okay?"

"Okay," Caitlin whispered.

The tears started to flow as she headed for the room she had taken from her brother. The adrenalin surge had abated and left her feeling weak. Caitlin felt a confusing twist of emotions and thoughts. She didn't want to tie Quinn down to being responsible for her. She felt terrible he had given up his room and now probably this duplex and the new basement room of which they were so proud. On the other hand, she couldn't let Bernie drag Quinn into the drug world because of her. But that could happen even if she were to leave if Quinn had no money. It was too much to think about. Caitlin fell into a fitful sleep on Quinn's mattress.

Chapter 16

February—Kansas City, Missouri

Beth wasn't surprised when she called Mark Overos and he told her the testing indicated traces of heroin in the hypodermic needle Arnie had pulled out of the drain trap.

"Were there fingerprints or DNA you could use?" Beth asked.

"Water in the drain washed away all traces of those."

"At least this proves what happened to the victim must have been drug related, doesn't it?"

"Not necessarily. We can't date the needle. Only your memory of how long you've had trouble with the drain indicates a relationship."

At least, to Beth's way of thinking, this find did help verify Mark's theory about the drug lord who had enough influence with the CSI Director or Chief of Police or someone to get the case dropped. Maybe he had supplied the drugs, and the drugs led to a murder or to an overdose. Lots of maybes. She wondered about the identity of the drug lord.

"Is the drug lord someone whose name I'd recognize? Has his name been in the papers?" Beth asked.

"I couldn't give you his name if I wanted to," Mark said. "Remember, I told you this person's identity is only my hunch. I'll put this evidence in the case file. Contact me if you find anything else in the duplex."

"I will," Beth said. "Thank you for taking the time to test the needle. My cat sort of pointed the way to it. He might find something else."

"Ha. If I remember correctly, that big yellow cat helped discover the body. We could use a cat like that in crime scene investigations."

Friday was only a day away. Beth didn't mention to Mark her upcoming evening with Talia Johnson. He probably wouldn't want her to go around interrogating people any more than Detective Rinquire would, but that is exactly what she intended. How could she learn anything if she didn't ask questions? Beth worked all day on her duplex projects. The physical work meant plenty of time to think of questions for Quinlin—Talia had called him Quinn—Turley who lived next door around the time the crime occurred. If he had moved out just before the murder was committed, he wouldn't be able to answer some of the questions. At least, her trip to hear Quinn Turley's band venue would give her the opportunity to find out.

Normally, several days passed after a lease terminated before Beth began her work on a rental unit. Sometimes she had to give the people time to return and clean, and many times it took a few days for them to remove all of their possessions. She figured she'd have at least a month, more if word of the skeleton spread, to apply some spit and polish to the current units since no one had signed a lease yet. When Quinn Turley and Bernie Landoff moved out, she couldn't remember how long it had been before she came in and smelled the awful odor. And how long had it taken to rent the unit out again? Seven years was long enough for her to forget details.

~~~

Friday arrived, and Beth still hadn't prepared an exact list of questions for Quinn Turley. Earlier in the week, when she'd told Arnie about her plan with Talia to hear Quinn's band, she'd said she intended to ask Quinn whether he remembered the terrible smell from the attached duplex seven years ago. A positive answer to that question would only verify the year. She needed more. Formulating substantial questions about a murder turned out to be harder than she thought.

As it turned out, Arnie planned to fly to Texas to play in a golf tournament Friday through Sunday. "I'm not sure two women will be safe around that club at night, especially if you're asking questions about a murder. I know you've made up your mind to go. I'll call off my trip and go with you," he had said.

"Oh, Arnie, you know I love you for worrying about me. Talia's experienced at rock concerts, but she hasn't seen Quinn Turley's band, *Novel Invasion,* for a while. When I showed interest, Talia jumped at the chance to hear his band play again. I'll have fun with her. That's my priority. Asking about the dead body smell is secondary. I'm just curious. The police have probably already questioned him, anyway."

"Just remember, it's up to the police to investigate."

"I'll remember that. You can go ahead to your tournament without a worry, I promise.

~~~

Having Arnie out of town gave Beth some time Friday morning to examine the side of the duplex Quinn Turley and Bernie Landoff had rented seven years earlier. She'd almost finished working on Side A where the body was found, but she had not shown either side to a prospective renter yet. Okay, it was winter, when fewer people looked for housing, but a week of advertising and no calls about the place was worrisome. The bathroom on Side B needed a new lavatory and some tile work on its walls. The kitchen had already been updated and was sparkling clean, due to the departing tenant's good care.

It was when Beth surveyed the basement she remembered her amazement at its condition after Quinn and Bernie left. How could she have forgotten the clean walls, painted floor, and handmade curtains she found here after they left? The basements had never been her priority when it came to fixing up the duplexes. Back

102

then, she thought they'd probably cleaned it up to use as a recreation room but was astonished two young men could leave it so nice. Now it made sense. If a young sister lived here, they must have transformed it into an extra bedroom.

More questions for Quinn Turley. Beth needed to write them down. With her mind on the mystery, she dashed up the stairs to the kitchen, tripped, fell down two steps, and cut her knee open on the edge of a step. Why did she have to be such a stumblebum? It was smart of her to always carry first aid supplies in her purse.

After bandaging her knee, she pulled a small notebook from her purse and contemplated writing a list of questions that might turn out to be useless. She had no idea how much time Quinn would be able to spend talking or any idea how much he'd remember or be willing to talk about.

A person who took on a third roommate without telling her? He might not be trustworthy. The lease expressly stated... What was she thinking? It happened all the time—people didn't pay a bit of attention to the wording of the lease after they moved in. They needed reminders. Beth had no idea a teenage girl had been living here at that time. On the other hand, to be generous, Quinn Turley may have forgotten he needed to let her know.

To the question for Quinn about the smell, Beth added questions about his sister, the basement, Devon and Essie Wild, drug use, and about anyone who had disappeared. She stood for a minute, leaned an elbow on the kitchen counter, pressed her pen against her lips, and contemplated what else she should ask. A sudden thought hit her. The fact that Quinn Turley and his roommates moved out just before or after this thing happened made them prime suspects. Her eyes grew wide. Maybe it *would be* dangerous to question Quinlin Turley! She scanned her list of questions.

No, she rationalized. The Wilds had lived in Side A for about a year after Quinn moved out of Side B. Quinn would've had to have a great deal to hold over their heads for them to stay quiet about him hiding a dead body in their attic. At the time, Beth thought the Wilds agreed with her about the probability of dead animals being there or in the walls. At least that's what Devon had indicated. She remembered talking to him one time while he was working on a car during the roof replacement, and he appeared to concur on the probable source of the smell when she discussed it with him.

But then, she wasn't looking at him as a murder suspect at the time. Beth couldn't remember seeing Essie again after Quinn and Bernie moved out, and her records showed she had mailed the deposit return to the order of either Devon *or* Essie Wild. Had Devon received and cashed the check after he killed...?

And how about Bernie Landoff? She didn't see him again after the young men moved out, either. Quinn turned up to collect the deposit she normally sent by check through the mail, one check made out to Quinlin Turley for the amount of the original deposit, which had been paid in cash. Well, she believed people when they told her who should get the returned deposit money. But, what happened to Bernie?

This line of thinking scared Beth—suspects, victims—but finally she decided it couldn't be too dangerous to interview someone in such a public place as a music club, and she was burning to learn some answers. Her hand could hardly keep up with her mind as she thought of questions and jotted them on her notebook paper. She wouldn't bother to call and run the list by Arnie since he was already out having a good time on the golf course.

Talia was ready to go when Beth reached her condo, and she looked much as Beth remembered her. She was dressed in tight black pants and a long red, white, and black diagonally striped sweater cinched at the waist with a wide belt. The outfit showed off her figure and complemented her smooth café au lait complexion and coal black tresses smoothed back into a sophisticated chignon on the back of her neck.

Beth felt frumpy in comparison, dressed in jeans, collared white shirt, and sweater vest, but Talia hugged her and started chattering like she would with a girlfriend rather than with an older acquaintance. The enthusiasm infected Beth so much she lost her purposeful attitude and looked forward to the music and musicians they were going to hear. She already loved R&B music, and Talia's company promised to make this an enjoyable evening, with or without the information she sought.

Spending an evening at a bar or club when she was younger, Beth recalled, meant entering a dark, hazy, noisy den of cigarette smoke, loud voices, grease and beer odors, and music that could barely compete with the people noise. It meant shouting across a table to one's companions and asking them to repeat themselves every time they spoke. She enjoyed live music, but she'd probably missed many of the subtleties in such boisterous, eye-stinging atmospheres.

This evening promised to be different from the first minute they stepped inside the club.

"Smokers have to use the back deck," Talia said, "even in this cold weather. And this club serves delicious food."

Through a window near the restrooms, they could see people outside on a kind of deck, puffing into the frigid air of the back alley.

They were seated at a table not too far from the small dance floor below the stage, and the folks around them were having calm conversations and partaking of such greaseless fare as turkey sandwiches and tomato-basil soup. Talia and Beth left their coats over the backs of their chairs and made their way to the food window. A waitress took their drink orders, and they had about half an hour to eat and visit before the band came out.

They discussed how surreal it seemed to find a body in an attic trunk. Beth told Talia everything she knew about the case.

"The investigation has screeched to a stop now, though," she said. "The police and the crime investigators were told to concentrate on other, more current, cases."

"What?" Talia leaned forward and put her elbows on the table. "Why would they do that?"

"I'm not sure, but I've learned there may be someone high up in the system who doesn't want the case solved. There could be some drug connection."

Talia's eyes showed a resolute spark. "It's not right. I admire you for trying to find out as much as you can. I'll help with anything you need for me to do."

"Nice of you to offer, but you don't have a lot of spare time, I think."

"I have lots more than I did when I lived in your duplex. Back then I worked full time and took a full time class load, some at the university and some online during evenings and weekends. Now that I've completed my master's degree and have advanced in my field of technology, I have a *little* more time to call my own." Talia smiled and lowered her gaze. "Maybe even time for a boyfriend, if the right person comes along."

"You haven't dated while you were earning your degree?"

"I came close to being engaged a couple of years ago. It was my fault we split up. He was in his early thirties and ready to settle down and have a family. I was bent on staying late at work every night and studying for my master's classes during much of my spare time. At that period of my life, marriage wasn't a priority. It didn't occur to me I should spend more time on my personal life and could work on an advanced degree at a more gradual pace. Ambition has its drawbacks. I miss the guy still, or, perhaps more so, I miss the idea of having a special someone to plan and share with."

"Timing is important in relationship building," Beth said. "But if that young man had been the one for you, you would still be together. You are what, twenty-six, twenty-seven? If Mr. Right's out there, you're now ready to find him."

As *Novel Invasion* warmed up, people finished their conversations. But on the opening note of the first number, voices died down, and the audience, seated at tables, in chairs on both sides of the room, or standing at the back, turned its attention to the music. Beth didn't recognize Quinlin Turley, but when moon-eyed Talia, after the first song, asked her how she liked his voice, Beth identified him as the poised young man on stage announcing the next number. The tall, lanky lad she remembered had matured into a good-looking man with an incredible voice and undeniable musical skill.

After the first set, during which Beth swayed and tapped her foot in time to the soul-penetrating music, Quinn announced the band would sell its CDs during the break. Beth and Talia joined a line of people waiting to buy the music and talk to the band members. When they finally reached the front, they had to wait a few minutes to talk to Quinn, who seemed to have the largest number of people milling around him. Finally, they got his attention.

"Hi, Quinn," Talia said. "I'm Talia Johnson. Do you remember me?"

Quinn's eyes lit up. "Of course I do. How are you?"

"I'm fine. And do you remember Beth Stockwell? She was your landlady and mine at one time."

He hesitated for only a split second, and then stuck a hand out. "It's so nice to see you again, Mrs. Stockwell."

"We would love to talk to you for a few minutes," Beth said. "Would it be possible for you to visit our table during your next break?

"It'll be my pleasure to join two such beautiful ladies," he said, his eyes resting rather longer than necessary on Talia's face, which, even in the artificial light, Beth could see turning pink. "I'm glad you came, Talia. I haven't seen you at one of our performances for a couple of years and thought maybe you'd found another group you liked better."

Talia looked down for an instant before she regained her composure. She recovered with a bright smile.

"I was just drawn away from your music for a while by a— uh—different concern. It's so good to hear you and your band again, and I'm glad to be able to introduce a new fan."

Beth smiled and nodded.

"I've loved your music ever since that summer evening on your patio," Talia said. "Do you remember when your sister invited me over for cold drinks and talked you into giving us a violin concert? I expected some blue-grass fiddling, but you played enchanting classical violin solos, all from memory, for over an hour as the sun set and the first stars appeared. It was so beautiful it brought tears to my eyes. I've enjoyed your band's music over the years, too, but your sound has matured. I loved your first set."

Quinn seemed to be struck dumb by this speech. He merely regarded Talia with an unfathomable expression until a small drumroll reminded him the second set was about to begin.

"After this set," he said over his shoulder as he returned to his place on the stage.

Quinn slid past the dancers returning to their seats and showed up at the beginning of the next break. Beth offered to buy him a drink, but he declined, holding up a bottle of water.

"For me, drinking and singing is as dangerous as drinking and driving," he said quite seriously, then grinned. "And water hydrates better than colas."

Talia and Quinn appeared ready to make more chitchat, but Beth remembered how short the breaks were. She was so eager to ask her questions that she rushed to blurt out the story about Psycho Cat leading Clay to the mummified body in the attic of the adjoining side of the duplex where Quinn lived seven years ago and the probability of the body being stuffed into a trunk and hidden in the attic about the time he left. Beth paused to take a breath, and Quinn stared at her, his face a mask.

"But the police," Beth said, "have dropped their investigation. Someone in charge designated this case low priority. They quit before they identified the victim or any suspects, as far as I know, and even before they questioned everyone who might know something. I mean, have you even been contacted by the police about this?"

Quinn shook his head back and forth several times and rubbed his hand through his hair as if he had walked into a spider web and tried to break free of the sticky threads. "No, this is the first I've heard about it. They might have tried to get hold of me, but I live with another band member, whose name is on the lease. Both of us have only mobile phones. Besides, the band has been out of town this past two weeks. It's possible the case was dropped before detectives were able to locate me. I'll be glad to talk to them if you'd like, but I don't think I'd be able to help."

"You don't remember any ghastly stench in the duplex before you left?" Beth asked.

"No, no. I would remember that, no matter how much turmoil my life was in at that time. If there was a dead body smell, it wasn't when I lived there. Did someone else report the stink?"

"My husband and I both smelled it after you moved out. We had the roof replaced, thinking it was a dead rodent. The problem is, I can't remember how long it was after you moved before I went in to clean and paint. The skeleton was found in the attic next door to yours. The smell was stronger, I imagine, on that side. But no one there complained. That seems strange to me. The couple who lived there hasn't been located. Can you remember any suspicious behavior from Devon and Essie Wild? Do you think one of them was capable of killing someone and stashing the body in a trunk?"

Quinn frowned, and a sorrowful look appeared in his eyes. His expression changed to disgust when he started recalling Essie Wild and her wild ways. "Essie Wild was a slut who had an alliance with a drug ring leader called Double M. She sold drugs and must have done more than that for the guy. I don't think Devon was involved."

"Do you have any idea where the Wilds are now?"

"I haven't a clue what happened to her and her poor bastard of a husband. I hope to hell he left her."

Quinn shot a look toward Talia. "Sorry about the language."

Talia waved her hand. "Couldn't have described them better myself."

"The worst thing about living next to them was what influence it had on my roommate, Bernie. He inclined toward drinking and drugs, anyway, and Essie grabbed him by the…. I mean, she got him hooked and also selling drugs for her. That made her even more important to Double M."

"Double M? Do you know what that stands for?" Beth asked.

"No. I tried to forget all of that after I moved. They almost railroaded me into their disgusting trade. I was having trouble making ends meet after I lost a job. The luck of the Irish was with me, as my mom would have put it. I found a job at a music store teaching guitar lessons and was able to make enough to live on just in time to be relieved of the temptation to make money Essie and Bernie's way. It was at the start of the big recession. It was a low time for me, but it was bad for lots of people that year."

"I remember. I had trouble finding tenants who could pay the rent." Beth said. "Where is Bernie now?"

"The band kicked him out when they found out about his drug dealing during our gigs. I couldn't help him talk his way out of that one, and we had already moved separately away from the duplex. I only saw him a few times after that. He charmed his way into another group, but they put up with him only for a short time. I got a letter from him a year after he left, and then I heard from one of my friends in Arkansas who saw him in our hometown a couple of years after that. Maybe he got himself straightened out and is making a life back home. I hope so. Bernie and I were on the outs after he was told to leave the band. It's a long story."

"So you're both from Arkansas?" Beth said.

"A small town in the Ozark Mountains," Quinn said. "It's nice, I guess, but I haven't been back in several years."

One of the other band members arrived at the table just then. Quinn introduced him to Beth and Talia and then apologized for needing to get back for the third set. Beth gave him her business card and asked him to please call if he thought of anything else that might help provide clues to the mystery. Talia followed suit. Quinn told them he was obligated to help break down after the last set but might have a few minutes to talk later.

As soon as he left, Talia slapped her hand to her forehead. "I forgot to ask about his sister Caitlin," she lamented, "again."

After the show, they talked to Quinn for only a minute before the eleven o'clock band started warming up, just long enough to say goodnight and thank you.

As they were leaving their table, Talia shouted over the sounds of the instruments, "Say hi to your little sister for me!"

Quinn frowned, shook his head, and gave a wave. It looked as if he didn't hear what Talia said.

Chapter 17

February—Kansas City, Missouri

On the way home, Beth and Talia discussed the music, Quinn's talent, and the information he'd given them. Beth couldn't pass up the opportunity to tease Talia a little about the effect she'd had on Quinn, but Talia dismissed it with a wave of her hand.

"I'm sure he shows the same interest in every young woman who buys a CD, compliments his music, or asks for his autograph," she said.

"Maybe, but I doubt he remembers it's been exactly two years and two months since those other women came to hear the band."

Talia sniffed, reddened a little, and then changed the subject back to the crime investigation. She admitted to being shocked by Quinn's description of the illegal drug trade that took place practically in her back yard for a couple of years. Even though she'd seen Essie receiving male visitors while Devon was working and knew Essie to be rather flamboyant and moody the few times they talked, Talia hadn't suspected drug abuse.

"Sometimes I think I'm stranded inside my own head," she said, "a head full of technology details and class projects. Those are the issues that came between my ex-boyfriend and me."

"I can assure you, you're one of the friendliest and most caring people around, and if anyone should have been aware of drug dealings in that duplex and done something about it, it would be their landlady. Me." Beth sighed.

"How could you have known?"

"Well, I had some suspicions, but I let them drop as mere musings until Arnie discovered the hypodermic needle. Now, seven years later... Well, those people were just too good at plying their trade in secret. Quinn is the one who should have reported Essie to the police, since he knew what she was up to. I wonder if his sister knew what was going on."

"Caitlin? You realize I forgot to ask about her again, and I don't think Quinn heard me say to tell her hi."

"We didn't get his phone number, either, did we? Great investigator I make. Well, maybe he'll call. We'll ask about her if he does. I'd like to be able to ask Caitlin what she remembers about the Wilds. She could have noticed something that will give us a clue."

At home, Beth pondered Essie Wild's and Bernie Landoff's drug history. It would be important information for her to give Mark Overos. Although those facts verified what they already suspected about drug use in the duplex, now they had a witness who could name names. It brought her no closer to knowing who was murdered and why, but the crime must have been drug related if an influential drug lord had made the case go away. More questions came to mind. Did Quinn tell them everything? He said he didn't think Devon Wild was involved, but Beth wondered if Devon knew about his wife's liaison with Double M. There were so many possibilities and lots more questions.

Arnie's golf tournament lasted for the rest of the weekend. So on Saturday morning Beth left a detailed report on Mark Overos's work phone with pertinent information from her discussion with Quinn Turley. Then she called Janae to ask if she needed any help unpacking. Helping her kids seemed more important than going back to the duplex to begin working. No one had jumped at the chance to rent either side so far, but she could almost see Janae leap at her offer of help right through the airwaves. Apparently,

Janae's overtime and Clay's piles of homework left zero time for them to organize their new apartment.

Psycho Cat ran a circle from the living room to the dining room and back into the kitchen and then tried to climb Beth's leg when he noticed her heading for the door. She gave him a belly rub and lots of assurances she would not be gone for long. For her efforts, she received a sad-eyed stare and a discontented meow before she closed the door. It was due to her imagination, she knew, but the cat often succeeded in making her feel guilty about attending to any need but his.

Beth abandoned her cat concerns as soon as she entered Clay's and Janae's new loft apartment, entirely a shambles of boxes and pieces of furniture that hadn't been moved two inches from where they had landed the previous weekend. This promised to be another full day of menial labor. Oh, well, what are mothers for? She mentally rolled up her sleeves and asked Janae where she'd like for her to start.

Janae had a sparkle in her eyes and a voice full of enthusiasm, for a change. "Oh, Beth, thank you so much for coming. I'm organizing the kitchen shelves that you lined last week. It'd be great if you'd unpack the boxes of dishes, pans, and silverware and rinse them in hot water." She set some dry tea towels on the counter. "You can just lay them on these, and I'll put them away in the cabinets and drawers as I dry them."

"Will do. I'll unpack this box full of glasses first. We'll get through this in no time."

"I hope so. It's a lot more fun to decorate than it is to unpack and store all this paraphernalia."

It looked to Beth as if Clay and Janae had eaten mostly microwave dinners and fast food for the past week, and now Janae anticipated being able to use her new kitchen. She didn't chat about food preparation while they worked, though. Instead, she told Beth all about the people they'd met in the building and the wonderful space in the loft.

"At the duplex, I had to alternate work on my metal sculptures from soldering in the basement and designing upstairs in the bedroom, then down in the basement, and again upstairs in the bedroom. Here we have brick walls and huge windows in the front room. I'm designing a screen to divide it into a living area and a studio. Then I'll be able to use my torch, my polishing tools, and my colors all in one place. I plan to put the studio space in order today after we finish the kitchen. That way I can soon go back to work on a sculpture I started at the duplex before the, well, you know...the *discovery*."

"That's a good way to put it. The discovery."

"Again, it's so nice of you to help me get this done," Janae said. "Clay had to be at the lab most of today."

"I'm glad to help," Beth said. "May I see the sculpture you've started?"

"Oh, I'm sorry. I can't bring myself to show my work to anyone until it's finished, at least until it's finished enough to make me proud of it. Then I'll be glad to show it to you. Actually, two of my small works have been accepted at a gallery and will be on display during First Friday in the Crossroads next month. I hope to be able to add this new one." Janae spoke in a matter-of-fact manner, but her eyes shone.

"That's terrific, Janae!" Beth dried a wet hand on her jeans and gave her daughter-in-law a one-arm hug. "Congratulations."

Down deep in her selfish heart, Beth had wanted Janae to be sorry she and Clay had moved out of the duplex and left her with empty rental property in the middle of winter. Now, she became excited that so much had happened for Janae's art career in such a short time, and she felt delighted to see her so energized. Good things could result from catastrophe.

Beth and Janae were filling the linen closet when Clay arrived home from his new job as a lab assistant at the pharmacy school. The part-time employment was a great opportunity for him to earn some money while learning more about his field. He had assured

Beth he'd still be available to help out at the duplexes when Arnie and she traveled. Such an eventuality wouldn't happen any time soon, it seemed, but Beth was glad to know he was willing.

As soon as he entered the apartment, Clay exclaimed over how much better it looked. Beth and Janae had folded empty boxes and stacked them in a corner, moved furniture into a semblance of order, and made room for the art studio. Janae had placed the covered sculpture against the far wall.

"Do you think Arnie will mind if I use your basement and his tools to build a wooden frame for the screen I'm making to hide the work area?" Janae asked. "I already found some dynamic fabric for a mosaic pattern."

"He'll be overjoyed to let you use anything," Beth said.

Clay moaned with fake agony when Janae asked him to help her haul her work table into position near the huge window.

"Look at the kitchen," Janae said. "You won't believe it."

"Wow, you could get a job as an interior designer and space organizer," Clay said and then entered the hallway and found his mother folding the last of the towels. "I guess it was a team effort. You two are amazing!"

"All the decorating was Janae's vision. I'm just the helper bee," Beth said. "How was your day, Clay?"

"Up to your old name rhymes, huh, Mom? Does she do this to you, Janae?" Clay yelled into the other room.

Both women giggled.

"Well," he said, "lab work can be a little tedious, I've learned, but the stuff happening in that lab is incredible. I have the good luck to be working for one of the top research pharmacists in the state, and I'm planning to let as much as I can of his knowledge and creativity seep through my hard skull into the gray matter. It'll be a terrific background for whatever kind of pharmacist I become."

While Clay changed clothes in the still disorganized bedroom, Beth and Janae finished the bathroom cabinets. It was almost dinner time, and Clay had the good grace to ask his mother to stay for dinner. They discussed going out, but Janae wanted to use her newly functional kitchen. She made a big salad out of fixings on hand, Clay went out to get a roasted chicken, a loaf of French bread for garlic toast, and a bottle of wine from the big downtown grocery store several blocks away, and Beth set the table. The only missing ingredient was a bouquet of flowers for a centerpiece, but Janae set a trio of candles there instead, and they sat down to a delightful meal made even more special by the feeling of accomplishment after a long day's work.

During dinner, Clay asked his mom if she had learned any new information about the attic mystery. Janae hadn't mentioned the duplex all day, and Beth hadn't brought it up. To answer Clay, she told them about the syringe Arnie found in the drain and about her experience at the music club the evening before.

Since she supposed Clay would be as against her sleuthing as Arnie, she tread lightly by trying to make it sound as if her former tenant Talia and she were merely catching up with another former tenant, someone Talia valued as a friend and as a talented musician. Beth's description of the band *Novel Invasion* and of Quinn's performance intrigued the music-loving duo, and she dwelled on that subject, especially Quinn's vocal range and his expertise with various instruments.

"He sounds great," Clay said.

"I'd like to hear him sometime," Janae said. "Are you and your friend going to another performance?"

"Well," Beth said, "Talia might want to make a return visit. She regretted forgetting to ask Quinn about his sister, Caitlin, and she doesn't have Quinn's phone number. What if I arrange for us all to go together? I bet your dad would consent to join us, too." She winked at Clay.

"Sounds like fun," Janae said. Clay nodded and headed to his computer to find out where and when the band performed next.

Meanwhile, Janae asked Beth about Quinn's sister and how Talia knew her. Beth explained about Caitlin's short time residency at the duplex.

"Talia wants to find out how Caitlin is doing and maybe get in touch with her," Beth reflected further, almost to herself. "Caitlin lived at the duplex just before the body was hidden in the attic next door. Maybe she observed something or someone, anything that might help us figure this out."

"Wait," Clay said from across the room, "Is this more of your detective work we're getting ourselves into?"

Recognizing she had given away her original motive for her musical outing, Beth came clean with the whole story. "It's intriguing, don't you think? The police don't seem to be doing anything to solve the case, and I'd like to know who the victim is and to see the murderer brought to justice. It'd be best for you, for Arnie and me, for the family of the victim, and for the reputation of the neighborhood to know the killer isn't out there somewhere able to do it again. In fact, after seven years, the killer may have already committed more murders."

Neither Clay nor Janae had any comment. They just stared at her. Beth went on, "There are four possible victims, or suspects, who have not been located yet, as far as I know—Essie Wild, Devon Wild, Bernie Landoff, and now Caitlin Turley. And I found out there's a drug dealer called Double M. If the death was drug related, he's indirectly involved. I'm just asking questions when I get the chance. Anything I discover, I tell the authorities."

"You know a lot about this," Janae said, looking impressed.

"Some. But the main reason to go hear the band is for the music. Also, I think Talia will welcome another opportunity to visit with Quinn, and, if I'm not mistaken, Quinn won't be adverse to another talk with Talia, either."

"Okay, Mom, you sound as if you need some company," Clay said. He tilted his head toward Janae, and she nodded. "The band sounds terrific, and maybe we can help keep you out of trouble."

Beth grinned. The mood turned celebratory, and they gathered around the computer to plan their musical evening. When Beth called Talia, expecting to leave a message on a Saturday evening, she was surprised when the young lady answered right away. She sounded eager to hear the band again and pleased Beth was including her family.

Talia was slightly older than Clay and vaguely remembered him helping at the duplexes before he left to serve in the military. Beth believed the young people would enjoy knowing each other. They all made a date for the following Thursday evening when *Novel Invasion* would be headlining at a fun casual pub out in the suburbs. It was left for Beth to entice Arnie, but she guessed he'd jump at the chance to spend an evening with his son and daughter-in-law without breaking his back carrying furniture.

While they cleaned up the dinner table, Beth noticed Clay deep in thought. Finally, he asked her why no one had been able to locate the people who lived in the duplex at the time of the crime. Beth told him about the curbing of the investigation and about CSI Supervisor Mark Overos's suspicion of a drug cover-up.

"Maybe Detective Rinquire was about to locate Devon and Essie, or actually did locate them before he was told to work on other cases. I don't know for sure," Beth said.

"So shouldn't we be trying to find them?" Clay asked, with a frown.

Beth smiled at the word "we." Somehow she'd won another ally in her quest.

"I am hoping Quinn or maybe his sister can give us not only some clues about how to find the Wilds, but also some ideas whether one of them or someone they knew might have the motive to commit murder," Beth said.

"Are you sure Quinn and his sister aren't suspects?"

"They aren't crossed off the list, for sure," Beth said. "I haven't met Caitlin yet. However, Quinlin didn't give me the impression he could have murdered anyone."

Clay gave her a know-it-all look and said, "In the heat of passion, people do acts not within their normal character."

Beth agreed with Clay, of course, and told him more about the drug connections and Quinn's admission of being at odds with his roommate Bernie before they parted ways. Then she remembered to ask a question she'd wanted to ask since this all started.

"Is there anything you noticed that may have caused Psycho Cat's crazy preoccupation with the attic door? I mean, at home he'll nose around a cabinet door or at a crack in the basement wall, but after a short time he loses interest. You told me he kept at it for days before you checked out the attic, right? And it turned out there weren't any rodents up there."

Janae, who had been avoiding this conversation, spoke up as if suddenly seized by a stroke of inspiration.

"*Sylvester*," she said with a prim look, "came downstairs with a piece of fabric the same evening he started stalking the attic door. He dropped it near me, like he was bringing me a gift. I looked around in the closet where I found him later, thinking he may have torn some of our clothing. Instead I found some strings, fibers of the same material as the gift, hanging on the head of a nail sticking out near the attic opening. It wasn't from any of our clothes."

After some questioning, Janae described the fabric as a nice wool blend, not from clothing a person would ordinarily wear when climbing into a dusty attic. She said she threw the fabric scrap away but thought the multicolored strings hanging off the nail formed an interesting design. She pulled the nail out of the ceiling and stored it with her artifacts for future art ideas.

"Did you tell the police detectives about this?" Beth asked.

"No, I didn't think of it," Janae said, scrunching her face into a worried look. "I'm sorry. We were so sure Sylvester was after rodents up in the attic, and I was so upset by the whole idea of a dead body being found above my bed."

Chapter 18

August, Seven Years Earlier—Kansas City, Missouri

"Hey, Caitlin!"

Devon Wild stood in the driveway wearing dirty jeans and a ragged T-shirt, his sweaty hands on his hips, a grease smear and a grin on his round face. Barefooted, Caitlin approached the garage across the August-dry grass. She wore short shorts and a tank top, as befitted the hot weather, and her brunette hair was pulled back into a braid, which flipped across her back as she tripped excitedly toward her neighbor. The young woman exhibited no awareness of her appeal.

"Hey, Devon," she greeted her mechanic neighbor. "You look like a cat that just swallowed a mouse. I guess this means you were able to fix my clunky car—within my budget, I hope."

"Give 'er a try." Devon held out the keys for Caitlin's twenty-five year old sedan. Caitlin gave a whoop, grabbed the keys, and drove the car up and down the long driveway a couple of times. She would no more drive into the street without shoes or license than she would rob a bank. Devon stood watching, and then gave the hood a pat when Caitlin pulled to a stop and emerged smiling.

"The temperature gauge is normal, and there's no smoke!" she said.

Ever since the trip from Frog Springs to Kansas City, the car's temperature needle headed toward the "H" immediately upon pulling away from the curb. Caitlin had tried to ignore the small gray puff that rose from the edges of the hood after as little as a three block trip to the grocery store. This past week, Devon had noticed the smoke and offered to look at the engine. Caitlin told him she didn't have much money to pay for repair work, but, after looking under the hood, Devon told her he could replace the cracked hose at a discount by getting the materials from the repair shop where he worked. When Caitlin asked how much she owed, he told her ten dollars would cover it. Devon felt the white lie act like a miniature brush scrubbing clean a tiny portion of his sooty soul. He intended to throw in the rest of the money for the new hose. The job at the shop paid less than his skills were worth, but he couldn't afford to lose it by stealing.

Caitlin realized any auto repair would cost more than ten dollars at a garage, but since Devon had supplied the labor free of charge, she handed over a ten dollar bill with a sigh of relief and no idea the materials cost more in the range of fifty dollars. She felt like hugging her chivalrous neighbor. Instead, she took his hand, gave him a radiant smile, and thanked him. He colored, awkwardly patted her on the shoulder, and told her to be sure to tell him if she had any more trouble with her car.

"I think you're an amazing auto expert," Caitlin said. "Just in the last couple of weeks, I've seen you bring in an old junker and a newer car that looked like it had been hit broadside, and by the time you finished with them, they were both like new."

~~~

It was true. Devon grew up with an auto mechanic dad who taught his son everything he knew. They rebuilt cars together long before Devon could legally drive. After high school, the already skilled young mechanic attended two years of technical school and then completed an apprenticeship with a topnotch import car service center.

It was after that, when Devon landed a high paying job at a Lexus dealership and found himself on his own with plenty of money, he started hanging out with a group who gambled, drank, and bought drugs until their money ran out. Then they became willing to do whatever it took to get more.

He met Essie, a flamboyantly striking girl who actually paid attention to him. He was shy of girls during high school, and there were few women in his vocation. Essie provided his first love affair. He became hooked on her, as well as on the addictive lifestyle. However, several months in jail for drug possession dried him out, and Devon determined to reform. He asked Essie to marry him and renounce the old lifestyle. He had skills. He could support her. He was in love with her.

She agreed to the marriage—the security appealed to her. She'd had many "boyfriends," she called them, since junior high school, but not one of them wanted to marry her, until Devon. He was sweet, and being married to him would give her a little respectability, for a change, and a family. As for giving up her old friends and the highs, her way of life since age fourteen, she'd give it a try.

It was possible she meant to try, on some level, but life with Devon left her wanting more—more money, more highs, more excitement, and more rough sex. Devon lost his job at the Lexus service shop when he was sent to jail, and his prison record, combined with having been fired from his previous job, barred employment at every dealership and large auto repair shop to which he applied. Finally, he was hired to help out in a small garage owned by one of his father's old friends, a man who had known him since he was a kid and didn't look into his recent background. The pay was low, the hours long. To make ends meet, Devon found old or wrecked cars to fix up and sell. Essie was left to her own devices, and she became more and more drawn to her old hangouts.

It made sense to Devon that Essie would seek employment, at least until he could find a better position. His wife told him she found a job that would help pay the rent and buy her the clothes and jewelry she craved. She explained how she had talked to

Double M, a wealthy restaurant owner and importer they knew from one of the dive restaurants where they used to hang out. He gave her a job that would allow her to work from home—keeping books for his import business. Essie was supplied a laptop computer loaded with the software she'd use to keep the records, and Double M's people taught her the program. Double M or one of his employees would bring the billings and receipts to the house, and she would input the numbers.

Devon liked the bottles of wine, the gourmet import foods, and the special pot Double M sometimes left for them. Essie became bubblier than ever. Her over-the-edge personality swings didn't make Devon suspicious. He expected it. It's the way she'd acted since he met her. Naturally, she swore she wasn't using drugs any stronger than marijuana, and Devon didn't notice her needle marks when they made love, less and less often, in the dark. He was busy trying to be a good mechanic, a good citizen, and eventually, he hoped, a good provider for his own family.

Essie pulled Devon out of his reverie. Spying Caitlin and Devon talking in the driveway, she hollered out the back door. "Devon, come on in here. You've been out there all day. I need for you to go to the store for me. We need some stuff for dinner." She yelled past Caitlin, as if she wasn't there.

"I'll go see what she needs," Devon said. "You take care of that little car and it'll last you another ten years."

"I'll do my best," Caitlin said. "Right now I'm going to pull the garden hose over here and give this old car a good washing. Then it'll look as good as it runs."

~~~

Less than five minutes after Devon left, Double M pulled into his spot in front of the garage. He nodded at Caitlin, who was carrying a bucket of soapy water out of the house. She noticed him walk right into Essie's back door without knocking, and it crossed her mind how coincidental it was Devon was sent away just before this man appeared. Then she forgot all about it until Double M materialized beside her when she was bending over scrubbing the back bumper of the car, a sponge in one hand, the hose sprayer in the other. He jumped back out of the way when she stood and turned the nozzle on to rinse the back of the car.

"Oh, I'm so sorry," Caitlin said, "I didn't see you there."

She thought she saw a frown of anger pass over the finely groomed features of this short, pompous person. He controlled himself quickly and laughed it off as he flicked the water off his pants.

"Well, I won't melt. It's a hot day. A shower feels good. I was on my way back to my car and stopped to admire your work. Thought maybe you'd wash mine next." He pointed to his Porsche, and his grin looked friendly.

"Well, I, uh… sure," responded Caitlin, unused to teasing.

"I'm just kidding," said Double M. "The boys down at the car wash do a good job. Not as good as you, but I think you have more potential than resorting to car washing for a living. Essie tells me you haven't found a job yet?"

"No, not yet."

"It's tough in this economy. I'll let you in on a little secret. Sometimes it's not what you know. It's who you know. Now here's the deal. I happen to have an opening for a hostess at one of my restaurants, and I can tell by the way you work around here and the way you hold yourself, you're a good candidate for the job. I pay eleven-fifty an hour to start, and the pay rate can climb depending on your performance."

Caitlin was speechless. Here she stood in flip flops and wet clothes, her hair in disarray, exactly zero of her multiple job applications having been even acknowledged, and suddenly someone was offering what sounded like a good job. She thought about her first impression of this man and immediately discarded it as unfair. However, she told herself to act responsibly and professionally and not to dance a jig and shout out with joy, which would have been her reflexive reactions.

"That's very kind of you, sir," she said. "I'll go get some paper and a pen, if you'll wait just a minute, to write the address and phone number where I can go to fill out an application."

"No need. You see. I'm right about you. You're as polite and polished as you are lovely. Here's my card. Be at this address tomorrow morning at eleven o'clock and ask for me. I'll show you around personally. Do you think you can find it? I know you're from out of town."

"Yes, sir, I can find it," She looked at the card. "Thank you again."

Caitlin watched Double M back his sports car out of the driveway, a different car than she'd seen him drive before. She was still dumbfounded by the unexpected offer of a job—a job that paid an acceptable beginning wage and promise of more! Caitlin had no doubt she'd be earning a good wage in no time. She giggled a nervous giggle to herself as she realized she still held the running garden hose in one hand and the valuable business card in the other.

~~~

Quinn and Bernie slept until early afternoon after a long exhausting night with the band. When Caitlin saw Quinn emerge from his basement room and head for the shower, she warmed a can of tomato soup and prepared a grilled American cheese sandwich, which she placed on the small kitchen table for him as soon as he came downstairs. She was bursting with excitement to tell her brother about her job offer and with it her opportunity to help them stay in the duplex or at least stay together. She wanted him to know he didn't have to think about selling drugs to make ends meet. He had time to wait for a day job or to just work on making more money with his music. Caitlin sat down at the table with Quinn and asked him about his latest gig. She listened carefully to his analysis of the previous night's performance and was delighted to hear his upbeat stories. Finally, she blurted out her news with a huge grin on her face.

"This guy owns several restaurants and imports wine and fine foods," she explained to her brother, showing him Double M's business card.

Quinn sat with a look of total shock on his face, not at all the reaction she'd expected.

"Devon told me Essie keeps books for Mr. Martin. She works at home, and he or one of his employees brings her the records she needs," Caitlin said, attempting to induce Quinn to be as excited about her news as she was. "He talked to me and thought I'd be a good hostess. He'd rather hire someone he's met rather than someone who just sends in a résumé, I think."

Quinn put down his spoon and shook his head back and forth without saying a word. Caitlin didn't understand and started to grow impatient with her brother.

"It's okay," she said. "I know it's not a job leading to a good office position like I was hoping, but it'll bring in money for the time be...."

"No!" Quinn said in a quiet but emphatic way, causing Caitlin to stop her chatter and stare at him in confusion.

"It's not..." Quinn detested having to quell his sister's joy. "Caitlin, listen. Mr. Martin is known as Double M. He might bring some receipts to Essie for inputting data, but he also brings the drugs she sells through people like Bernie. Essie wants me to help sell, and Double M, by hiring you, will make me indebted, or at least give him a means to ask for favors from me in exchange for not hurting you."

Caitlin's jaw dropped. Her eyes started to water. She didn't want to believe Quinn.

"What do you mean by hurting me? He offered me a job as a hostess in one of his restaurants—a good, honest job," she said.

"Yeah, I've been in two of those restaurants," Quinn said. "The hostesses are offered a good wage, right? Believe me, they have to do a lot more than guide people to their seats and hand out menus in order to make the money—stuff you would not ever get involved with, unless you were threatened, or blackmailed, or whatever other means that drug lord uses on people."

Caitlin drew her brows together. She believed her brother now. His account coincided with her original impression of Mr. Martin and with her observation of his extended visits to Essie. The thought of the offer he made out of the blue and her innocent acceptance of his benevolence infuriated her. She shook, thinking how close she'd come to showing up at an appointment with the man the following day and beginning a job that would trap her in his filthy web. Her young mind started whirling with ways to get both Quinn and herself far out of the reach of this horrible man.

Chapter 19

February—Kansas City, Missouri

"Here it is," Janae said, holding the pointed end of a nail off of which trailed several lengths of gray, black, brown, and blue threads. Clay and Beth had watched her look for this dubious artifact, kneeling on the hardwood floor and searching through several still unpacked boxes, for the past ten minutes. Janae considered her prize. Beth's fingers itched to grab the nail and take it to her CSI contact, Mark Overos, as soon as possible.

Janae said, "If someone tore clothing on this nail, it's possible that person ripped some skin, too. There might have been blood on the nail head. Do you think it's possible to test such an old DNA sample?"

"Probably," Beth said.

"Absolutely," Clay said.

"We shouldn't get too excited," Beth cautioned. "There may have been no blood. Or Psycho Cat—sorry, I mean Sylvester— may have diluted any blood when he tore the fabric away from the nail. Um, then, too, I suppose the torn clothing could have been from someone other than the killer."

"No, I think this nail has the killer's DNA on it. I do," Janae said. "Can we get it tested?"

"The police have dropped the case," Clay said.

"Fortunately," Beth said, "there is a CSI investigator who, I believe, will help us. I can take it to him."

~~~

After Beth explained her discovery of possible new evidence over the phone, Mark Overos agreed to a meeting on Sunday afternoon. They met at a frozen yogurt shop, where Beth arrived a few minutes early and loaded up a small cup of nonfat yogurt with all kinds of decadent toppings. She did feel a little guilty when Mark arrived a few minutes late and ordered a cup of low fat yogurt with no toppings. Why should she care if Mark thought her a healthy eater? She considered the question for just a moment before she turned all her attention to the reason for their meeting.

Beth showed him the nail and strings of fabric she had preserved with care in a plastic bag—knowing full well the bag wouldn't do much good after several years of aging, attack by a cat, and Janae's handling. Mark looked at the nail through the plastic without expression.

"Do you think you can get any DNA off the nail or the fibers?" Beth asked.

"I'll take it in and test it for blood," he said. "I can't guarantee this will help track down our killer. Even if there is a testable DNA sample here, the DNA might not be in our system."

Mark gave her a doubtful look. "Also, you must have considered the fibers may have come from someone other than the person who put the body in the attic. There must have been dozens of people up there over the years."

Beth screwed up her face. Then she echoed Janae's stand on the issue of whether or not the fabric came from the killer. "I don't think anyone, other than the guilty person or people, has been up there since we've owned the property. Most of our tenants have used the closet, including the shelves, not even aware there is an attic access in the ceiling."

"Well, it's worth a look. I'll test it, and we'll go from there."

"Are you sure there is a killer? It couldn't have been an accident, or maybe a drug overdose?"

"There are multiple wounds on the skull. It wasn't necessarily premeditated, but it was a murder."

"I guess I expected as much."

Mark verified the information Beth had given him about her visit with Quinlin Turley and what he had to say concerning Devon and Essie Wild. She repeated the information she'd given him over the phone about Essie's drug dealing and Bernie Landoff's participation, and then she remembered what Quinn had said about Essie's supplier, someone called Double M.

"Quinn thinks Essie was trading sex with Double M for drugs as well as getting drugs for Bernie. She tried to talk Quinn into selling, and Quinn thinks she might have had other sellers, too."

Mark's eyebrows shot up the minute she mentioned Double M. He asked Beth more about the man, but she had only heard the name one time from Quinn and couldn't tell him anything more.

"I do know Quinn and Bernie moved away before I noticed the putrid smell in that duplex, but I can't remember how long it was after they moved that I went in there. Quinn may have moved away because of the drug dealing. He may have been concerned about his teenage sister being exposed to that atmosphere. I'd like to talk to his sister, Caitlin, if I can locate her."

Beth didn't tell Mark about her plan to question Quinn Turley again. There was a high probability they wouldn't find out anything more from Quinn, and his sister could have gone back to Arkansas. Beth decided she could always let Mark know later if they learned more.

When Beth returned home, a slow Sunday afternoon still loomed ahead. She considered going to the duplexes to begin her planned project on the side where Quinn Turley had lived so many years ago. The bathroom tile project seemed a little like overkill to her, though, since that rental already looked presentable. New tiling would create added sparkle, and she knew it was something she could accomplish, but a new look wouldn't make much difference if the ghostly shadow of a spirit at unrest remained. At least the remains were gone—ugh, such dark puns should never enter her mind.

She decided to put the work off until Monday, and with unaccustomed impulsiveness, Beth called her young friend, Talia Johnson. Clay and Janae had offered to help, but they were quite busy, and Talia had already shown her enthusiasm for solving the mystery. Beth told Talia she needed her assistance to research the whereabouts of Devon and Essie Wild.

"I think you can find them, because you found Quinn Turley super-fast. I don't know if detectives have questioned or even found Devon and Essie yet, and they are the people I believe to have been living in the duplex when the murder took place," Beth said.

Even to herself, she sounded a little desperate and pleading, but Talia didn't hesitate for a moment. In fact, she invited Beth to visit her condo where they could collaborate on the search more easily in front of her computer screen rather than having to make phone calls back and forth.

While Beth gathered together what information she had about her former tenants, Psycho Cat decided he needed her attention. While she rummaged through the file cabinet, he leaned his front paws against her leg and addressed her with a guttural, "Meow." Ignoring him never worked when he was in this mood—so she patted his back and scratched him under the neck and behind his soft ears.

"I don't have time to hold and brush you now, you Psycho Kitty," Beth said. "This is important business. I need to help find the people who may have been involved in the murder of the skeleton you discovered."

The cat looked at her with big, inscrutable eyes and grew quiet.

"It could turn out to be dangerous. You didn't let that stop you when you leaped into the attic, did you boy? I'm not sure why either of us thinks this is so important, except for our own peace of mind. Nevertheless, I'm committed to finding out what happened and bringing the culprit to justice. What do you think of that?"

Psycho Cat seemed to give her the go-ahead as he executed a graceful jump from her leg onto the chair at her desk and sat like a guardian sphinx as she drew out the file folder with its scanty information about Devon and Essie Wild. This was his sophisticated Sylvester side, as opposed to his Psycho Cat side.

~~~

When she met Beth at her door twenty minutes later, Talia apologized. "Excuse my appearance. I've just been hanging out at home today." She wore a T-shirt, plaid drawstring pants, and house slippers, no make-up, her hair pulled into a pony tail.

Beth blinked. "You are lovely as usual."

Talia led the way into a bright room decorated in what Beth designated a sleekly ultra-modern style. Above a sculptured gray leather sofa, flanked by two box-like black end tables topped by lamps stolen from George Jetson's apartment, was mounted a stunning five-by-three mosaic. It's monochromatic stone, ceramic, and glass tiles in dozens of shades of red faintly suggested a city scape. From the subtle print in the gray, black, and red area rug in the middle of the shiny black hardwood floor, to the geometric easy chairs, the room dazzled with complex harmonious components. Beth stared from the room to Talia, back at her décor, and then at her face.

"A beautiful hostess in a gorgeous setting," she said. "Do you have a decorator, or did you do this?"

"It was me."

"Wow! Multi-talented. Talia, I've never asked about your heritage. You must have good-looking, creative parents."

"Thank you. It's nice of you to say that," Talia said, taking Beth's jacket and motioning her toward the sofa, which turned out to be as comfortable as it was sleek. "My dad married my mother in the Philippines when he was stationed there as a young serviceman in the early 1970s. Polynesian, Southeast Asian, Arab,

133

maybe a touch of Chinese, Spanish, and probably other European blood ran in her veins."

"How about your father?"

"My dad's father emigrated from Denmark—thus the Johnson. His mother's heritage is European, too. She's an English, Irish, French, and German-American mutt." Talia grinned. "A mutt like me."

"I'm impressed you know all this genealogical information about your relatives," Beth said. It astounded her how much this young lady had it together, whether she thought so or not.

"I started asking about my parents' backgrounds when I was very young," Talia said. "At school in the southern Kansas town where my parents inherited a small farm, kids tended to shun anyone who might be the daughter of a seasonal Mexican harvest worker or maybe a Native American girl. My older brother looks like our father and avoided much of the spitefulness, but even as early as kindergarten I remember running into the house from the school bus, holding back sobs, and questioning my mother about what kind of girl I was."

Talia brushed a stray strand of hair away from her face and smiled. "My mom was the best. She told me about her family of doctors, lawyers, and university presidents in the Philippines . Anyway, she convinced me I'd be okay if I held my head high, did my best in school, smiled, and treated everyone the way I'd like to be treated. She was right. It pretty much worked for me."

A slight frown crossed Talia's face, and she lowered her eyes. "Um, lately I've been thinking my mother's advice may have worked a little too well. I need to lower my expectations for myself enough to let others in—to care more about other people and not about what they think of me. I might still have my boyfriend if..."

"No. Allowing you to get away was that young man's loss. When you meet the right person, you'll care about each other in equal shares. Look what you're doing right now. Helping with this case, which has nothing to do with you, *is* caring about other people. It seems to come naturally to you. Your mother sounds like a smart lady. Do your parents still live on the Kansas farm?"

"My dad does," Talia said. "My mom died of cancer when I was in high school. Then Dad married a lady who has three children younger than me. My brother was out of the house by then." She grinned. "He's a bio-chemistry professor at Kansas State University.

"Dad's new wife didn't have much use for me, but I was there with her family for only my senior year of high school. Then my father gave me the deposit for the duplex I rented from you, and he paid the tuition for my first two college semesters. After that... Well, you know. I worked full time to pay my own way. It took me longer to finish school that way, and I scrimped along through the tight times, but, hey, some people don't even have anyone to help them get started."

"Your mother would be proud of you," Beth said, "and your father..."

"...lets my brother and me know how proud he is," Talia finished for her. "But you didn't come here to talk about me. We'd better get busy seeing what we can find out about your former tenants."

They sat in front of a large computer monitor in Talia's brightly-lighted home office, Beth answering questions and feeding information from her rental records, Talia translating the known facts into relevant searches. From her records, Beth knew Essie was short for Estelle and Devon's middle initial was R. The search of social networking sites revealed nothing conclusive, but Beth gazed in amazement as she watched Talia use AND, OR, parentheses, brackets, and all manner of advanced search techniques on a variety of search engines and government directories. In a little less than fifteen minutes she found a promising listing. On the website of an auto shop in Belton, Missouri, a suburb southeast of Kansas City, Devon Wild was mentioned as one of their master mechanics. Current information about Essie Wild or Estelle Wild remained elusive, but if the mechanic in Belton was truly their Devon, then they'd found Essie, too, Beth hoped.

Chapter 20

August, Seven Years Earlier —Kansas City, Missouri

On Monday morning Caitlin debated whether to call and cancel her appointment with Double M or just not show up. She waited until ten-thirty to wake Quinn. That was early for him after the late nights of his weekend band performances, but she needed his advice. He knew about this guy and would know better than she how to handle the situation. They decided together. She should take the high road by notifying the restaurant she wasn't going to be there for the interview. It was the way she would handle any appointment she couldn't keep, and besides, being polite might keep the gangster from getting mad and retaliating in some way. What things drug lords did to people who didn't show up for an appointment, Caitlin wasn't sure, but she thought it could be bad for her or for Quinn or for both of them. Before the eleven o'clock appointment time, she left her cancellation message with the receptionist, hostess, or whoever answered the phone, and figured she'd done her duty.

To take her mind off her disappointment and to feel industrious, Caitlin went to her bedroom and dressed in a summer skirt, a nice blouse, and flats, preparing to revisit some of the businesses where she had filled out applications in the past couple of weeks. Follow-up visits would let employers know she was still interested.

"Be proactive." That's what Quinn had said. It worked for him two years ago when he found his job at the home improvement store. Of course, this summer neither Quinn's good résumé nor his persistence had paid off. Most of his online applications yielded no response at all. Only a few were confirmed, but when he sent follow-up inquiries he discovered the positions had either been filled or the companies had decided not to fill the slots after all. That the nationwide recession could have such a dismal effect on their personal lives and need for employment had begun to sink in so far that a murky bottom threatened to swallow them.

"I'm going to make use of my newly renovated car for some job application follow-ups this morning," Caitlin said, trying to appear cheerful. "First I'm going to that Taco Bell over on State Line Road. I applied there almost a week ago for a job I am totally qualified to do. After all, I worked at a Taco Bell in Frog Springs during the summers after my sophomore and junior years and on evenings and weekends during the school year. I've done every job there is to do at a Taco Bell, except manage the place. It's better to have a fast food job than no job, right?"

Quinn looked up from the application in front of him on the kitchen table. He looked impressed by the comeback his little sister had made from the funk in which he'd put her yesterday afternoon. She'd not only survived her disappointment, but also she had gained spunk.

"Go for it," he said. "You look so pretty, they'll probably hire you just to bring in customers. I mean, besides the fact that they are probably going to hire you anyway, with all your experience."

"You look pretty" was a comment uncharacteristic from her brother. Quinn was trying to make up for bursting Caitlin's bubble about the hostess job. But Caitlin didn't quibble with the remark. She felt energized. If not today, then tomorrow she'd find a job, any job for the time being. She'd go from business to business and beg for employment, if she had to.

"Thanks for your kind remarks," she said while spinning around to let her skirt swirl about her legs. "You're right. They'd be crazy not to hire me."

The upbeat mood lasted through her visit to the Taco Bell, where she had responded to a *Become Part of our Team* sign in the window last week. Mr. Crewman, the general manager, had taken her application and told her he'd be in touch. The job was a part-time position, and Caitlin wanted to assure the manager again that she was fine with part-time, that she was experienced, and that she would be the hardest worker he could hire. It wasn't to be. She entered and told the young man at the counter she wanted to talk to Mr. Crewman about her application for the job opening.

"Mr. Crewman isn't here right now," the young man said, leaning over the counter in a confiding manner. "But if you're talking about the job advertised in the window last week, it's already taken. In fact, the new kid started last night. Marcia, one of our evening workers, is going off to college, and he's her little brother. I didn't think anyone else had applied. I guess Mr. Crewman didn't call to tell you he hired someone else, did he?"

"No," Caitlin said, trying to maintain her composure. "Thank you." She walked toward the door but stopped and turned back. "Please tell your manager Caitlin Turley is okay with part-time or full-time work if he has another opening."

She understood. They always hired relatives of good employees at the Taco Bell in Frog Springs. It was easier than hiring someone they didn't know anything about.

Caitlin drove to a drugstore where she'd applied for a job five days before and was told the opening had been filled by one of their part-time employees who wanted full time work. At a clothing store, she wasn't able to speak to the manager because she didn't have an appointment, but one of the ladies in the office told her they had at least forty-five applications for the job. She tried two more follow-up visits, which gave her similar results. Her jauntiness diminished.

Then, she inquired at the ice-cream shop in the mall, where she had applied for a position a week and a half previously, and was told, with a trace of irritation by the manager on duty, there had been no job opening at that location for several months. She thanked the man for his time, set her mouth, and pointed her feet in the direction of the mall exit.

The carnival-like atmosphere, women swinging their purses, folks talking and laughing with each other, people in happy moods examining shop window displays, clerks making money by pushing their wares, all sent Caitlin's spirits reeling farther than ever toward depression. When a young woman stepped into the aisle to entice her to try a hand cream infused with miraculous minerals from the Dead Sea, Caitlin stopped and gave her an incensed look that caused the woman to back into her booth.

Late in the afternoon, having eaten nothing since her toast and jelly that morning, Caitlin parked at the curb and trekked in a dejected way toward the front door of the duplex. She stepped onto the porch practicing a brave smile. Through the screen door, she heard the din of raised voices from the kitchen. Stepping inside without a sound, she stopped to listen when she recognized Essie's shrill insistent speech. Essie was lecturing Quinn about the money he could be making if he would sell drugs directly to his music venue admirers instead of sending them to talk to Bernie. Bernie sneered smugly that Quinn would have to do that, because he was doing a shitty job of sending more customers to him.

"Hey, man, what do you want me to do, use the microphone to announce to the crowd they should see our drummer for their drugs after the show?" she heard Quinn ask.

Essie nagged some more. Bernie cussed at Quinn. Quinn wavered, said he'd try to send some people Bernie's way but wouldn't sell outright. As she left by the back door, Essie called him a pussy and more Caitlin couldn't hear. Caitlin was about to go into the kitchen when she heard Bernie blasting her brother, telling him he was already a part of the drug deals and could go to jail as fast as any of them.

"Ya know, man, Double M won't be happy about you knowing what's going on and not doing your share. The guy has people. Big guys who rough up anyone who doesn't cooperate. He's going to blame me, too, for not keeping you in line. I'm the one who gave you this job."

Bernie went from a growl to a bellow. "It's your fault we have to move. From this duplex into some ratty apartment. What kind of place can we find with what we make from our gigs? You don't have any money coming in, and now you've got your sister here. I'm trying to help you, man. You owe me enough to put a deposit on an apartment if you're going to refuse to help make money."

Quinn kept his cool and replied in an even tone Bernie would have enough money for the deposit if he didn't shoot up everything he earned. Bernie spat out a few more epitaphs and threats, and Caitlin thought the encounter might come to blows.

Instead, Bernie rushed out of the kitchen and past her to the stairway. He paused for less than a second to cast what seemed to Caitlin the most hateful look she had ever seen, worse than she had ever received from her father. Bernie climbed the stairs two at a time, and Caitlin stepped outside onto the front landing, leaned against the house, and took some deep breaths.

In her shaken state, her depression over the day's rejections and her youthful need to create a fair world led her to believe she was the cause of this whole situation. Her entire adolescence predisposed her to self-blame. First, her mother died, and she felt somehow responsible. Then her father turned into a cruel substance abuser, caused her brother to leave home, and blamed it all on her. Now this. It had to be her fault. If she hadn't come here, her brother would not be in this situation.

With hardly a thought about what she was doing, she went to Essie's door, opened it, and screamed for the floozy. Essie appeared in the kitchen doorway with a surprised look that turned into a smirk. She leaned against the door frame with one hand on her hip and turned her head to a mocking tilt. Someone on the outside would have seen her as she was, a painted tart trying to bully her way out of her guilt-ridden circumstances. To Caitlin, the older woman with her derisive expression represented all of the girls in high school who seemed to look down their noses at her after her mother died and her father became an infamous drunk in their small town, the employers who turned a deaf ear to her pleading for a job, and, in some ways, the mother who left her to face all this on her own.

"Leave my brother alone," Caitlin yelled, "or I'll call the police and tell them everything I know about your drug dealing."

"Ha, the police," Essie said with derision matching her expression. "Double M owns the police, you know. Nothing's going to happen to me. It's Double M you need to worry about, Missy. You had your chance to be helped, but you blew it. Now go on home and stop butting into other people's affairs. I hear you've got less than a week left to live here anyway. When you're gone, you won't be able to eavesdrop on my conversations, will you?"

Essie turned her back on the desperate teenager. Caitlin stood for a moment, her hand on her abdomen, feeling weak, as if the air had been crushed out of her. If adrenalin had kicked in right then, she might have advanced on the woman, maybe even hit her. Instead, she rushed through the front door across the front stoop and put her hand on the handle of her brother's screen door. She pulled away and started toward her car, but she realized there was nowhere to go. Caitlin sat on the front step for a few minutes and then headed toward the back yard. She needed to talk to someone good, someone she trusted. It was impossible for her to confront her brother at this time. She heard him say he would help sell the stinking drugs. What was she going to do?

Caitlin headed toward her backdoor neighbor. During the few weeks she had been here, she'd become friends with Talia

Johnson, who was about her brother's age and lived in one side of the duplex behind them.

She and Quinn had invited Talia over to their patio one evening, and she'd spent money she could not spare to purchase hamburger, buns, and chips. Remembering her mother's trick of fancying up hamburger meat with an egg, bread crumbs, and ketchup, Caitlin had fried the meat in the kitchen, since they didn't own a grill, and accepted praise for her cooking while the three of them ate outside sitting on rickety lawn chairs that must have been left by previous tenants. The enjoyable evening, full of conversation, laughter, and music, floated in Caitlin's memory like a lovely little white cloud flying around the black stormy clouds in her gloomy sky. It wasn't Caitlin's habit to talk to others about her problems, but this time she couldn't think of anything else to do. The thought turned out to be another dead end. Talia was not home. She was probably at work or at school.

Caitlin sat on Talia's back step until summer twilight darkened the sky. Then she saw Bernie bound unsteadily out the back door, stumble to his car in the driveway carrying a bag of something, and pull away. Finally, thirst and hunger drove her home. Also, she needed to talk to Quinn before she wavered from the decision she had made while sitting there. She'd go to California for sure. There was room in the back seat of her car to sleep, and she'd drive as long as she could each day. She had an address and a phone number for Aunt Sharon, her mother's sister, and she had that memory of an offer for help tucked away in the back of her mind.

Quinn would have no reason to have anything to do with the drug world after he moved away from here and didn't have to worry about supporting her. He could concentrate on his music, recruit more students for guitar lessons, and maybe take some classes himself. Caitlin became almost cheerful at the thought.

Chapter 21

February—Kansas City, Missouri

Arnie didn't congratulate Beth or act interested in her weekend activities and discoveries, as she expected. Instead, he became almost confrontational. He sounded a little like the Monday morning quarterback he became when the Kansas City Chiefs lost their games, and a little like a jealous kid. He dismissed the importance of Janae's thread-trailing nail, insisted it must obviously have lost any traces of blood if there were any to begin with. When Beth told him she and Talia had tried to locate and wanted to question Devon and Essie Wild, Arnie lectured her about getting Talia mixed up in her harebrained schemes.

He seemed especially upset by Beth's description of her meeting with Mark Overos earlier in the afternoon. She was astounded. She felt so proud of the steps she had taken over the weekend to try to get to the bottom of this mess, and she'd become entirely convinced she was doing the right thing. Clay and Janae, Mark, and Talia Johnson all supported her purpose, too. Now here was her own husband, offering only hostility.

Disappointment hit Beth in the gut. She felt wounded. She tried to argue Arnie into understanding her position, but he wouldn't listen and went back to his original position—she shouldn't be working on a police case.

"It's not only dangerous, but also it could hurt the detectives' investigation."

"There isn't an investigation," Beth said. "The case has been dropped by the police."

"Not dropped, just temporarily postponed while they work on more pressing cases," Arnie said with a stern frown on his face.

When Arnie got that know-it-all look, Beth realized her arguments would be like reasoning with Psycho Cat about the innate freedom birds have to land on the bird bath without being chased by a cat. She gave up and entered her silent mode. It's not a technique she was proud of—she wouldn't advise her daughter to act in this childish way—but when she found her position opposed so vehemently without room for argument or reasoning, she closed down.

Beth spent an hour or so avoiding conversation with her husband and staying out of his way by cleaning up the kitchen and reading, until her mood began to soften and she felt bad about having a fight with Arnie after not seeing him for three days. She curled up on the couch with him and kissed him on the cheek. They watched a show and the news on television together before going upstairs, but neither of them mentioned her weekend activities. They both acted as if the issue had been resolved. It hadn't. Right then Beth didn't understand Arnie's emotional reaction, and she couldn't think of a way to resolve the stalemate. Later, she'd realize they should have continued their discussion.

~~~

On Monday morning, the sleuthing wasn't mentioned. When she didn't see any resentment or blame on Arnie's face, Beth pushed their argument to the back of her mind. The TV weatherman forecasted one of those unseasonably warm days Kansas City folks enjoy sometimes in February. The two decided to don jogging gear and go for a fast walk on the Trolley Track Trail before breakfast, but, even though the forecast called for a high of 58 degrees in the afternoon, Beth felt her nose and cheeks stinging from the morning chill.

"I know it's in the high thirties," she said as they turned toward their house, "but with the wind in our face it feels like it's in the teens."

"No kidding," Arnie said. "I felt my muscles loosen up on the outbound, but they're going to freeze up again before we make it back against this wind."

"Argh, we should have worn parkas instead of running suits."

Beth felt the cold wind strike her teeth when she smiled at Arnie, and she closed her mouth. Arnie gave her shoulder a hug. "Come on, we're almost home." He jogged a few steps backwards and motioned to her.

She broke into a jog with a grin and beat her arms across her body until they reached the warm house. After the two ate a hot breakfast and read the morning paper, Beth sensed a joint convivial mood.

It wasn't until Arnie received a call to meet with one of his consulting agents Beth felt a twinge of guilt. Her first thought edged on being deceptive. Now she could go to Belton to talk to Devon Wild without having to argue again with Arnie about it. He could just assume she would head to the duplex and her bathroom tiling project.

The duplex is where she'd go after her interview with Devon. If Arnie asked her about her plans for the day, she wouldn't lie. She'd merely omit the part about her intention to visit Belton.

As it turned out, she didn't need to say a thing. For years they had gone about their daily work routines without explanation beyond the casual "How was your day?" questions and the stories they told each other about their funniest or most frustrating experiences. Arnie, his mind on the information he needed to gather for his impending consult, didn't query Beth about her intentions for the day in regard to the inexpert investigation she'd been conducting. She breathed a sigh of relief as soon as she kissed her husband good-bye and shut the door behind him.

Now, how would this work? Beth paced back and forth in front of her phone debating whether she should call or show up unannounced at the shop where Devon worked. She could make an appointment to have her oil changed. But that wouldn't guarantee Devon would be the one to work on the car or would even be there. If she called and asked for Devon, what could she say that would convince him to visit with her? She didn't want to flat-out lie, but she couldn't come right out and ask him if he knew who killed someone and put the body in the attic where he lived. He wouldn't agree to see her unless she had a reason which sounded innocent.

Beth didn't want to ask questions over the phone. She wouldn't be able to see Devon's reactions. What to say? Then she thought about the roof replacement. She could tell him she was contacting former tenants to ask about the long-standing rodent problem on the roof. It wasn't entirely untrue. She intended to talk about how she thought a squirrel died in that attic, and she *had* contacted other former tenants.

Beth waited only about two minutes for Devon to answer after he was called to the phone in the service department. After her short explanation of the reason for calling, Devon sounded pleasant and agreeable. They decided to meet during his coffee break at a Wendy's across the street from where he worked.

Beth started half an hour early, stepping with determination past Psycho Cat. She detected disapproval in his wide green eyes. "Don't look at me that way," Beth said as she bent down to give him a head rub. "You started this. I need to find out how some unfortunate person ended up as the skeleton you found in the attic at the duplex. If you hadn't led Clay into that attic, we'd all be fat, dumb, and happily spending our winter playing rather than trying to solve a murder." The cat made a little growling noise in his throat. "You're right. I'm being a little sneaky, but Arnie will be as thrilled as I if I can get this figured out."

Even with a GPS to guide her, the way to the expanding suburb of Belton seemed to follow a challenging path a terrific distance out into the countryside, although, in reality, it was closer than several other Kansas City suburbs. Beth arrived at the fast food establishment and selected a somewhat private table in one corner some minutes before Devon had promised to meet her. She ordered coffee and jotted some questions to ask Devon.

Beth sat in the booth intent on plowing through the unfamiliar territory of interrogation when, with a sudden jolting thought, her shoulders tightened. What was she doing? It was evident Devon Wild wasn't the victim, but he could very well be the perpetrator. Of all the residents of both sides of the duplex during the year the crime must have been committed, he was the biggest and strongest. Also, she still could not remember whether she ever saw Essie during or after the time she detected the bad smell. Devon's courteous and innocent-sounding demeanor on the phone could have been an act. He could be a wife killer!

Beth shook her head and tried to get a grip. After all, what could he do to her in this public place? However, just to feel safer, Beth picked up her belongings and casually moved to a table in front of the window, a table visible to almost everyone in the restaurant.

Devon approached the table with a friendly smile. "Hi, Mrs. Stockwell! You look the same as when you were my landlady. I spotted you right off."

To Beth, startled out of her reverie and a little uneasy about the meeting, at best, the greeting sounded too cheerful. However, the young man appeared anything but scary. The shaggy locks she remembered were trimmed into an attractive style capping his clean-shaven face, Devon's dark pants and long-sleeved uniform shirt were spotless, and the nails on the hand he offered for a shake looked clean and neat.

"Please call me Beth. I almost didn't recognize you. It looks as if you might be a supervisor or the boss at your shop. I've never seen such a clean-looking mechanic."

Devon smiled. "As a matter of fact, I was promoted to supervisor of the entire auto service operation just a few months ago."

"Congratulations," Beth said. "How long have you worked there?"

"Four years, but I had a number of years of previous experience."

"I knew you were a super auto mechanic when you and Essie lived in my duplex. I remember seeing cars in the driveway that started out as wrecks and ended up looking great. I suppose you and Essie live here in Belton now. It's a long drive out here from the city."

"Oh, I guess I thought you knew. Essie and I broke up several months before I moved out of your duplex. She and I haven't been together since then. I live in Belton now, but I've actually lived a couple of places since that time."

Devon paused, and Beth remained quiet, nodded and tilted her head as if asking for more information. Now she knew why she couldn't remember seeing Essie after Quinn and Bernie moved out. Essie wasn't there. Was it because she left, or because she was killed and her body jammed into a trunk—an eerie, hateful trunk that had since gathered dust in the attic for seven years? Beth's heart started pounding, but she strove to remain calm on the outside. None of her questions seemed right. What could she ask—did you kill Essie and stuff her in a trunk?

Finally, Devon broke the silence. "I recently moved in with my fiancée. It took several years for my divorce from Essie to be finalized. I couldn't locate her to sign the papers. It took even longer for me to get over the experience, but Angela—she's my fiancée—has helped me put it all behind."

"I'm glad you're ready to move on," Beth said, holding out hope this seemingly nice guy wasn't a killer.

"Thanks. Me, too. It took a long time. It wasn't the marriage so much as the reason for the split. I found her in bed with a-a (Beth could tell Devon was trying to find a polite word, for her sake) jerk, a guy called Double M—Double Malignant, I'd say. He was supposedly her boss, and I learned he supplied drugs she used and sold. They must have been sleeping together for a long time. Anyway... the marriage wasn't a good one to begin with. It just took me a long time to realize it."

"So, you haven't seen Essie since?"

"Not even once. Shortly after I found them, she packed up all her things and left while I was at work. I figured she went off with *him*. I ran into one of our mutual acquaintances when I went to one of our old hangouts to try and find Essie a year or so after she left. He told me he thought Essie might have taken the name Estelle Sun, or Estelle Shine, or maybe Star, to be an exotic dancer at some club on the East side. Essie loved to dance, and her given name is actually Estelle. It made sense. I went to the club to look a few times, but I never found her." Devon shook his head. "I wasn't motivated to find her because, by that time, I didn't want to see her, and there was no pressing reason for me to get the divorce finalized quickly."

Beth decided Devon was either innocent, or he was a good actor. "I'm sorry you had such a bad experience," she said, "but congratulations on your engagement."

"Thank you," Devon said. "And excuse me. I didn't mean to bore you with my sad story. It's just, I mean, you're easy to talk to. On the phone you said something about a rodent problem on the duplex roof?"

"Yes, the roof." Beth said, remembering the pretext she'd used for contacting Devon. "I know you don't have a lot of time, but thank you for telling me about your life since I last saw you. I'm very interested."

She manufactured her roof question as she talked, "About the duplex roof—you see, during the time you lived in the duplex the roof was replaced with what was supposed to be one that would last for at least twenty years. But since then—remember the big pin oak trees out front?—the branches have spread over the roof, and they hold tons of bird and squirrel nests. After only seven years, now the roof's starting to get... that is, it's covered with moss, sticks, and rodents and may be rotting again. We had it replaced back then because there were rotten places in the old roof. Maybe rodents chewed through. Do you remember hearing squirrels on the roof?" Beth hoped that didn't sound like a lame reason to be here. "Do you remember the roof replacement at all?"

"I do remember," Devon said. "It wasn't long after Essie left, and I was really down. There was a terrible smell in there before you had the roof replaced, and I stayed at my parents' house for a couple of nights. They tried hard to get me to talk about my break-up, though, and I went back to the duplex and slept downstairs, probably too drunk to let the odor keep me from sleeping. I worked long hours and wasn't at the duplex much during that time. But, yeah, I thought some animal had chewed its way into the attic and died there. I don't remember hearing them, but it sure could have been a squirrel. After the roof was replaced the smell went away."

"Do you remember when you smelled the bad odor, the approximate date, or time of month?"

"It must have been the end of August or the first part of September. Essie left near the end of August in 2008," Devon said. "I had to dredge up that information for the divorce papers, and it'll be hard to ever forget. I stayed on for several months, nearly a year, after that, even though I could hardly afford it. I was just... I know I'm not the only guy who was ever kicked in the rear by a woman, but I took it hard. Anyway, I never smelled a dead animal again during those few months' time. The roof was brand new then, though. I bet it's easy for a squirrel to jump on the roof from those Oak trees. Maybe you should have the tree branches removed. If the shingles aren't strong or are falling off, those rodents could chew holes in the underlayment."

Beth nodded. She needed a moment to think. If Devon was the killer, he knew what made the smell in the attic. If he was not (and he certainly seemed sincere), should she be the one to tell him? Would he be able to help identify Essie's body, if it was she in the attic? It didn't sound as if the body would look like anyone now. Would he even have anything with her DNA on it? Unlikely.

Did this information prove the body was Essie's? No, but it didn't prove it wasn't Essie. Could Essie still be working somewhere as an exotic dancer, if that part was true? And there was this Double M name again, associated with sex and drugs and...murder?

"Thanks," she said. "Your memory of the roof replacement matches mine. I'm just trying to get my facts right. I'm going to hire a tree specialist to remove those branches and go from there."

"Is that all you needed? I need to get back to work. Sorry to hear about the roof. A twenty-year roof should last longer than seven years, even if squirrels are crawling around on it."

Beth reflected for a minute as she lifted her arm to shake Devon's hand. It wasn't her intention to tell Devon about the body in the attic, but this interview had left her only with questions, no answers. She peeked around at all the people sitting in the restaurant and felt safe enough to see how Devon reacted when she confronted him with a specific question about the attic.

"By the way, did you have anything stored in the attic at the duplex or go up there to look for the dead animal?"

Devon frowned. "In the attic? No, I didn't store stuff there. I never went into the attic, not even to hunt for dead squirrel carcasses. I just waited for the smell to go away. And..." He averted his eyes for a second. "Well, I don't know for sure, but I don't think Essie ever put anything in the attic, either. We had plenty of storage space in other parts of the duplex."

Devon sounded truthful to Beth. But then again, what did she expect him to say?—Oh, yes, I left a body in a trunk in the attic. Can I get it back? Or—Essie didn't store anything there, but she's been stored there for the last seven years. Beth was not a trained interrogator, that's for sure.

"Okay," Beth said. "I just thought you might have seen some holes in the roof or something."

A spark of inspiration hit—she could at least use this opportunity to gather more DNA samples for Mark, couldn't she?

"Thank you for meeting me," she said. "I know I've kept you too long and you need to get back. Just leave your tray. I'll take your stuff to the trash with mine." Beth grabbed Devon's coffee cup and napkin and transferred them to her tray before he could protest.

Chapter 22

February—Kansas City, Missouri

Turning Devon's story around in her head while on her way to the duplex, Beth couldn't think of anything she might report to Mark Overos about Devon that would be of much help. Since she wasn't sure whether Essie was alive and dancing exotically or not alive and lying around in the CSI morgue, she could only report the possibility of the corpse being Essie Wild—which the police investigators had probably already considered. That is, they might have considered it when they were still working on the case. She decided she'd do some more investigating before she called Mark again.

She stored Devon's napkin-wrapped coffee cup in her glove compartment feeling a little silly. When the CSI investigators looked for DNA in the duplex, they must have looked for Essie's and Devon's in particular, since that couple lived there when they thought murder was committed. But then, what if neither Essie's nor Devon's DNA was in any of the data bases? She'd better keep the cup and give it to Mark when she had more to report.

It was somewhat of a relief for Beth to go into Side B of the duplex to work. Side A still made her uneasy. She understood the feeling was completely illogical, but there it was. Beth cleaned windows and made a list of the materials she needed for the bathroom tiling project. Snippets of her talk with Quinn Turley and Talia Johnson came to mind.

Her meeting with Quinn Turley gave her more reason to feel comfortable on this side of the duplex, where he had lived. With only the short visit, she respected the young man, for some instinctive-feeling reason, and was glad she had plans to attend another one of his concerts and talk to him again.

Beth knew she was also being a romantic. She recognized a spark between Quinn and Talia. It would be fun to see something come of it. Besides, there was a possibility Quinn could get her in touch with his sister and with his old roommate and band member, Bernie Landoff. One of them might be able to provide more information about Devon and Essie's relationship and Devon's character. Not that they would be able to tell her whether Devon murdered Essie... But Bernie, at least, might be able to tell her more about this Double M character. After all, Double M could be the murder victim. Devon wouldn't be the first man to kill someone who slept with his wife. She wondered if Double M was a man small enough to fit into the trunk.

There were too many questions. Beth felt a stiff neck coming on. She finished her supply list and went home for lunch. She retrieved the coffee cup from the car, placed it in a plastic bag, and hid it in one of her desk drawers.

Arnie wasn't there, but Psycho Cat greeted her at the door and followed her through the house. She'd been so preoccupied she hadn't given much time to her pet. Relieved to have an uncomplicated, relaxing chore, she hefted the big yellow cat onto her lap and brushed him until his fur shone. Her anxiety eased somewhat. Solving this case was not her responsibility. She had her job, her home, her husband, and this crazy pet to care for.

She remembered a line from *The Adventures of Huckleberry Finn*, one of Mark Twain's books she'd read many times. When Huck and Jim found a dead body, Huck told the reader: "...I didn't say no more, but I couldn't keep from studying over it and wishing I knowed who shot the man, and what they done it for." That's exactly how she felt. Huck didn't act on his inclination to find out the truth, but she knew he would have if Jim hadn't held him back. It was the right thing to do. She, Beth Stockwell, had people willing, perhaps eager, to help solve *this* murder mystery. The first most enthusiastic and willing helper she thought of was Talia Johnson.

She knew Talia spent long hours at her job, but, while she fixed a quick lunch, she left a voice message for her young friend. She hoped Talia would be willing to use her research skills again to locate Essie Wild. With the new information Devon had given her about the possibility of his ex being an exotic dancer with a stage name, there'd be a better chance of finding Essie, if she was alive, just as they were able to find Devon because of his occupation. Talia didn't return the call immediately, as Beth expected.

"My friend, Talia, must be busy working today," Beth said to Psycho Cat, the fur-piece sliding around her legs and rolling on his back demanding more tummy rubs. "Working is exactly what I need to be doing. I know you want me around here, but what if I take you with me? It won't be the side of the duplex where you stayed with Clay and Janae, but you'll find plenty of places to explore or to sleep in the sun while I work. Would you like that?"

As if he understood, the cat raised one paw to her knee and delivered a short, "Meow."

"Sounds like yes to me," Beth said.

The afternoon sped by. All of the supplies and equipment had been stored in her basement since she started updating the rental units with tile a few years before. She purchased several boxes of the same kind of tile for the bathrooms, basic white tiles that, when installed from the floor to above the sink and toilet, gave a clean fresh look to the old rooms. Only the trim tiles were unique, and Beth had fun each time deliberating over all of the new options before choosing edging pieces that added a bit of elegance to the otherwise utilitarian spaces.

She prepared the wall, marked the plumb lines, spread out her materials, and set several rows of tiles into the adhesive on the wall before she realized she'd not spent any time banishing Psycho Cat from the room. That was unusual.

Beth pushed to her feet from a kneeling position beside the partially tiled wall. She stretched, acutely aware that prolonged periods of time in bent positions are not friendly to aging joints. With only a small grimace and a vow to be more diligent about stretching after her walks, she treaded down the stairs to hunt for the cat.

The cat would normally be curled in a corner catnapping or stretched out in a ray of sunshine in front of one of the windows. At the bottom of the steps, she turned into the living room and stopped. Psycho Cat paced around the fireplace hearth, emitted small cat yelps, and then sniffed at various spots before he repeated the routine. Beth approached the fireplace.

"What have you found there, Kitty? We don't have a bug infestation, I hope. The exterminator was here just last summer."

She examined the places where Psycho Cat sniffed and pawed. The wide hearth was low, only a brick's width above the wood floor. It had been swept and dusted clean, but evidence of its many years of use showed. There were chipped bricks, discoloration in the mortar, and black singe marks from errant sparks, but she spotted no evidence of insects, spiders, or even cobwebs.

Meanwhile, the cat assumed a sphinxlike stance on his haunches and stared wide-eyed at the brick fireplace. Inside, the firebox was black, but it had been shoveled and vacuumed clean, thanks to the most recent tenant. The chimney bricks and the high wooden mantel exhibited their age, scratches and blotches here and there. A decorative, black metal insert below the mantel and above the firebox still shone. Beth had sanded the sharp edges and had given it two coats of rust-retardant paint just a couple of years before. Nothing seemed amiss. She stood with her hands on her hips and regarded the cat.

"Is this just another instance of psycho behavior from you, Mr. Cat? Oh, well, you're entitled to act goofy sometimes, just like the rest of us. Isn't that right?" Beth squatted to stroke the kitty. Of course, the cat rolled over and groveled for more. "Don't worry, little pal, I'm going to heat some water in the microwave for tea and apply a few more tiles. Then we'll clean up and clear out for the day."

~~~

At dinner, the atmosphere was warm again between Beth and Arnie. He recounted the gossip from the office and made her laugh when he used a decrepit old-man voice to tell about a young woman who'd started working there right out of college, when he was already middle-aged, and now was a mother with three children. Beth enjoyed seeing Arnie excited and happy about his job and his old friends at work.

In the same vein, Beth described her afternoon of constructive renovation work and her bafflement about Psycho Cat's behavior around the fireplace. Arnie kiddingly chided the cat for his nutty antics, as Beth had. She thought about telling Arnie about her morning's adventure. But she hesitated. She didn't want to start more quarrels. After dinner, while they tidied the kitchen and went to the living room to relax, she forgot to bring it up.

Only when her phone rang and she saw it was Talia Johnson, did the meeting with Devon Wild come back to mind with sudden clarity. Yikes! She glanced at Arnie sitting in his easy chair with a book in one hand and the TV remote in the other. He would think she was trying to keep secrets from him if he heard her tell Talia about Essie before she told him. Beth pointed to the noisy television for an excuse and took the phone into the kitchen to talk.

Talia sounded impressed by the way Beth followed-up their research by visiting Devon in Belton early that morning. Without hesitation, Talia agreed to search for any reference she could find on the internet for Estelle Sun, Estelle Star, or the name Estelle followed by a variety of other astrological terms combined with exotic dancer, strip club, gentlemen's club, etc. The search sounded impossible to Beth—too many terms to navigate, but if Talia wanted to take on the task....

Beth declined Talia's invitation to hop over to the condo and participate in the search. She needed time to explain all this to Arnie. The problem was, right now everything appeared calm and normal between them again. She was not anxious to trigger a repeat of his reaction when she told him about her weekend sleuthing. It crossed her mind to wait to tell Arnie about her morning visit until she knew more. Beth returned to the living room, picked up her book, and plopped into her easy chair without a word, still unsure what to do.

"Who called?" Arnie asked.

It was not an unusual question. Arnie and Beth had never had reasons to keep secrets about phone calls. Who called, what they said, whether it was an invitation from a friend, a call from a tenant, news from one of the kids, or whatever the subject of the phone call, had always been important, or at least interesting, to both of them. Beth looked up from her book, trying to appear casual, but Arnie frowned and looked a little hurt as soon as he saw her face.

"It was Talia Johnson," she said, eyes lowered, thinking how much she did not want to hurt her husband's feelings by keeping secrets from him but unsure how to tell him about her most recent sleuthing efforts. She peered at Arnie. He closed his book and gave her his full attention, a serious look on his face. Arnie's face and her guilty conscience at that moment caused Beth to want Arnie to know everything. She'd feel truthful, for one thing, but also she needed to be able to count on him to be a level-headed sounding board. She took a deep breath.

"I'll tell you all about the reason for the phone call if you'll promise to let me tell you the whole story before you respond."

"Okay, shoot," Arnie said in a casual tone. He looked anything but relaxed, however. He looked stiff. And—sad.

"This morning, after you left for your consultation at the office," Beth said, "I called the phone number Talia found for me, the number for the auto shop where Devon Wild works."

She described her visit in detail, emphasizing the public meeting place and the innocuous reason she gave Devon for the visit. Arnie watched her closely as she talked and shook his head just a little at her audacity. Beth noticed and hurried on, hoping to win him over with her upbeat telling. Finally, she revealed how Talia's phone call fit in.

Arnie's shoulders had relaxed just a bit by the time she finished, but his question startled her. "So.... You're telling me that wasn't your CSI buddy on the phone?"

Chapter 23

August, Seven Years Earlier—Kansas City, Missouri

Everything seemed calm and normal the morning after Caitlin informed her brother of her determination to go to California. Bernie's door was closed. Quinn hadn't appeared from the basement. Caitlin had been awake since dawn, determined to put her decision into action before she lost courage.

In the kitchen, she poured herself a half glass of milk and filled it to the top with water, a practice she'd adopted since their funds had dipped so low. The food supplies had dwindled to almost nothing, partly because of their lack of money, but also because Quinn and Caitlin had agreed they didn't want to have to transport a bunch of provisions when they moved. Bernie hardly ever contributed groceries, since he mostly ate at his clubs or at fast food establishments. He didn't seem to have a problem helping himself to Quinn and Caitlin's food, though. Caitlin's leftover piece of frozen pizza, the slice Quinn would never have eaten because he knew she was saving it for herself, was missing from the fridge. With a sigh of resignation, she spread some peanut butter, excavated from the bottom of the jar, on bread for a sparse breakfast.

During high school, Caitlin had sometimes worked on food and clothing drives for some of the poor families who lived in the Arkansas hills, but she'd never imagined she might someday be this needy. In spite of his delinquent ways, her dad had always managed to get enough employment, or perhaps use up funds from the sale of the hardware store, to provide her with money for necessary clothing and groceries. In fact, Caitlin had become a respectable cook since her mother's death. Her father appreciated her home-cooked meals when he was sober enough, and nothing had pleased Caitlin more than to see her brother eat seconds and thirds of dishes she'd spend so much time preparing when he still lived at home.

Caitlin daydreamed with nostalgia about the good times as she ate her peanut butter bread and drank her watered milk. A noise from outside brought her back to the present. Out of the kitchen window, she could see Devon Wild leaving for work.

Immediately, her spirits sank. Leaving for work—if only Quinn and she could lead normal lives, going to work in the morning, cooking and eating a good meal together in the evening, she keeping the house in order and doing errands on the weekends while Quinn performed with the band. It would be the kind of pleasant life she remembered from her early childhood, when her dad still attempted to be a good husband and father. She had tried to fulfill her promise to her mother by taking care of her father and her brother, but it looked as if she had failed at both.

Maybe she should go home, Caitlin mused. Going to California had been her back-up strategy, but she had no organized plan, beyond contacting her Aunt Sharon, for getting there and making a life. On the table in front of her sat the atlas she'd used to find her way from Frog Springs to Kansas City. That trip played like a nightmare in her memory. Now, planning another journey of escape held as much appeal as scheduling a visit to the hospital for a vital organ removal.

The fantasy of a comforting homecoming flitted out of her mind as fast as it had entered. Reality set in. Caitlin had called her father twice during the past month. The first time, three days after she arrived in Kansas City, she'd only left a message, a request for him to call back, and the phone number for Quinn's mobile phone.

He didn't call. Two weeks later, thinking he might have regrets but feel ashamed to call because of the way he had hurt her, she called again. Rob Turley answered that time but only scolded her in an incoherent tirade and never once asked her to come home, never mind ask how she and Quinn were doing. In truth, she knew it would be the same as always if she moved back to Frog Springs.

With determination, Caitlin began studying the atlas and the major highways that would take her to Los Angeles. That her aunt might not be able or willing to take her in didn't occur to her. Caitlin kept the cards and letters Aunt Sharon sent after her sister's death, less frequently as the years went by, in which she gave Caitlin and Quinn offers of help. Over the years, after they never accepted the overtures, her aunt had quit making them. Good will and kind spirits remained in the correspondence, however, and Caitlin perceived it all as an open invitation.

Last Christmas, eight months ago, was the last time she'd heard from Aunt Sharon. The return address had remained the same for the past several years, but the only phone number was old. Caitlin didn't own a cell phone to use to call her aunt, and she couldn't even start to imagine where to find a public pay phone or how to make a long distance call on one. Quinn had to keep a mobile phone to call and receive messages about band rehearsals and schedules. She'd have to ask to use Quinn's phone to try to contact her aunt. She needed to let Aunt Sharon know she was coming, get directions to the house from the highway, and...

Steeling herself for another argument with her brother about leaving made it hard to concentrate on plotting her journey. She looked in the back of the atlas for information about the distance between cities, calculated the miles by two different routes, and then leaned an elbow on the table and thought for several minutes about how to soften a confrontation with her brother. When she looked back down at the atlas, she forgot the calculations she'd already made and had to start over. After several rewinds, Caitlin started getting bleary-eyed and gave up—decided she would plan the route tomorrow or maybe as she travelled.

A few minutes later, a more immediate worry replaced all other thoughts. Caitlin started toward her bedroom, intending to tuck the atlas into one of her travel bags, when she heard Quinn burst into the kitchen from the basement doorway. He stormed past her up the stairs, and she followed him to the second floor hallway where he pounded on Bernie's door.

"What's the matter?" Caitlin asked, and cringed at the furious expression on her brother's face.

Quinn ignored the question. "Come out here, or I'm coming in!"

They both stood watching the door for half a minute. "Maybe he's stoned and can't wake up," Caitlin whispered.

Quinn glanced at her, turned the knob, and pushed the door open with ease. It opened into an almost empty room—only a smelly mattress, some scattered magazines, and a pair of dingy undershorts on the dust-bunny-covered wood floor. The faint odor of pot and dirty socks hung in the air. Nothing else remained. Caitlin's first thoughts revolved around how long it might take them to haul the old mattress to the curb for trash pick-up and how much work it would be to clean the filthy room for the landlady's inspection so Quinn and Bernie wouldn't be charged part of their deposit money. Her brother's thoughts, obviously, didn't have anything to do with cleaning.

Quinn wandered into the room with drawn brows and tight lips. He kicked some of the papers around and looked into the closet as if hunting for a clue. Caitlin stood by the door and watched, wondering what had precipitated the door pounding and anger. Not wanting to upset her brother further, she stayed mum while Quinn searched the room. The three of them had discussed the moving plan. They'd help each other load their few pieces of furniture into car trunks and backseats on Friday. Then they'd have time to clean and carry unwanted items out for trash pickup. It was now

Thursday. Caitlin wasn't surprised Bernie didn't wait to help Quinn, but at least he hadn't taken Quinn's TV or microwave. The old mattresses and lumpy sofa were going to be thrown out anyway, and she could help carry them out. She didn't know why Quinn seemed so distressed.

"I saw him leave last night," Caitlin said. "He was carrying something, but he must have been taking things out gradually over the past few days. I didn't know he was leaving for good."

"Yeah, and whatever he was carrying last night included all the money I've been saving for the move-in deposit and first month's rent for the new place."

"Bernie stole your money?" Caitlin said, incredulous. She had never liked the guy, but he and Quinn had played music together and hung out with each other since fifth or sixth grade. Not only that, but Quinn had always stood up for the punk, always made sure he was part of every group. It was misplaced loyalty now, for sure, since Bernie had been using and selling drugs so heavily. The fight they had last night must have something to do with this.

"Are-are you sure it was Bernie? How could he…?"

Quinn was so angry he had to take a deep breath with which he seemed to control himself enough to keep from screaming. He explained the whole thing to his sister in a flat, patronizing tone, as if she were a small child needing to learn the cruel facts about the world.

"Yesterday, Bernie and I had a big blow-out."

Caitlin nodded. "I know. I heard a little bit of it."

"Well, he told me I owe him money. How he figured that is another story, but he came up with a large sum. He said it could all be forgotten if I will help him with his drug sales. When I tried to back off from the job, he and his little friend next door threatened me with all kinds of stuff. Getting the money from me any way he could was only one of the threats."

"Where was the money? How did he find it?"

"I had it hidden inside a box in the bottom of one of the tubs I use for my clothes downstairs. I wouldn't even have noticed if I hadn't opened it up this morning to get some clean pants. It was obvious someone had rummaged through the contents, but I checked for the box of money and couldn't find it."

He looked at Caitlin with eyes full of sorrow as well as anger. "This isn't the Bernie I grew up with. God knows, that Bernie was always self-serving and devious enough, but he wouldn't have stolen money from his best friend and threatened you. The drugs and alcohol have claimed him and changed him." Quinn gazed into space. "Those greedy dope sellers are pushy. Robbing him of any morals he had."

"How much did he take?"

"Seven hundred dollars and change, the six hundred I need for the apartment and the rest for expenses. I have about thirty dollars in my wallet, and that's it until the band gets paid."

"So—so what are you going to do?"

Quinn started down the stairs before he answered, as if giving himself a minute or two to consider. Caitlin followed close behind. Over his shoulder, he said, "Don't you worry about it, Sis. I'll work it out with him. We have a performance tonight in Westport, and I'll see him at our rehearsal this afternoon. He'll come to his senses and give the money back—if he didn't already spend it all on drugs and booze last night."

"And what if it's gone and you don't get the money by tomorrow for the new landlord?"

"The landlord seems like a reasonable guy. He'll probably let me pay him a little at a time if I have a good explanation." Quinn's voice faded, and his steps slowed. "I'll find a way to get the money."

He stopped in the living room, turned around to face his sister, and put his hands on her shoulders. "I know you've decided to go to California, and I know you'll be eighteen tomorrow and are old enough to do as you want. You don't need to go. We'll be okay.

Aunt Sharon is a good person—probably not as good as our mother was, but kind and thoughtful. I'm sure she'll let you stay with her family for a time. But it may not work out. If you're determined to go, you know you can always come back here and stay with me if you're not happy, right?"

"I know," Caitlin said. She gave her brother a tight hug. "I can't believe you're thinking of my welfare when you've just been robbed, you idiot. I'll think over your offer to stay, but I'm not sure I can take living with you in a studio apartment." She grinned. Quinn held her out by the shoulders, started to say something, and then turned away.

While Quinn showered and dressed for his afternoon and evening with the band, Caitlin opened the last can of soup for lunch. She ate a couple of spoonsful and gave him the rest, telling him she'd just eaten breakfast. After he left, she packed what remained of the kitchen paraphernalia. She finished before she started thinking again about her decision to go to California. It was hard to concentrate on planning when deliberations about how Quinn might be planning to work things out with Bernie kept nagging at her.

Chapter 24

February—Kansas City, Missouri

"You're telling me that wasn't your CSI buddy on the phone?"

What on earth had Arnie meant by that? Why would Arnie question if her phone call was from Talia Johnson? What made him so sensitive about the CSI Supervisor's interest in the case? She put her book aside, folded her arms across her chest, and slumped in her easy chair for a moment or two, thinking how to respond to his insinuation. He might as well have asked, "Are you sure you aren't lying?"—an undeserved accusation in her estimation!

On second thought, she had to admit she lied by omission when she didn't tell him about her morning meeting with Devon until after the phone call from Talia. Maybe she deserved his doubts about her truthfulness. Could be her efforts to keep Arnie from being upset had backfired.

"I haven't yet called Mark Overos about my visit with Devon Wild," she said. "But, I do have the coffee cup Devon used today and plan to give it to Mark so he can test whether Devon's DNA matches any DNA he finds on the nail Janae took from the attic entrance or on the hypodermic needle you found in the sink, or— on the trunk and the dead body. So far I haven't heard about any DNA matches at all. Anyway, first I want Talia to help me find out about Essie Wild. I called her earlier about it, and Talia called to say she'll start working on the research tonight."

"What if you and Talia don't find Essie Wild? What if she isn't alive to be found? What if you've alerted the killer by asking about the roof and the attic?" Arnie's voice rose higher with each question.

Of course, Beth had no good answers. She had been asking herself the same kinds of questions all day. Especially, she worried about Devon pulling up stakes and moving away to hide from the police investigation if he was guilty.

"Beth," Arnie said, "whether the killer is caught or not isn't so much my concern. Your safety is what I'm worried about."

"Oh, I don't feel threatened by Devon Wild. His demeanor today was friendly and sincere. I didn't tell him we found anything in the attic, and he told me he had never been in the attic. As far as I know, he believes my story about us having a roof problem and trouble with squirrels." She attempted to convince herself and Arnie at the same time.

It occurred to her, if she thought Devon believed her story, then why would she be afraid he might bolt out of town? Devon could be a mild mannered auto repair supervisor—or—not.

Wrapped up in their thoughts, Beth and Arnie sat in silence. Beth tried to read and snuck glances at Arnie every so often. Maybe part of his objection to her collaboration with Mark Overos was because he thought she was pestering him and should let the law enforcement professionals pursue the case on their own time frame.

She didn't blame him for being upset and worried, though. After all, Devon Wild, the big, strong mechanic with an ex-wife who must have been unfaithful, lived in the duplex at the time they all believe the murder was committed. It was crazy to have sought him out and met with him alone!

Not until almost ten o'clock did Beth get another call from Talia. This time, she stayed in the living room where Arnie could hear every word. Talia apologized for calling so late.

"Don't worry about that. I'm glad you called. Have you learned anything helpful?"

"I've been searching all evening," Talia said, "but I haven't found our elusive Essie Wild, or Estelle Sunspot, yet. I'd keep at it tonight, but I need to be at work by seven-thirty tomorrow morning for a meeting, and I don't do meetings well without enough sleep."

"Oh, my goodness," Beth said. "If I'd known you were sitting at that computer this long, I'd have begged you to quit a long time ago. I'm not sure we'll find Essie at all. She may have been the murder victim, and, if so, we'll probably have to wait for the police to prove it."

"It's possible," Talia said. "There's one part of the story that could be true, though. You told me Essie may have taken the name Estelle Sun or Star and be working as a dancer. Well, I found the name Estelle Star. She was touted as a highlighted dancer at a gentlemen's club on the East Side a few years ago. Unfortunately, the club's Web Page was last updated three years ago, and I could find nothing to prove Estelle Star is actually Essie Wild."

"You're so good at this!" Beth said. "I realize that name doesn't prove Essie's still alive. Devon even told me he only heard about Estelle Star from an acquaintance, who could've just assumed it was Essie. However, it proves at least part of Devon's story is true, and it gives me something more to tell my CSI contact about our duplex duo. What's the name of the club?"

"It's called the East Side Gentleman's Club. I'll do some more searching if I have any time the next two days. My work, as usual, is keeping me busy, but I hope you and your family still have plans to go with me to hear Quinn Turley and his band Thursday evening. Maybe Quinn will remember some more about Devon and Essie."

"We're looking forward to Thursday evening," Beth said, shooting a questioning look at Arnie and getting a short nod. "I hope we can talk to Quinn long enough to ask him about the Wilds and about his sister."

"I do, too! I mean, if I don't remember to ask about Caitlin right off, I deserve a swift kick. I've been wondering about her for years. Meanwhile, I'll call you or send off an e-mail if I find out any more about Essie Wild before Thursday. Then we can ask about all of them when we talk to Quinn, maybe find out more about Bernie, too."

After the phone call, Beth told Arnie everything Talia'd told her. He said little. The only time he perked up enough to add a comment was after Beth related the name of the gentlemen's club.

"I remember seeing that place," he said. "We've driven past it before on the way to Kauffman Stadium."

~~~

For the next two days, Beth installed tile at the duplex without Psycho Cat's company, since Arnie was working at home. Arnie understood she intended to contact Mark Overos, but she knew he didn't want to be reminded. With only a small pang of guilt, Beth decided not to bother Arnie with the details. She arranged to meet Mark Overos during his lunch break to hand over Devon's coffee cup, tell him about her conversation with Devon, and pass on Talia's findings concerning Estelle Star. CSI Supervisor Mark Overos, up to now mild and supportive, greeted Beth at a sandwich shop near the CSI building with a stern talk about the dangers of dealing with a possible murderer.

"You're right," she said, and looked him in the eye. "I realized after I was there what a stupid thing it was for me to do, but it was too late. Even though I didn't sense any danger from Devon Wild while we were together, he could've followed me or found out where I lived and—and done something terrible."

Mark gave her a stern look. "He could still do something, you know. I can't promise to help with this if you're going to put yourself at risk. Your instincts about this guy could be wrong."

"I promise to question no more people who might be killers, and I'll give you any more clues I find in the duplex or from research. If I learn the whereabouts of any other possible suspects, I won't try to talk to them. I'll let you, or Detective Rinquire, interview them." Beth felt as if she should cross her heart and hope to die. "It makes me shiver to even think about talking to a possible murderer."

"You'll have to be patient if the investigation doesn't get started again as soon as you'd like. I'll help as much as I can, but I can't spend my days on it. That doesn't mean you should be out there detecting. Remember, there may be a drug link here, and people in that world won't think twice about harming a pesky landlady if they sense trouble."

"Good advice, taken."

Like a peace offering, Beth handed over the preserved coffee cup that she hoped contained Devon Wild's fingerprints and DNA. She told Mark about her conversation with the young man and added the information about Essie Wild's possible stage name, unable to hide a note of triumph in her voice.

Mark took the coffee cup from Beth and ascertained she had not touched it with her bare hands before she placed it in the plastic zip-lock bag. He told Beth he'd finished analyzing the DNA samples she provided earlier, but none of the samples collected so far—from the body, from the dried blood on the nail head, or from other DNA found in the house—matched anything in the national database. Devon Wild's fingerprints were on file—but not his DNA.

Beth raised her eyebrows, "Maybe Devon's DNA from the coffee cup will provide a breakthrough."

"Breakthrough or not, it does provide one more piece of the puzzle," Mark admitted.

Finally, after Beth related Devon's depiction of Double M as Essie's lover and drug supplier, Mark sat forward in his seat and expressed the same interest as before at the mention of the mysterious Double M. "Did he describe this Double M?"

"No. I didn't think to ask what he looked like. I just imagined this huge, hairy guy with bad teeth, I guess."

"Okay. Did Devon Wild know what kind of drugs Double M supplied to his wife and where he got them?"

Beth thought back to what Quinn and Devon had said about Double M. Not much.

"I didn't ask. But it sounded like Double M was the boss. I guess that would be the drug boss—drug lord. I'm not sure. And, no, he didn't say what kind of drugs." Beth screwed up her face. "This Double M person—who is he? Do you know his real name? Is he the one who would likely harm me if he thinks I'm finding out too much?"

"I'll say it again. You need to be careful not to get involved."

Chapter 25

Double M—Kansas City, Missouri

Myron Martin won his seat on the City Council with ease. Loved by the people in his district, valued by his fellow council members, and respected by the Mayor himself, his re-election four years later was a shoo-in. Myron, in fact, spent more of his time dealing with city business than any other council member. He attended every council meeting, represented the city at meetings with business, arts, and non-profit leaders, and competently lobbied on behalf of Kansas City around the country.

This diminutive powerhouse of energy and impressive double talk put twinkles in the eyes and tickles in the hearts of leaders of both political parties. Myron Martin's name shot to the top of their lists of possible candidates for mayor, congressman, governor, and beyond. A relatively young man, he had years of politicking left in him. However, no one in any political party had actually dropped Myron's name into a particular race, as yet. The current mayor of Kansas City was popular enough to win a second term, and Myron seemed eager to cement his local influence and power, for the time being, by working with the mayor as a member of the City Council.

Popularity in the political arena scored as only the latest in a series of successes for Myron. His first victories gladdened his greedy little heart when he was only a youngster, the son of a burly blue-collar bully and a tiny, uneducated, kowtowing mother. The boy inherited his mother's small stature along with an intellect miraculously preserved for him in a recessive gene bequeathed by some ancestor, which progenitor may have forgone having children had he known how his legacy would be sullied.

At age five, he was playing in the backyard with his younger brother and baby sister when the family dog got in the way of their game. Myron grabbed Blacky's tail and pulled until the dog yipped. Dad appeared and smacked Myron, who fell to the ground with a bloody nose.

"What's the matter, you little shrimp? Ain't tough enough to tackle boys your own age, so you go and pick on the dog?"

Myron was furious, but he kept his cool. "No sir," he said, "Anita pulled his ears, and Blacky was going to bite her. I was just pulling him away to protect her." He shot a warning look to his doting brother, Leonard, a year younger and three inches taller than him, to keep quiet.

"Okay," Dad said. "Just go easy on the dog." He stomped back into the house without an apology.

As soon as their father was out of earshot, Myron whispered, "You know Dad's uniform Mom just washed and ironed? Well, I have a black crayon. Wouldn't it be funny to mark all over the back of it and fold it up so Dad won't know? The guys at work will laugh their butts off."

His siblings thought that would be a fun trick. The pattern was not new, even for the five-year-old. Myron, the small son, had already learned how to protect himself when his father started picking on him. He had already become an expert at redirecting the blame and at exacting revenge.

To his kind and forbearing mother he was not so malicious, but neither was he particularly loving. Rather, he found it easy to talk her, his adoring protector, into giving him whatever he wanted.

Most of Myron's teachers liked him because he acted unfailingly polite and obedient when they were watching. Only a few times was an educator observant enough to catch his mischievous dealings with his playmates. Teachers reported to his parents Myron's lack of living up to his potential. In truth, he was living up to the potential he saw for himself. He became the king of the playground, the cool guy who could get away with almost anything, and the ruler of his adoring sidekicks.

Instead of the feisty bantam rooster a weaker intellect might have become, Myron maneuvered himself into his leadership position with his smarts. He suffered a snub, a threat, or the unforgivable snide remark about his name from playmates only once. Offenders would immediately find themselves tripped and trampled on the playground, hit in the back of the head with a kickball, or, most vile of all, shunned by all the other kids, while Myron stood by, smiling his approval at his cohorts and smirking at his antagonist.

He awarded each of his lieutenants according to individual circumstance. Poor kids got snacks, maybe a cupcake or cookie made by Myron's mom, in later years a hamburger after school. Lousy students got a homework assignment completed by Myron, in later years even a research paper. In a couple of cases, Myron talked girls into kissing or going on dates with shy boys who provided Myron with needed services. Most kids, however, were entirely satisfied with Myron's approval and the privilege of running with his crowd.

It was hard to tell whether Double M, as Myron Martin renamed himself, ever valued any of his conquests or if the stimulation of controlling others displaced any need for friendship. Whatever the underlying cause, his reputation was never besmirched by his followers, boys or girls, no matter how vile the deed he required from them in order to receive his approval. In high school he was elected class president two out of the four years, and his high school counselors outdid themselves finding him the best possible college scholarships—because of his charm and that potential they ascribed to him.

Double M magnanimously agreed to attend a university after it offered him a scholarship for full tuition plus room and board. There, neither the faculty nor the student body fell at his feet. However, while attending college, Double M discovered the means of using his talents to create wealth as well as popularity. Drug dealing—he was a natural. He identified weak people with the need, finagled deals with supply people, and found willing patsies to do all of the work collecting and selling in exchange for individualized compensation of narcotics, money, women, or status—all maneuvers similar to the smooth talk and double dealing antics he had already perfected. After setting up his drug operation, Double M spent much of his considerable proceeds to expand, to ensure loyalty, and to divert suspicion.

His new career supported other successes at school for the young man. It provided money for clothes that gave him a particular aura, access to certain fraternity men who introduced him to their girlfriends or sometimes their sisters, and the realization that learning to speak well, excelling in his classes, and impressing the right people would lead to a promising future.

Girls and women had always fallen at Myron's feet—some quite literally, for one reason or another. They continued to be easy conquests. A particular type of college woman succumbed to addiction both to Double M's charms and to the easy access to drugs. The classy chicks (as Double M termed them only when bragging to the old gang during his infrequent visits home) were impressed by his intelligence, his quick wit, and his confident demeanor. The talented Mr. Martin, known as Double M on the dark business side and as Marty to his legit, high society acquaintances, somehow managed to glide from one side to the other without damaging either image.

When it came time to choose a wife—whom he married three years before being elected to the City Council—Double M did not go for the tall, blond bombshell a man of shakier ego might have chosen. Rather, he married an equally small, attractive, ambitious, risk taker. Marilyn Martin, known back in her rough neighborhood as Lynnie, became the supporting, hard-as-nails, second Double M. She helped drive the behind-the-scenes business while charming the leaders of society, both men and women.

Not long after they were married, Marty told Marilyn about the money he gave to charity. The practice helped keep his image clean, not to mention that it laundered money at times. The next day, Marilyn volunteered with the Happiness Fund for Children and soon became a board member.

One afternoon she said, "Marty, we received an invitation to a dinner party at Sam and Charlotte Ward's on Friday evening."

"I have business with the boys at the Front Street Grill on Friday night. You know Fridays are always busy for me."

"Well, you might want to reschedule this time. Sam Ward is President of Ward Industries and not only one of the leading philanthropists in town, but also a huge political backer."

Myron swiveled his desk chair around and pulled Marilyn onto his lap. "Lynnie, my love, you do know how to charm the right people."

"We're in this together, Babe."

It was only after marriage that Double M somewhat curtailed his frequent sexual affairs and spent more time being Myron, or Marty, Martin, the upstanding businessman and citizen. The legitimacy of his restaurant and import business was seldom questioned for long. Police who might have looked into his businesses were well-paid or well-threatened to leave them alone. Each time questions were raised about his import business, the investigation was squelched. DNA samples gathered from him mysteriously disappeared before they could be processed into the system. Photos were never published.

Almost all Marty's drug smuggling and rough dealings were left to underlings. With the help of his paid cops and political access to top investigators, he had no problem implicating certain criminal associates, when it served his need, without his name being mentioned. Marty and the Director of the CSI interacted socially. Marty and his charming wife used their philanthropic and social connections to plant the impression that they were upstanding citizens, ethical to the bone.

All in all, Mr. Martin considered himself free to enter the world of public service with the same self-serving attitude he had held his entire life. However, although their status and connections kept them free of prosecution, they were not free of suspicion by those who dealt with the dirty underworld of drug racketeering.

Chapter 26

February—Kansas City, Missouri

"**I**'m serious about this," Mark Overos said. "I can't name names, but if Double M is the guy I think he is, he has wide connections and will find out if you start questioning the wrong people. I'm not a detective, but I have detective associates who've been on this guy's case for years. They've never been able to pin a thing on him. He has friends in high and low places, and people who cross him have been known to disappear. An investigative news reporter got too close and was snuffed out with no forensic clues left behind. You would be no exception. You need to back off."

Beth nodded. "So you think this Double M is the guy with enough clout to put this case on the back burner? But if he had Essie selling drugs for him and providing other, um, services, why would he murder her? And why would he protect Devon if Devon is the murderer?"

"You aren't listening. These are questions for the police investigators to solve."

Beth opened her eyes wide. "Wait. What if Essie is the killer and the victim is some underling drug dealer who threatened to tell? Double M would be protecting Essie. We need to follow the lead about Estelle Star. And we haven't yet found Bernie Landoff, Quinn Turley's roommate. According to Quinn, Bernie became hooked on drugs and drug dealing by Essie, who got the drugs from Double M. We need to…"

"Hold it," Mark said, getting red in the face. "*I* need to pass this information on to Detective Rinquire as part of the case. *You* need to stay away from possible criminals. Don't go poking around any gentlemen's clubs or meeting a drug-dealing roommate to question him about your duplex attic. You have to swear."

Beth didn't say anything for a minute, feeling stubborn, but she knew he was right, and she promised, "I won't make contact with those people, but I will keep trying to find out more about them—and pass the information on to you, of course."

Mark looked disgusted, as if he'd been pushed far enough. "I'm telling you to quit now. If you find anything at all, let the police do the investigating."

"Okay. I understand." Beth didn't want to be in danger, nor did she want to harm the investigation. If only there was an investigation. At any rate, she couldn't be cited for hindering a non-investigation, now could she?

~~~

Beth wished she knew what Double M looked like. Then she'd have a better picture in her mind about the goings-on in that duplex. She figured she should be able to find a picture of an important city leader online. She could print it out and ask Talia or Quinn if it matched their memories of Double M. A police chief, city council member, head of the CSI, even the Mayor, for crying out loud—her first priority should be to find a city leader with two names beginning with M. Oh, yeah, come to think of it—it couldn't be the mayor.

At home, she went straight to her computer. She'd learned a few things from her session with Talia Johnson, and it didn't take her long to find Marvin Marshall, Max Munroe, and Myron Martin in her search for Kansas City law enforcement and political figures that might influence an investigation.

Max, a man in his late seventies, was a retired Police Chief who sat on the police board, but, according to one report, he hadn't been present recently because of a debilitating disease. Not a likely candidate. Marvin, age thirty-one, must have been a political prodigy. At such a young age, he already served as a councilman. However, Beth couldn't find any mention of the young man having influence beyond his own district. That left forty-three-year-old City Councilman, Myron, or Marty, Martin, a well-known businessman and second-term councilman with lots of clout.

Funny thing—no photos of Mr. Martin popped up. The side of his face around a council table seemed to be the best Beth could find. It wasn't enough for a clear identification.

Then an idea struck, and Beth scrolled back toward the beginning of her search results. She clicked on a link to a charity event to benefit Children's Mercy Hospital. The event involved golfing superstar, Tom Watson, one of Arnie's heroes, and other golfing greats. Myron and Marilyn Martin would chair the event at the Green Hills Country Club in Kansas City. Arnie would love to see the golf champions play, and he might be able to get autographs from some of them.

Beth read the details. Levels of participation required different donation amounts, starting with seventy dollars a person for a chance to see a pro-am golf tournament, weather permitting, and meet the stars at a reception, and on up to two hundred fifty dollars or more per person for those activities plus a black tie dinner dance later that evening and more hobnobbing. Well, a hundred forty dollars for a good cause might be within her means, and they would have the chance to observe Myron and Marilyn Martin—two double M's.

Arnie walked in from the garage while Beth was still looking at the computer screen. Beth called to him from the den with such excitement that Arnie rushed in, dropped business folders on his desk, and peered at the screen from behind her chair.

Beth held nothing back. "Arnie, I took the coffee cup used by Devon Wild to Mark Overos today. He grew interested when I mentioned a man nicknamed Double M. Quinn Turley, Talia

Johnson, and Devon Wild all talked about him. He might be the person who squelched our skeleton in the attic investigation.

"Look here. I found this charity golf tournament chaired by Myron and Marilyn Martin. Myron Martin is an active City Councilman. Get it? Double M. It could be the guy.

"Tom Watson will be there and everything. It would be fun, and we could take pictures of all the golfers *and* Myron Martin. What do you think?"

Arnie glanced over the information on the screen and didn't respond. His expression was flat.

"What's wrong?" Beth asked. "Oh wait, will you be out of town again next weekend? I could ask Talia Johnson if she'll go with me instead."

"Will your debonair CSI buddy be at the event?"

Beth's mouth opened, and she stood rooted to the floor for a few seconds, in shock. She felt her face burn, and then she felt remorse.

"So that's what's been eating you?" she said. "You think I'm... No, sweetie. You're wrong. I only saw him today to give him the cup, the coffee cup with Devon Wild's DNA. I'm not interested in him or trying to do his job. In fact, he's your ally. He gave me a harsher scolding than you do about getting involved in police work. I didn't realize you thought I...that is...I'm sorry I...."

Psycho Cat appeared in the doorway and crept toward them. Beth and Arnie turned toward their furry feline friend and then back to each other. Arnie's eyes looked moist, and Beth bit her lip. Arnie reached out to touch Beth's shoulder, leaned over to kiss her forehead, and nuzzled her hair. The cat rubbed his body around and through their four intertwined legs, feeling to Beth like a mother smoothing the hair back from the face of her sad child. Beth and Arnie both peered downward and giggled in harmony.

Beth spent some minutes cuddling with Arnie and poured through her memories of Arnie's reactions the past week or so. She should have understood sooner.

Arnie cleared his throat. "So tell me more about the charity golf event."

Beth explained how she found the golfing event while searching for Double M's identity. She told Arnie all she'd learned from her various tenants' descriptions of Double M and the possible link to Myron Martin. By the time she finished her explanation and revealed her vow of no contact with the suspects, Arnie was not only eager to attend the golf outing, but he also became fervent about hearing everything Beth knew about the connections between the Wilds and the man known as Double M.

After dinner, as Beth began to clear the dishes, he motioned her to stay seated, and, with his elbow on the table and his chin on his hand, started spouting his own guesses about the identities of the killer and the victim. Beth's cheerfulness bubble inflated.

Chapter 27

February—Kansas City, Missouri

Since the golf tournament wouldn't take place until Saturday, Beth set her sights on Thursday evening plans to hear Quinn's band. During breaks in her tiling job, she called Clay, Janae, and Talia, reminded Arnie (so many times he finally crossed his two forefingers in front of her to X out the over-enthusiastic chatter), and e-mailed them all to confirm the time and the strategy for snagging a good table.

The event appealed to Beth. She liked good music. Arnie had agreed to go. He disliked crowds but enjoyed going out with their kids. It would be fun to introduce Talia to her family. Also, now that Beth knew more, she hoped to be able to ask Quinn Turley more questions about the people and events at the duplex around the time the victim was chucked into the trunk in the attic.

True to plan, Beth and Arnie picked up Talia, met Clay and Janae, and then found a table in a great spot a little to the left of and a couple of tables away from the band. While the warm-up group played, the hot, cheesy tavern food and the drinks were delivered without delay. A friendly neighborhood feel permeated the room—dark wood with layers of shellac, flirty waitresses, creamy draft beers, dim lighting except for the spotlight on the band, and speakers kept at a low enough level to allow conversation.

After introductions and some initial chatter, Beth sat between Arnie and Talia listening to her husband and son talk sports and politics while Janae and Talia, having established their mutual computer interests, broke into twenty-first century tech talk Beth could barely understand. She watched them all with a warm feeling while tapping her toe to the music.

At eight o'clock the host announced, "Ladies and gentlemen, please welcome one of our favorite groups *Quinn Turley and Novel Invasion.*"

Beth and Talia looked at each other in pleased surprise. Quinn's name led the group. It was appropriate. He was that good. Beth studied her family from time to time while enjoying the music. Arnie grinned at her and nodded his head to let her know she didn't exaggerate the band's excellence. Talia's eyes shone. In the midst of a particularly moving ballad, during which Quinn displayed his three-octave vocal range, Janae smiled up at Clay and took hold of his hand. It felt almost like a letdown when Quinn announced the first break.

Talia waved to Quinn. He let his band mates handle the CD sales and headed directly to their table. Arnie gave Quinn his chair and found a spare stool at the bar to haul over for himself while Beth doled out more introductions and waited a few minutes while everyone complimented Quinn.

At the earliest opportunity, Beth changed the subject from music to the skeleton mystery by telling Quinn how Clay and Janae became involved in the duplex investigation. She followed with one of her burning questions.

"Quinn, did you ever see Essie Wild after you moved out of the duplex?"

"No, I never saw her or her husband after that."

"We know Devon Wild is still alive but claims not to have seen his ex-wife since they lived in the duplex. How about your roommate, Bernie, did he continue to associate with Essie?"

"I don't know for sure. I know he still had drugs. He got them from somebody, and I assumed it was probably from her. Like I told you before, Bernie and I were at odds with each other after we moved out of the duplex into different apartments. After my sister left, I acquired some guitar students to ease my money problems. He and I hardly spoke for the months he remained with the band. Then he moved back to Arkansas, and I've only heard a bit here and there about him since then."

"How many months did he stay around after you both moved?" Beth asked with raised eyebrows.

"It was only a couple of months. Why? You're not thinking he could have anything to do with the dead body, are you? I mean, Bernie had problems, but I don't think he could have murdered anyone."

"He would've had to kill the victim just before or just after you moved," Beth said, "in order to fit into the timeline we've determined. I'm just trying to eliminate possible suspects and victims. He could have qualified as a victim, but since you say he was still around for a couple of months after you moved, his body couldn't have been in the trunk when we cleaned the duplex. As for Bernie being the murderer, it's still possible, since he was drug dealing. I remember him being a fairly large young man." She paused and looked around the table for input.

"Yeah. Size would be another reason to eliminate him as the victim," Clay cringed. "The dead body was small enough to fit into the interior of that trunk."

"Clay saw the skeleton. I didn't." Janae said. Despite the pronouncement, her face took on a green tinge.

Quinn looked troubled. "Well, I can't think how Bernie would've had a motive to kill Essie Wild, or anyone else, for that matter. Unfortunately," he said with a wry face, "he was usually either high or hung over, and getting stoned didn't make him combative, as a rule."

"As a rule..." Beth murmured, half to herself.

"Quite a few rules have been broken in this case. Do you have anything of his that might still have some of his DNA on it?"

"I don't have anything at all that belonged to Bernie," Quinn said. "He took his drums and everything he owned with him. We had to find a new percussion player fast when he left. I'd have to go find him in Arkansas to come up with a sample of his blood or saliva."

"That's the job of police detectives," Arnie said. "Any information we get will be reported to the police," he added, with an eyebrow cocked in Beth's direction.

The group grew silent for a moment until Talia piped up. "I heard you say your sister left before Bernie did. Did Caitlin go back to Arkansas, too? I've been wondering about her all of these years."

"No, as far as I know, she didn't ever go back home…" Quinn said, just as a woodwind player from the band stepped back onto the low stage and played a jazzy scale on his saxophone. "Woops, I need to get back up there before they play the second set. They'd probably be better off, but I can't let them find out they can do without me. I'll catch you at the next break, if you're still here."

"We'll be right here," Talia promised with a smile.

At the second break, they all anticipated Quinn's immediate return to their table. However, he was stopped near the stage by well-wishers and fans, those who'd bought the band's CD during the first break, seeking autographs. The break was nearly over by the time he dashed over to the table, apologetic about being delayed.

"No problem, man," Clay said, "Those fans and CD buyers are your first priority."

The others nodded their heads.

Beth watched them. Her son looked impressed with Quinn's music. The kid always did admire talent. Janae appeared awestruck, also. There was no doubt Talia adored Quinn and his work. As for Arnie—well, one could never tell exactly what he was thinking, but he nodded approval along with the rest.

Beth was well aware Talia wanted to find out about Quinn's sister, Caitlin, and Quinn's explanation was cut short. Caitlin was a possible witness of the Wilds' complex relationships and activities. Beth hoped to find her, too. It seemed a little rude, but she wasted no more time on the niceties to bring up that subject.

"Quinn, you started to tell us about your sister. You said she left but didn't go back home. Did she move somewhere close to Kansas City?"

For some reason, Quinn looked sad and took a deep breath before answering. "She set out to drive to California. I don't know where she ended up. We have an aunt in California who had offered to help us, and Caitlin wanted to find her when she and I couldn't make a go of it here together. I begged her to stay and give it more time, but she was determined to not be a burden. She was like that."

"But—but, she didn't find the aunt? You don't know where she is?" Talia's voice was barely above a whisper.

"Caitlin didn't have a cell phone. We hardly had an extra penny to our names for food, let alone extra phones. I knew when she left I probably wouldn't hear from her for a while, and I was busy moving. Then, after a week and a half passed with no contact, I researched our aunt's phone number and called. The phone number was an old one and not in service. I found out later she had converted to cell phone only, and it's not easy to find those numbers."

Quinn looked at his hands. "My sister was angry with me, too, when she left. She thought I was going to help Bernie with his narcotics business. So I wasn't totally surprised she hadn't called or found an Internet connection and e-mailed me. Anyway, after another week or so, I called my dad, and believe me it takes a huge amount of pressure for me to do that. Dad hadn't heard from Caitlin, but he had Aunt Sharon's address.

"Long story short, I contacted the authorities in California, and they contacted my aunt. She hadn't seen or heard from Caitlin. We filed a missing person's report, which supposedly went to all the jurisdictions between Missouri and California, but she's never been found. Maybe she changed her name and found a new life. That's what I hope. She was distressed about booze and drugs in the lives of our father and me. Maybe she wanted to completely block us out of her life. I just wish...."

"You're sure she took off for California?" Beth asked.

"I'm sure. She told me she was going. Her belongings, her old car—everything was gone when I came back to the duplex the night before I moved out. Caitlin even left me some of the money she saved for her trip so I could move into my new apartment." Quinn paused and set his mouth for a moment before continuing. "What happened on the way to California, I don't know. I'm ashamed to remember how I felt when I realized she'd actually left. I was upset but also a little relieved. I'd just turned twenty-one years old and could hardly take care of myself, let alone my sister."

They all remained quiet. Beth contemplated this sad story. Then Quinn was clapped on the shoulder by one of his band members. None of them, including Quinn, had registered the cue to return to the stage for the final set. The music took a back seat to Beth's thoughts for the rest of the evening. She pondered the fates of the three people, Bernie, Essie, and now Caitlin, from her suspect/victim list who were still missing. Quinn was too busy to talk again at the end of *Novel Invasion's* performance, but he rushed over to give one of his cards to each of them before they left.

"Please keep me in the loop about this—this—skeleton in the attic case," Quinn said.

Chapter 28

February—Kansas City, Missouri

On Friday morning Beth got to the duplex late. Arnie and she had slept in and skipped their morning trail walk. Beth was not in any particular hurry to finish her work at the duplex, since there had been no rush of people wanting to rent either unit. At this point, the ceramic tile was set into the adhesive, the grout had dried, and she had only to seal and polish the finished job to call the duplex as ready to show as it would ever be.

When she finished, after surviving her usual dropping and retrieving of tools, she stood back and admired the new look. The tile was variegated rust and tan with an integrated mosaic trim near the top. This kind of work provided Beth with immediate satisfaction. She knew herself to be the kind of person who needed to see a job through to the end and receive positive feedback. As if in response to her uplifted spirits, her phone rang with its cheery little ding-a-ling-a-ling.

"We saw a For Rent sign at your duplex. When will it be available, and can we take a look?" the caller asked.

"Both sides are available immediately." Beth said. "I can show them today or this weekend. What time is convenient for you?"

A pause while the person on the other end consulted someone else in the room. "Sunday afternoon at about two o'clock would be good."

"Two is fine. Will it be just you?"

"No, my husband will be with me."

Beth collected a phone number and some cursory information about the couple's ability to pay the rent and recorded the appointment on her calendar. She decided it was good karma kicking in. She could show both units, because both sides were fixed up and ready to rent.

Even with the good news to tell Arnie, during her drive home Beth couldn't help feeling a bit edgy. She thought about the story Quinn had told about Caitlin. His business card peeked out from the side pocket of her purse. Beth glanced at it. If she were to call him, what would she say, or ask? Would she ask him why his sister might have murdered Essie Wild and then disappeared? On the other hand, had Caitlin threatened to expose Essie's drug dealing? Could Essie have killed Caitlin and then disappeared with Caitlin's belongings?

As soon as Beth thought she had the victim and suspects figured out, another possibility showed up. Did Devon know more about this than he told her? Why did Bernie leave the city? What did Double M have to do with the body in the trunk, and why might he be protecting whoever put it there? Beth tucked Quinn's card into the purse. She needed to think this through and decide what to do.

Arnie showed infinite patience while listening to her rambling thoughts. He had done a complete turn-about in his attitude concerning their part in discovering the secret of the skeleton in the attic ever since he discovered how wrong he was about the Mark Overos business. Beth couldn't help putting her arms around his neck and kissing him when she saw how concerned he looked. Surprised, he kissed her back and then laughed.

"What brought that on?"

"It's a thank-you for being you," Beth said, realizing she had been a little upset about being mistrusted but also a little flattered about his jealousy. Marriage certainly had its ups and downs.

~~~

On the way home from the music club on Thursday night, Beth had asked Talia if she wanted to accompany them to the charity golf tournament on Saturday afternoon, Beth's treat. Talia accepted only if she could pay her own way. She wanted to see Myron Martin for herself even if she wasn't sure she could identify him as Double M.

On Saturday morning, Beth received a telephone call from her young friend. "I won't be able to make it this afternoon," Talia said. "I'm going out of town. That is, Quinn and I are driving to Frog Springs, Arkansas today to see if we can locate Bernie and find out what he knows about Essie and Caitlin. We might talk to Quinn's father, too. Will you take pictures of Myron Martin at the event to show to Quinn and me?"

"Absolutely, I will. How did this trip with Quinn come about? You're traveling together?"

"I just couldn't stop thinking about Caitlin. So yesterday I called Quinn to ask more about her. Since Quinn doesn't have a performance, we decided to make this trip. I'm going along as moral support, mostly."

"That's great."

"I hope we can find something with Caitlin's DNA on it and maybe Bernie's, too."

"Be careful, Talia. You don't know exactly what you're dealing with. Bernie could be…"

"I feel safe with Quinn."

Beth was dumbfounded by Quinn and Talia's sudden solidarity of action but couldn't wait to hear what they'd learn. She didn't feel completely comfortable with Talia's plunge into the same kind of snooping she'd been doing, but she admired Talia for following up with Quinn. There wasn't much she could do to stop them, anyway, now that the two were on their way to Arkansas.

~~~

"You golfers are absolutely nuts!" Beth whispered to Arnie on Saturday afternoon while they stood in the smallish crowd on the damp grass of the country club golf course sidelines, shivered in the forty-five degree weather, and watched famous and not-so-famous golfers drive balls down the fairway.

"We've been to Chiefs football games in much colder weather than this," he whispered back.

"Yes, but there I spend the time jumping up and down and screaming," Beth whimpered.

Someone hit a good shot, and the audience clapped politely with gloved hands. A couple of spectators nearby glanced her way with sympathetic looks and pulled warm scarves tighter, but they, like Arnie, gave most of their attention to the golfers on the course.

In the past, when driving past golf courses in the Kansas City area, Beth had seen people out there at all times of the year. Arnie was often one of them. They played unless there was snow, ice, or water on the greens and fairways. The only way this event could have been planned for February, though, was with contingency dates earmarked in the spring. The pros were to be commended for being there on such a chilly day in the name of charity. Beth figured they could all have been playing on some beautiful warm course in Florida or Hawaii right now. She picked up her stride when the crowd moved to the next viewing area. It was fine weather for a brisk walk but much too cold for standing around.

Myron Martin had introduced himself and the professional and amateur golfers at the start of the tournament. The City Councilman didn't look familiar. Beth had guessed she might have seen a photo of him in the *Kansas City Star* sometime during his tenure, but the man must have always been extremely careful not to have his picture published. Maybe he bribed people.

She focused her camera lens with the zoom. Perhaps Talia or Quinn would be able to identify him as Double M. If Martin was a drug kingpin, Beth could understand why he recruited other people to do his dirty work. From a distance, he didn't look at all dangerous—closer to her size than to Arnie's and clean-cut to boot.

Arnie put his arm around her shoulders and whispered in her ear, "Don't be obvious about your picture-taking."

She looked around. "There are lots of cameras out. Everyone wants photos of the golfing stars."

Arnie followed her gaze. "Okay. You're right. Get some good ones for me."

At the end of the tournament, Arnie was ready to go home. Beth had other ideas.

"We paid for the reception. Let's attend for a little while. I want a closer look at this Myron Martin, and maybe you'll have a chance to shake hands with some of the pros."

"One drink and a handshake, then."

There were dozens of people already at the party when they arrived—wives of the tournament attendees and participants, older people, and smartly dressed people who hadn't cared to stand in the cold during the tournament. The dress was supposed to be casual, but Beth thought some of the women made a more stylish appearance in their casual outfits than she did in her finest party dress. Tight pants, flowing tunic tops of silk and fine wool and other lovely fabrics she couldn't name, costly jewelry, expensive shoes, and hairdos that were not styled at the neighborhood Quickie Cuts Salon made her want to hide behind the nearest buffet table in her last year's woolen slacks, tailored sweater, and the black flats she had changed into from the sturdy walking shoes she wore outside during the tournament. She sighed. At least she had thought to bring those shoes along.

Some of the men wore short-sleeved golf shirts that bore the logo of the exclusive country club. The shirts must have been given to each of the tournament participants, and maybe some of the club members were wearing theirs, also. Beth noticed Myron Martin wore one of the shirts and was holding court among a group of people near the two-story glass windows that separated the reception gallery from the huge pool and patio area dimly illuminated during this cold season with white lights strung around the perimeter. He drank from a Coke can rather than from a wine glass or cocktail glass as did most of the rest of the crowd. Beth eyed the pop can. As long as she was collecting DNA samples, perhaps....

As she and Arnie circulated around one of the tables in order to sample some of the delicacies, Beth discovered they were in speaking distance of Tom Watson. "Mr. Watson, she said, "I'm Beth Stockwell, and this is my husband, Arnie. He's a huge fan. Would you mind posing for a photo with him?"

"Of course not, I'll be glad to. I appreciate having fans, and I appreciate your donation to Children's Mercy."

Arnie thanked the famous golfer, shook his hand, and gave his wife an appreciative hug after Mr. Watson moved on.

In short order, Arnie and Beth found a small table in a corner where they sat in comfortable upholstered chairs with their drinks and small plates of goodies within easy reach. To Beth's great delight, they sat beside another wall of windows outside of which the beauty of a spectacular sunset adorned the western horizon. She gazed at it until the twinkling lights of the palatial room and the fire in the massive stone fireplace outshone nature's picturesque display.

Beth turned her attention to her camera's display window and showed Arnie the pictures she had taken during the day. They admired the photos of Arnie with Tom Watson and then peered at the zoom photos of Myron Martin.

"Good try, Babe, but I don't know if Quinn or Talia will be able to identify this man from these shots," Arnie said. "Some are a little fuzzy, and the others show the backs of spectators' heads more than they show your subject."

"Hm, you're right. I couldn't get a better shot out there. I don't know if the pictures will look clearer on the computer screen, or..."

"Arnie Stockwell, I'm not surprised to find you here." A golfing friend of Arnie's approached their table with his hand out.

Arnie stood to shake hands. "Brett, how're you doing? Beth, you remember Brett Rodgers."

"Nice to see you, Brett. Did you watch the tournament?"

"Yes, Ma'am. Wasn't that golf amazing?"

Arnie and Brett broke into hole-by-hole analysis, and Beth's attention turned elsewhere. Out of the corner of her eye, she noticed a figure, grabbed her camera, told the men she'd be right back, and darted across the room. She'd just seen Mr. Martin set his pop can on a tray, a tray that was bound to be collected by one of the caterers at any minute.

When she came close to the tray with the pop can, Beth slowed and picked up a cookie on a small plate and a napkin from one of the tables as she passed. She wandered over to the tray table, nibbled at the cookie, and then, looking around to make sure no one was looking, she set the cookie plate on the tray while folding the napkin around Myron Martin's discarded pop can and sticking it into her handbag. She felt like a private eye who gathered such clues every day. Thank goodness she wasn't carrying one of those tiny evening bags.

She shifted her eyes from side to side and then over her shoulder before she headed to the lady's room. No one seemed the least bit interested in her recent stealth, and she relaxed a bit. Halfway to the lobby, where she'd noticed the restroom signs when they entered, Beth spotted Myron Martin, his arm around the waist of a small woman—Marilyn Martin, perhaps?—and deep in conversation with Tom Watson.

Her only thought was that this might be her only chance to get a good picture of Mr. Martin. Beth went into a silly star-struck fan act. "Excuse me, Mr. Watson," she said, interrupting his conversation, "you were so kind to let me take a picture of you with my husband, but it isn't clear. Do you mind if I take one more photo of you? It'll just take a second."

Tom Watson, used to such interruptions was quite cordial. "Of course. Excuse me just one minute, Marty."

He smiled and posed for Beth, although she noticed a disdainful look on Myron Martin's face. Beth snapped the photo and thanked the group of people gathered around the golf star for so graciously allowing her to intrude. She reached the restroom in two shakes and checked the photo she just took. Sure enough, she was able to get half of Tom Watson and all of Myron Martin, his face toward her, holding a drink in his hand. It might have been Beth's imagination, because of who she believed him to be, but his dark eyes looked menacing to her even inside the camera display. A shiver ran down her spine.

Chapter 29

February—Frog Springs, Arkansas

Talia and Quinn felt comfortable with one another—traveling together, discussing their lives, exchanging driving duties, formulating a plan for what they would do after they reached their destination. Neither of them understood exactly why they weren't tense and uneasy in such an odd situation. They were barely acquainted. They had such dissimilar occupations and educations. Talia had been acquainted with Caitlin Turley for only a few weeks, many years ago. Yet, here they were with a common purpose, and it didn't seem strange or unreasonable to either of them.

Like Beth, Talia also hadn't been able to get Quinn's story about his sister's disappearance out of her mind after Thursday evening. Unlike Beth, Talia had pulled out the business card she'd been given and used the phone number to call Quinn on Friday morning.

"I hope I didn't wake you," she'd said. "You were probably up until all hours with the band last night."

"No, I've been up for a while preparing for a student. I cleared out right after our last set. Thursday night gigs don't go late, and my band members don't party afterward. I might have been in bed before you were last night."

"Oh. I mean, I'm glad I didn't disturb you. I-I called because— well, because all these mysteries are driving me crazy. First, Beth's skeleton, then the disappearance of Essie Wild, and now your sister. Your ex-roommate, Bernie, too. I'm not sure why he skipped town. At least, that's what it sounds like. These things all happened around the same time, and Caitlin is…"

"I can't stop thinking about it, either, since the whole episode has come up again. I need to find out what happened to Caitlin, once and for all. Her disappearance has haunted me all these years. Sometimes I think she must have broken down in some little town, found a job, married, and is now living happily with a kind husband and their cute babies."

"Then why wouldn't she have contacted you?"

"Fear, resentment, pride… I don't know."

"So you said 'sometimes' you visualize that family scenario. What do you think other times?"

"Other times, I think she must be dead. But I've always imagined her at the bottom of some ravine in Colorado where her car went off the road and crashed to the bottom in a blaze so bad that she and the car became unidentifiable. That would explain why she never called and why she was never found. I drove out to Colorado one time. No plan. No idea of what route she would have taken. I just drove around in the mountains for about a week and then headed home."

"At least you felt as if you'd done something."

"Maybe, but now this body in the trunk puts a whole new perspective on Caitlin's disappearance. I remember the precise circumstances when she threatened to kill Bernie for bringing drugs into our lives. Then, later, she found out about Essie's role in Bernie's drug trade and heard her threaten me. Caitlin had tons of reasons to hate that woman. What if it's Essie's body in the trunk? Should I suspect my sister? Caitlin a murderer—hiding out somewhere for the past seven years?"

Talia had remained silent for a long pause. "No. I can't believe that. Caitlin was too caring, too—I don't know—decent. Do you think Bernie could give you any information about what happened to Essie Wild? I'd be glad to help track him down."

"Would you? I'd like to talk to my dad, too. He might have heard from Caitlin sometime over these past years. It would be like him not to tell me. Could you, I mean, would you consider going to Arkansas with me to talk to them?"

~~~

Now they were on their way, Talia told Quinn all she knew about the skeleton mystery.

"Tell me about your little Arkansas town," she said. "For one thing, how in the heck did it get the name Frog Springs?"

"You like that?" Quinn grinned. "They say the English settlers mispronounced the French name for the town. The original name had to do with the forested hills, not frogs."

"So? Are there lots of frogs around there?"

"Tons. Bernie and I used to catch them by the bucketful. Do you like fried frog legs?"

"Sounds delicious—I think."

"And there are fresh water springs, too. Wait until you taste the good water in Frog Springs."

With plenty of time to talk, Talia learned much more about Rob Turley, Bernie and Caitlin's mutually disparaging relationship, the unsavory Double M, and the cruel facts about the siblings' dwindling means of support and futile job searches in 2008. Talia hadn't known Bernie back then, had only seen him play the drums in the band, but she was fascinated to hear Quinn describe him—partly best buddy and generous colleague, partly derelict druggie and despicable manipulator.

Neither Talia nor Quinn voiced the possibility of Caitlin being the victim, but the idea existed between them. During quiet intervals, that dark thought gloomed the air around them. At one point Talia turned up the volume on a bright, happy song in order to drown out their unstated misgivings. Quinn smiled at her from the driver's seat. Talia's heart bounced along with her tapping toe, and it took her a moment or two to bring her breathing back to normal. That a mere smile could cause such a reaction! Sparks of electricity vied with dread for control of their emotions—fear of what they might discover.

Having started out early in the morning, the two reached Frog Springs by mid-afternoon. The February landscape had appeared brown and scraggly for most of the drive, but the pines in the Arkansas woods added a bit of color, and the scope of the views from the tops of the hills opened up through the bare branches of the deciduous trees.

"We'll look for Bernie first," Quinn said. "Before anything else, I want to find out if Bernie knows anything about what happened to Essie Wild. I don't think he has any information about Caitlin, but I didn't talk to him much after the disappearance. It won't hurt to ask. We can just hope he's halfway communicative these days."

"Right," Talia said, "and then your father."

"Yeah."

Quinn didn't share with Talia his misgivings about visiting his dad. He hadn't seen his father since the year Caitlin disappeared. Seven years before, Rob Turley added his daughter's disappearance to his list of reasons for being vindictive toward his son. After a few phone call messages left in vain, Quinn continued his life sans hope of family relationships. Before going out to the old house, Quinn hoped to get a read from Bernie on how his father was doing and how he might receive a visit from his son—if Bernie was reachable these days.

During the drive to Arkansas, Talia told Quinn about her family and questioned him about his. They learned that they both lost their mothers as teenagers. Talia heard an exalted description of Quinn's mother. About his father, he told her of the early years but only hinted at a current substance abuse problem. Talia was driving as they approached the town of Frog Springs, and Quinn pointed to the home improvement store where he worked as a teenager.

"That's the company that put my dad's hardware store out of business," Quinn said. "My dad has never forgiven me for getting a job there. After working at his hardware store all through grade school and junior high, though, that job was a natural for me."

He turned to Talia with a wry smile. "You may not want to go with me when I visit my dad. I should probably attend to that little errand on my own."

For the first time in many years, Talia felt like the child who was shunned as different and therefore inferior because of her sun-kissed skin color, high cheekbones, and almond-shaped eyes. She responded in her accustomed manner.

"I understand. This is a small town. You may not feel comfortable introducing me to your father," she said, looking straight ahead at the road beyond the steering wheel.

Quinn regarded his beautiful companion who had set her soft mouth into a hard line. "No, I... It's not you. I mean, Talia, I'd be proud to introduce you to anyone in the world."

He felt his face turn pink and turned his head toward the passenger window to hide his feelings. "I don't know how my dad is going to... I—I just don't want to subject you to his abusive language," he said.

Afraid his excuse sounded a little lame, Quinn turned back to Talia with a worried look.

"Oh," Talia said, "I'm sorry. That's horrible of me to think of my own feelings at a time like this. It was a reaction to...to past experience. I'll do whatever feels right to you. But, keep in mind I'm here to support your effort to find out about your sister. No amount of foul language from your father will make me think less of you."

It was Talia's turn to blush. These compliments and admissions turned them into shy school kids experimenting with first love. They both remained quiet until Quinn directed Talia to turn off the county highway onto Main Street. He pointed out the homes of schoolmates, the shops he remembered and those that had changed in the town center, and the street that led toward Bernie's family home. Talia listened with a slight tilt of her mouth to Quinn's exclamations of surprise over changes and about how small and shabby his church and school looked compared to his memory of them.

She gave Quinn a knowing grin. "The buildings only look smaller and tackier because you are bigger and classier."

Quinn gave her a grateful smile and indicated the turn into the Landoff's driveway. "I'm a little nervous about just dropping in like this. I didn't pre-arrange the visit. They may hate me and kick us off the front porch if Bernie moved back here after our, uh, falling out, and blamed his failures on me. Then there's my dad. Maybe they won't want Bernie associated with someone from my family. Well, maybe they aren't home, or if they've moved, plan B is to find a local directory at the library or to ask some local official to locate Bernie."

Bernie's mom answered her door, stared blankly for a minute when Quinn greeted her, and then gasped.

"Quinlin Turley!" She gave him a long hug. "It's so good to see you. How are you, dear? You just got better lookin' with time. This is so unexpected. You must be looking for Bernie, aren't you? And who is this lovely girl with you? Don't tell me you're married and bringing your new bride home to meet your—uh...your dad. Oh, I'm so surprised. But I'm not remembering my manners. Come on in. Can I get you something to drink?"

Quinn broke away from Mrs. Landoff's hold, introduced Talia as a good friend and traveling companion, and returned Mrs. Landoff's big smile. Talia felt embarrassed but also oddly comfortable when Bernie's mother gave her a comparable embrace. Unsure what she expected, she was nevertheless somewhat surprised to be greeted by such a friendly, attractive woman. Mrs. Landoff, her tall, square figure enhanced by slim jeans and a bright pink jersey tunic top, short expertly-dyed hairdo neatly parted on the side and combed almost over one eye, looked more like a weekend business woman or society queen than a fiftyish small-town housewife.

After the effusive greeting, Quinn remembered how verbose his friend's mother had always been. He was relieved to be received in such a loving manner. It sounded as if Bernie's mom, at least, didn't have anything to hold against him and might tell him where he could find her son. He remembered her drink offer.

"We don't need anything, Mrs. Landoff, thank you. We ate lunch, and we don't have much time." Quinn looked at Talia and waited until she nodded her agreement. "I'll see my dad while I'm in town, but I'd like to visit Bernie, too. We had some hard spells when Bernie lived in Kansas City, and our parting was, well, not the friendliest. I was hoping you could tell me how he is and how to find him. Bernie was my best friend for so long, and you were like a mother to me after my mom passed away. I should have visited a long time ago."

"You're a good boy, Quinlin. Just sit for a minute, both of you, and I'll tell you how it is with Bernie."

"Thank you, Ma'am," Quinn said. He and Talia sat side by side on the doily-backed sofa while their hostess seated herself across from them in an overstuffed chair. Quinn looked around. "Is Mr. Landoff working today?"

"Pa always works on Saturdays, at least half a day. You remember he always went into the shop on weekends to get work done while there were not so many interruptions? Well, he's still doing it. I don't think that man will ever retire. He likes building his cabinets too much."

"I can understand how he feels," Quinn said.

"Of course you can. You and your music will never be parted, I'm sure. Well, back several years ago, when Bernie returned home, after his terrible escapades up north, you know, Pa took to working at his shop most of the time. He couldn't quite come to grips with Bernie's troubles, and any time they were together Pa was yelling and Bernie was hunkering down. Thank goodness, things are much better now. Bernie made a complete turnaround. Pa'll be home this afternoon, and we'll have some time before our cookout with the neighbors this evening."

Quinn was relieved to hear Mrs. Landoff refer to Bernie's sojourn in Kansas City as *terrible escapades*. He didn't know how aware she would be. "So what happened to make Bernie get clean?" Quinn asked.

"I was just getting to that," Mrs. Landoff said.

Talia observed with an inward smile that Bernie's mom was the kind of soliloquist not used to being interrupted. She could also detect the pride and excitement in the lady's voice. For Quinn's sake, she appreciated that this story promised to have a happy ending. Since they left home this morning, Quinn had acted determined but not delighted to connect with the people in his home town.

Bernie's mom continued, "Bernie came home in terrible shape. Not only was he addicted to drugs, but he was scared he was being chased, either by the law or by the people he got his drugs from. His dad didn't give him any slack, either, and the poor boy slunk into a depression, which, of course, required medicating with more drugs. It wasn't Pa's fault. He was just so frustrated with Bernie and didn't know how to handle it. Like I said, in order not to nag or yell at the boy, he started staying away. I was desperate to help but didn't know what to do until I attended an Al-Anon meeting and learned how to help Bernie help himself. With the resources I learned about in the training, I got him to go to a good program in Little Rock. He came back dried out, as they say, but it only lasted until he met up with some of his musician friends and got drunk and...you know. It wasn't my help, in the end, that turned him around.

"Are you sure I can't get you something to drink?" She paused, as if she just remembered her manners, and then grinned. "Non-alcoholic, I mean. There's some fresh homemade lemonade in the refrigerator."

With a quick glance between them, both Talia and Quinn assented at once. One thing was obvious—this wasn't going to be a short story.

Chapter 30

February—Kansas City, Missouri

On Sunday, Beth attached the camera to her computer, and she and Arnie studied the pictures of Myron Martin from the charity reception.

The evening before, after the reception, she had contacted Mark Overos, and she and Arnie, together, had given him the confiscated pop can. She had offered it like a little kid showing off her handiwork and expecting compliments. Mark had taken it from her with a grim, resigned expression.

"Okay, I'll see if I can find time to test this," he'd said.

Beth had deflated. Maybe his stoic reaction resulted from his disbelief that she'd go near a man she suspected of being a drug lord, after he'd warned her? And now he could see that Arnie had joined her quest. He probably wondered what the two of them could be thinking.

Beth hoped Mark would be able to match the DNA on the can to something found in the duplex, but she knew it wouldn't prove anything. Finding Myron Martin's DNA or his fingerprints in the duplex wouldn't prove he had anything to do with Essie's drugs or with the squelching of the case. But it would indicate that Myron Martin and Double M were names for the same person. That was something. And what if they could match his fingerprints to some found on the trunk?

"Look, Arnie, this picture is clear and detailed on the computer screen. I think Talia, or at least Quinn, will be able to tell from this if Myron Martin is Double M. Don't you?"

"The man is balding, and he's sporting a mustache. We can't be sure whether he looked the same seven years ago. But, yes, it's a good photo."

"I guess it depends on what kind of look they had of him back then. Talia only saw him from a distance, if she saw him at all. Maybe Quinn saw him up close. I don't know. Anyway, I'm glad I got the pop can."

The distance photos taken out on the golf course were fuzzier, because she used the zoom, but someone who knew the man might be able to identify Mr. Martin in them. Beth planned to print out a couple of the photos and show them to Talia and Quinn when they returned from their trip. Meanwhile she e-mailed the best photo to Talia. Maybe either she or Quinn would be able to identify the man from seeing the picture on Talia's phone—if she checked her e-mails while they travelled.

She hoped the two travelers would come back with some information that might help prove who the victim was. Also, it was hard to keep from wondering whether their joint venture would bring Quinn and Talia closer together or if the emotional turmoil might tear them apart. Beth leaned in for a closer look at one of the photos. She saw something she hadn't noticed before.

"I'm going to magnify this picture," she said to Arnie.

It was the picture she took of Myron Martin standing next to Tom Watson. In the photo, Myron wore the short-sleeved country club shirt, and on his bare arm Beth could distinguish what looked like a large faded scar, perhaps from a burn or from a deep cut. It was the shape of the scar that had caught her attention, a shape that reminded her of something she'd seen before. It appeared like a tiny ceiling fan on top of several concentric circles. Enlarging the scar didn't help. It merely appeared fuzzier. Beth stared at the scar until it began to look like a blob of red, but couldn't think of what it reminded her.

"It could be a birthmark," Arnie said while regarding the screen from behind the desk chair.

"That's probably what it is," Beth said. "Or it could be a rash that will heal and not be there in a week or so. This is like seeing Abraham Lincoln's image on a piece of soiled cloth, or a rabbit in a cloud, except I can't remember what this shape looks like. Maybe I'll think of it later."

Psycho Cat jumped onto her lap and nudged her hand with his head.

"I think ol' Psycho Cat wants to help," Arnie said.

"What do you think, Sylvester?" Beth asked. "Do you recognize this scar shape from anywhere?"

The cat turned his head toward the screen and hissed.

Chapter 31

February—Kansas City, Missouri

A few minutes ahead of schedule, Beth and Arnie arrived to show the duplex to the prospective renters. Arnie came to be Beth's calming influence. She was still a little nervous about showing the side where the murder victim was found. They planned to show the couple through Side B, the side Beth had recently finished renovating, and then offer to show Side A, where Clay found the skeleton in the trunk. The police hadn't told her not to accept new renters. For that matter, except for Mark Overos, no one had told her much of anything about the case, and Mark had said nothing about keeping their duplex empty.

"Arnie," Beth said as they stepped onto the back porch, "will you unlock and turn on the lights in Clay's side while I get this side ready to show?"

"No problem. You're still calling it Clay's side, huh?"

"Habit. It'll change as soon as I get used to someone else living there."

While Beth walked from the back door to the front switching lights on, three things happened in quick succession. First, the doorbell rang, a good sign of eager and punctual future renters. She strode toward the front door. Next, her dust-seeking eye passed across the fireplace, where Psycho Cat had performed his crazy antics. It was there she noticed the metal decorations on the bottom of the mantle. They triggered an instant mind picture of the scar she had seen earlier in the photo of Myron Martin. Finally, Arnie hollered in alarm from the back porch.

Arnie's shout reached her just as she opened the blinds and saw a smiling young couple standing on the front stoop. They had seen her, and she couldn't very well turn around and head back toward the kitchen to find out what Arnie was all upset about. It would also be impolite for her to leave the door to go over and investigate the fireplace while they were standing outside in the cold. Beth turned her head from the visitors to the back door and to the front again, unable to decide for a moment. Then, courteousness won out. Beth opened the door, put on a friendly face, and welcomed the visitors into the duplex.

Arnie entered the living room with a letter in his hand and a frazzled look on his face, a look that became gracious the minute he saw the young couple. Beth led the introductions and repeated the information about the duplex she'd given the young woman over the phone. She pointed out the appliances in the kitchen, the patio and garage out back, and the door to the full basement. Then she let the people look around.

At most showings, Beth listened for the comments people made. She heard, "The basement has tons of storage space. We could probably get a washer and dryer cheap through Craig's List. The kitchen is attractive. We'd probably need an area rug for this beautiful hardwood floor. Maybe we could ask my parents if they we could use the one they have rolled up in the attic." Those comments told her they were impressed, already seeing themselves and their belongings in the duplex.

This time too much weighed on her mind to grow optimistic at the chatter. Standing in silence beside Arnie, Beth at first studied the fireplace. Then she glanced at the pieces of paper Arnie held against his leg and presented a raised eyebrow to her husband, who seemed to remain expressionless and noncommittal with great effort. Staying quiet and relaxed with a dozen questions bobbing around in her head was almost more than she could handle, but

Arnie raised one finger slightly, nodded in the direction of the couple coming up from the basement, and raised his eyes toward the upstairs. Beth clamped her mouth shut and waited.

When the visitors appeared from the basement, they all exchanged polite smiles, and Beth directed them up to view the second story. At the last minute, she remembered she hadn't had time to turn on the lights upstairs and raced up ahead of the two. A minute or two later, she came down looking back over her shoulder and listening for the murmurs of discussion coursing down the stairway.

"Arnie," Beth whispered, "Come over here and look at this metal décor on the fireplace. It matches the scar on Myron Martin's arm."

Arnie squinted at the design and nodded. Just as Beth started to ask about the paper he held, however, the young couple appeared. While the wife revisited the kitchen, the husband asked what seemed like an endless number of questions.

His wife joined him with a smile and requested a rental application. Ordinarily, Beth would have offered to show them Side A as a second choice. This time, however, she was too anxious to finish the showing and find out what Arnie was holding onto so tightly in his stiff fist. When the couple announced they would return with the application fee if they chose to take the duplex after seeing the others on their list, Beth wasn't even disappointed. She gave them her business card and asked them to call when they decided. To think, just the previous week, getting new renters was the most important goal in her life. Now, that these folks were leaving without signing an application held secondary importance to her.

The minute the door closed, Beth and Arnie both spoke at once. Arnie let Beth speak first. He still clutched the paper.

She pointed to the metal fireplace decoration. "Don't you think Myron Martin's scar has to have been made by this metalwork? This not only proves Myron Martin is Double M, but also proves

Double M was sometime or other on this side of the duplex, the side where Quinn Turley and Bernie Landoff lived. And he either fell onto the front of the fireplace, or—or maybe someone pushed him, hard."

"Interesting reasoning, although that mark on his arm could still be just a birthmark," Arnie said in a monotone. He squinted at the metal. "And that metal doesn't appear sharp enough to leave a lasting scar."

"I spent hours a few years ago sanding it down with a metal sander. I did it so no one would get hurt on the sharp points. Guess I was too late."

Arnie turned his head sideways to give it another look. "We'll need to bring the picture over here for comparison, but it does seem to have the same shape and design as the scar." He held his papers out for Beth to take. "But before we go sticking our noses any farther into this thing, I think you'd better look at this note I found tucked between the storm and the front door on Side A."

Arnie handed her the paper and the damp, wrinkled envelope that was addressed to Beth at the duplex. The typewritten note, at first glance, looked like a professional business letter, folded into thirds. She thought it might be one of those notices from a utility company that tells people they've missed a payment or that a new meter will be installed. If so, Arnie made a huge deal over one little late charge in the midst of so much turmoil.

Beth skimmed the letter. Then, in an instant, panic hit as she registered its gist. She started reading again, word by word from the beginning, to make sure she understood. When she finished, she looked up at Arnie. Adrenalin caused an almost nauseous feeling, and Beth searched her brain for a way to deal with the import of the letter she held rigidly with both hands. She looked down at the printed page again.

Be advised,

The murder case you are attempting to solve is
none of your affair. You are putting yourself and

your family in grave danger by pursuing your present course of action. Cease and desist your questions and your gathering of evidence immediately.

This part could be from the police if the language had been more professional. They had told Beth as much before. The "cease and desist" part made an attempt at sounding official, but it wasn't on police department letterhead, nor was there a signature at the end. The remainder of the poison pen letter contained veiled threats, each of which sent a shiver through her. It said there were worse things that could happen to the duplex than finding a body in the attic. A gas leak could be ignited and explode. A giant oak could be cut down and land on the building. Beth and Arnie's own home was mentioned with the possibility of it catching fire during the night. The last sentence held the most daunting threat.

For the safety of your children, Clayton and Janae Stockwell, your husband, and yourself, end your involvement and your meddlesome investigation immediately.

Arnie waited for Beth to react, she could tell. He looked as if he'd already assessed the situation and made a decision about what they should do but knew she needed to analyze each word and sentence before she would listen to his recommendation. Beth guessed he considered her a little stubborn. He could be right.

"Arnie, this is scary."

"Damn scary."

"It looks as if it's been in the door for a while, maybe a few days? I don't think it has anything to do with the golf reception we attended last night." Beth remembered Myron Martin's frown in the photo she pretended to take of Tom Watson.

"When was the last time you went through that front door?" Arnie asked.

Beth thought about it. "I've been working on this side all this past week, and even when I was working on Side A, I almost always went in through the back door. It could be two weeks since I've opened the front door over on that side."

Beth and Arnie discussed who might have put the letter in the doorway. Could it have been Devon Wild? Might it be someone else Devon had told about her clumsy meeting with him? Did Myron Martin have anything to do with this? The wording appeared too unsophisticated to be his, but he could have paid someone to threaten them. It could've been Quinn Turley! Or, someone in the nightclub might have heard her question Quinn and told Bernie about it.

If Double M sustained such a scar-producing injury on Side A of the duplex, where Quinn and Bernie lived, then one of the two young renters must be involved. Caitlin Turley lived there at the time, too. And Essie Wild lived on Side B. Were they getting too close? Now the killer would try anything to scare them off?

This time Beth agreed with Arnie—with no second thoughts. They would hand the letter over to Detective Carl Rinquire and leave it to him to investigate.

Chapter 32

February—Frog Springs, Arkansas

Mr. Landoff came home while Quinn and Talia listened to his wife's story about their son. "Hold on," he said after fifteen minutes more non-stop chatter about the wedding, Bernie's work, and the grandchildren. "Leave something for Bernie and Serena to tell Quinn and his friend."

Pride showed in Mr. Landoff's eyes. He placed a gentle hand on his wife's shoulder and volunteered to call Bernie to ask if he would be home that evening. After a short conversation with his son, he handed the phone to Quinn.

Bernie must have inherited his mother's penchant for chatter. After Quinn said a few words of hello, he mostly listened and grinned, grinned and listened for the next ten minutes. Finally, the phone conversation ended and Quinn told Talia about Bernie's enthusiastic invitation to dinner at his home seven miles south of Frog Springs.

~~~

Quinn drove through town and onto a country road. On the way, he and Talia talked about how a woman can turn a man's life around. They both brought up their own parents as examples while they discussed Bernie's story.

Bernie's mom had explained, in great detail, what happened after Bernie rediscovered the neighbor girl he had a crush on in high school. Serena was two years younger than Bernie and had come home from school for the summer to stay with her parents. She started seeing Bernie while he was still struggling to stay off narcotics. Not long after they began dating, Bernie worked to become sober and hadn't had a real relapse since. Serena helped him cope with his increasingly infrequent depressions without resorting to narcotics. After she became pregnant, they married, Bernie finished technical school, and he settled into business as a successful electrician. He also played percussion with a local band that landed a gig once every month or so, and Serena attended his performances.

The women and children stood neglected while Quinn and Bernie shook hands, backslapped, congratulated, and hugged. Serena grinned and introduced herself and her two children to Talia.

"Oh, sorry. Didn't mean to be rude," Quinn said. "Bernie, this is Talia Johnson. Talia, Bernie Landoff. And this must be your wife, Serena, and your kids...."

"Yeah, this is..."

Talia and Serena laughed.

"We've already taken care of the introductions," Serena said. "Come on in and make yourselves comfortable, you all. It looks as if the guys have a lot of catching up to do. And I'd like to get acquainted, too."

Quinn noticed Bernie's mature features and good grooming, the softening of his jokes, and the twinkle he remembered in Bernie's eyes from childhood. He told Talia that, a year after leaving Kansas City, Bernie had sent money to replace what he stole. With a jiggling foot suggesting some embarrassment, Bernie confessed he had been arrested for possession before he left Kansas City. He admitted how often he had thought about getting in touch with Quinn beyond sending the money, but he'd felt too ashamed to do so.

Quinn felt his shoulders relax. "I've thought often of getting in touch with you, too. I guess it's just easier to let past differences rule our lives. I'm glad we're here now, anyway. And I'm proud of you for beating your devils."

"You can thank Serena for helping me with that," Bernie said as Serena appeared from the kitchen with a tray of appetizers.

After dinner, Quinn and Talia sat on a comfy sofa facing a wall of windows with a western view. They watched a bright water-colored winter sunset disappear behind the hills beyond the wide back yard. Quinn and Bernie joked and reminisced as if their friendship had never lapsed.

Talia played with the three-year-old and the baby on the carpet before their bedtime. She didn't seem to tire of tossing a soft ball and making faces which elicited giggles. "Goodnight, Sweetie. Thanks for playing with me. I had lots of fun." she told the little girl when Serena announced the kids' bedtime. Her huge smile and bright laughter proved she meant it.

"Say night, night," Serena said as she picked up the baby and took her daughter by the hand.

While Serena took the children off to bed, Quinn brought up the subjects he'd been waiting to discuss. He told Bernie about the dead body found in the trunk, and Talia chimed in with the reasons Beth Stockwell had for suspecting the murder took place around the end of August, seven years previous. Expecting Bernie to have some kind of shocked or at least disturbed reaction but instead seeing only nods, Quinn stopped talking and looked at his friend.

"Okay, what gives?" Quinn asked. "You act as if you know all about this. Do you?"

"I don't know *all* about it," Bernie said, "but I know a body was found in Essie and Devon's apartment. A detective, name of—Rinquire, called me a couple of weeks ago. He asked a bunch of questions and said I could be called for more information. I haven't heard anything since."

"Why'd they call you specifically?" Talia asked, mystified why Bernie would've been sought out and not Quinn.

Bernie looked sheepish but answered Talia matter-of-factly. "Remember my arrest for possession I told you about? Well, soon after my arraignment, Essie Wild was taken into custody and quizzed about her sources. She didn't give anybody up, as far as I know, but she and her drug supplier figured I was the one who fingered Essie. So. The cops were on me for information. The thugs were after me for snitching. I lucked out with a lenient sentence from the judge for it being a first offence, but I didn't think Double M would be so compassionate. I left the city and came home. Anyway, I have a police record in K.C. and a link to Essie Wild, you know, with the drugs and having lived next-door. That's why they questioned me."

"Okay," Quinn said with a frown, "that means Essie was still around when you left town."

"And Beth Stockwell believes the guy known as Double M might actually be on the city council now," Talia said.

Bernie snorted. "That's bullshit! He shouldn't be allowed anywhere but inside a penitentiary."

"Which brings me to the main question I need to ask you," Quinn said. "You remember my sister left for California right after you ditched the duplex and just before I moved out?"

"Yeah, sure. Listen, man, I'm sorry about the way I treated Caitlin. I was…"

"I know," Quinn said. "I'm just glad you've got it together now. But that's not why I'm bringing this up. I just need to find out if you know anything about what happened that day before she left. You weren't at the band's warm-up session that afternoon, and I thought maybe you went back to the duplex and saw her. You and she were not exactly… I mean, maybe Caitlin rushed out of there when you came back to see Essie—or—or something. I don't know. I'm just digging for info."

"Info? You mean you can't ask her? Aren't you in contact with Caitlin?"

"No, I haven't heard anything from her since the day she left Kansas City."

"Well, I didn't go back to the duplex, ever. Essie left there soon after that, and I guess she left her husband, too. It's been a long time ago, and I've tried to put it out of my mind, that is, the part I can remember from when I was halfway sober. I knew you hadn't heard from Caitlin by the time I left Kansas City, but... So, you haven't heard from her since? Wow. I'm sorry, man, I don't know anything about why she took off earlier than you thought she would or what happened to her after that. I wish I could help. I know how much you care about her."

Serena, Talia, Bernie, and Quinn parted with multiple ideas about how they might stay in touch. Quinn drove back toward Frog Springs with Talia lounging beside him. She looked dreamy.

"Bernie sounded as if he told the truth tonight," Talia said in a soft voice. "He was surprised to pieces when you told him that your sister disappeared."

"I agree."

Talia said nothing more. Quinn stayed quiet.

Neither of them broached the subject of lodging for the night, but when Quinn spied a well-lighted, new-looking economy motel on the outskirts of town, he looked at Talia. She smiled and nodded. They asked for two rooms and were assigned accommodations on the second floor across the hall from each other. Before going up to their rooms, they found a store where they bought some beer and microwave popcorn.

It was ten-fifteen by then, and the two spent half an hour deciding in which room they'd sit, which movie they'd watch, and who got the easy chair and who the desk chair. By the time they'd decided and arranged everything, they missed the first fifteen minutes of the movie. It didn't matter, because they spent the next hours talking and laughing and popping corn. They ended up on the bed with pillows behind their backs and the bedspread over their legs in Talia's room. It was late before the talk turned to the next morning's visit with Quinn's father. Quinn again admitted dreading the encounter and accepted Talia's offer to accompany him.

Their first kiss felt so gentle, so sweet, and so real it reached right into Quinn's soul, and the burst of passion he felt overrode his dread of seeing his father and of learning Caitlin's fate.

"Listen," Talia said at last, breathless, "We've been drinking beer, and we've shared our deepest thoughts. It'd be too easy to give in to passion and then regret it."

"I could never regret it."

"I mean… After this trip, if we still feel this way, we can…"

From outside the door as he left, Quinn peeked back inside the room, just in case. Talia gave him a sweet smile and began collecting empty cans. He shut the door with a soft click.

Quinn couldn't sleep until early morning. His thoughts and emotions galloped from desire to anxiety to sadness, from thoughts of the past to hopes for the future, from Bernie to Caitlin to his dad and back to Talia. The happy contemplation of their evening together finally let him slumber.

By the time they rose, checked out of the motel, and ate a light breakfast at a pancake house, noon announced itself on the car's dashboard clock. It was just as well, Quinn told Talia. Unless his father had changed, he wouldn't be up until twelve anyway. Talia drove to Quinn's dad's house. Quinn feared if he sat behind the wheel, he'd drive right out of town.

Rob Turley answered the door after the third push of the non-working doorbell and the fourth knock. His eyes looked bleary, with deep bags underneath. The thick brown head of hair Quinn remembered had faded to mostly gray and was longish and disheveled, and Rob's shave looked several days old, as old as his deodorant smelled. He wore a stained sweatshirt over a pot belly and a pair of scruffy house shoes. Quinn stared a little too long, and his father's sour look turned surly.

"Well, what is it?" he growled. "Are you two some kinda do-gooders from an agency, or are you sellin' something?"

"I'm..." Quinn began, but faltered.

"This is your son," Talia said, "and I'm Talia. May we come in and talk to you?"

"Quinlin?"

Rob stared for a few minutes at his son, and his eyes started to turn liquid. When he spoke, his voice sounded more like that of a croaky old man than like the strong voice of a fifty-seven-year-old.

"Quinn. You came home. I'd given up ever seeing you or your sister...." He turned accusingly toward Talia and raised his voice, "Where's little Katie?"

"Dad," Quinn said with as much patience as he could muster, "we don't know where Caitlin is. We were hoping you could help us find her."

Rob looked confused for a few moments, and then his face soured again. He backed away from his visitors a couple of paces and left the door open. By the time Quinn and Talia entered the house and shut the door against the chilly February air, Rob had plodded to his shabby recliner. He regarded the two with a squinty frown without asking them to sit, and Quinn, feeling his neck and shoulders become tight again, peered around at the dusty and rumpled furniture to look for either a seat to offer Talia or a good excuse for asking her to wait in the car. Talia must have noticed Quinn's discomfort, because she sat on the edge of a sofa cushion and patted the spot next to her.

Quinn sat and faced the man who had not been a father to him for years, since before his mother died. All of his nervousness vanished as he gazed. When he was a kid, his father was his hero, a man respected in the community and liked by everyone. It was hard for the teenaged Quinn to disappoint and be ridiculed by his dad. He felt as if he were a failure. And he was never able to disassociate the hero father figure from the abusive addict.

The man before him now hadn't much to do with the father who could make him feel so inadequate. The old man made him feel nothing but pity. With a quick glance at Talia, Quinn saw that her face registered the same feeling, rather than the disgust he expected to find there.

"Dad," Quinn said, "I need to know whether you've seen or heard from Caitlin since she left, if you know where she is now."

"You took her away from me. She went up there when you told her to, and she never came back. She never even called or wrote. You told me she went to California rather than back here to be with her dad. First, Martha, then you, and then Caitlin left, too." Rob jerked out of his slump as if startled by a thunder bolt. He sat straight as a ramrod and stared at Quinn. "You never heard from her either? You swishy music boy, you stole my little girl away, and now you *lost* her?"

All the compassion Quinn felt evaporated. With complete confidence, he stood. "I think you know, deep down, how you drove us both away. Come to grips with that fact, Dad, and you might be able to get some help and turn your life around. Meanwhile, we have to find something of Caitlin's to take back to Kansas City with us. We're going to search Caitlin's old room."

Without another word, Quinn took Talia's hand, and the two of them entered the bedroom. It looked much as it had when Caitlin left. Under a coating of dust, they found clothing, books, papers, stuffed animals, and even cosmetics. In the back of a drawer of her dresser there was an old hairbrush with some of Caitlin's hair still stuck between the bristles. Quinn grabbed that, and Talia latched onto a tube of used lipstick. When they turned to leave they found Quinn's father standing in the doorway.

"Will those things help you find Caitlin?"

"Maybe they'll help us find out what happened before she left Kansas City," Quinn said. "I'll call you if we learn anything."

Talia turned to Rob as she stepped out the front door and said proudly, "By the way, Quinn Turley is known all over the Midwest…" She looked around at Quinn for a second. "No—all over the country—as a fine musician. You should order one of his CDs. Look for the music of the group called *Quinn Turley and Novel Invasion.*"

Chapter 33

February—Kansas City, Missouri

Beth could have sworn Detective Rinquire gave her an "I told you so" look after he read the threatening letter Arnie found in the duplex doorway. True to form, however, the staid law enforcement officer at once resumed his business-like demeanor and analyzed the letter and considered the best course of action.

"Do you have guesses about who might have left the letter?" he asked as he pulled the ubiquitous notebook out of his jacket pocket.

They ran through their list of possibilities, impossibilities, and maybes. Rinquire shook his head and rolled his eyes when Beth described her meetings with Devon Wild and Quinn Turley. Devon Wild topped her list of letter writer suspects, but she admitted the letter didn't sound like the man she interviewed.

Arnie brought up the scar they'd seen in the photo of Myron Martin and its uncanny similarity in pattern to the decorative metalwork on the duplex fireplace. Beth explained how she'd photographed Mr. Martin at the golf event he and his wife had chaired. Carl Rinquire assumed the same alert, yet cautious, expression Beth noticed on Mark Overos's face every time she mentioned Double M.

"What made you notice this scar?" Rinquire asked.

"It looked so familiar to me," Beth said. "Then, today at the duplex, I looked at the fireplace décor, and I decided the metal design must have made the scar. I guess I could be wrong. Arnie said the scar could just be a birthmark."

"Is there some reason you scrutinized Mr. Martin enough to notice a scar on his arm?" Detective Rinquire asked in a routine way. But he watched Beth closely.

"Well…" Beth hesitated, remembering Mark Overos was the one who gave her the idea to look up a city leader to find out if there was a connection to Double M. "Both Devon and Quinn mentioned a narcotics dealer called Double M when they told me about what went on at that duplex before the—that body was stuffed into the trunk. Then someone with pull caused the investigation of our case to be dropped. When Councilman Myron Martin was pointed out to me at the reception, it hit me, two names beginning with M. I heard some of the other golfers call him Marty—Marty Martin, still double M's. He is short and dark, the way Double M was described to me. So I looked him over. In fact, I took that picture of him in which the scar is visible. I have the photo at home, if it will help."

Arnie threw Beth a quick look of surprise, but he didn't mention her conversations with Mark.

"Whew." Detective Rinquire sighed, and he looked again at the letter in his hand. "I'll keep this letter and let my lab people examine it, but meanwhile do you have a safe place you can stay while we look into this?"

With a helpless look, Beth turned toward Arnie. He pressed his lips together and shrugged, as if to say, "We gotta do what we gotta do." Beth looked back at the detective. She struggled to keep her voice from shaking when she answered.

"My sister's house—she and her husband will let us stay there. Their kids are grown and out on their own. But my son and his wife are threatened in that letter, too. It doesn't mention their new address. Do you think they're safe?"

"If we are actually dealing with Double M, I wouldn't take any chances."

~~~

By the end of the day Beth and Arnie had arranged their *safe* housing. Beth's older sister, Meg, and brother-in-law lived across the state line in a Kansas suburb and were glad to take Arnie and Beth in. Beth wasn't eager to deal with all of the questions her sister would have and the mothering she'd attempt, but she felt grateful for the help. Even Psycho Cat was invited.

Meg asked Clay and Janae to stay at her house, also. Instead, after a short discussion, they decided to rent the inexpensive guest accommodations in a dormitory at the University for a few weeks. It would help Clay to be close to school and work. Then they'd go visit Janae's folks in Minnesota for the week of spring break. After that? They all hoped there would not be an after that.

The dormitory housing wasn't available until Monday. Beth and Arnie stopped in to help Clay and Janae pack up a few things to take to Meg's house for the first night and to commiserate about the necessity of going.

Their suitcases and cat paraphernalia were in the car, and Beth carried Psycho Cat in her arms when they arrived at the loft apartment. After Janae spent a few minutes cuddling the kitty, Psycho Cat made himself at home by sniffing around the loft. He paid particular attention to the art studio, and Beth had to slip behind the lovely screen divider to shoo him off Janae's box of found objects against his stubborn feline will.

Beth remembered the nail Janae had stored in that container. Was Psycho Cat still directing them toward artifacts having to do with the dead body? Mark Overos had the nail now, but its scent could still be in the box. In the process of capturing her big orange cat before he could knock something over, Beth noticed the covered sculpture and was tempted to peek. Instead, she carried Psycho Cat to the other side of the screen in time to see the kids appear from their bedroom.

Janae headed for the kitchen with a clothes basket. "I want to pack some of the boxed and canned food we'll need in the student housing so when we come back here tomorrow evening it'll be ready to go. We can put the cold food in our cooler then and…"

"Oh, I'm so sorry for all this," Beth said. "If I hadn't gone on a rampage to figure out whose body was in that trunk and who put it there…."

"Mom," Clay said, "You don't have to apologize to us. We'll be fine. You know, we found the skeleton, we gave you the nail, and we went to the band concert with you and heard Quinn's story. We'd be out there helping you track down clues if we had the time. Look, you've got the police back on the case. That's more than anyone else has done. Right, Janae?"

"Correct. I was a little upset at first, but I'm sure you're doing the right thing, and, like Clay said, if we had just a smidgen more time, we'd be doing more."

"You kids will make me cry by being so understanding." Beth gave Psycho Cat to Arnie and went into the kitchen to help Janae pack her basket.

~~~

All the way to the loft, and then again as Arnie drove toward Meg's house, Beth kept looking back and to either side of the car, expecting to find someone mean-looking following them or ready to bump them off the road.

"Get a grip, Babe. The letter sat in the doorway for several days, at least, maybe for over a week," he said. "We went in and out all that time, and nothing happened. That doesn't mean there's no danger, but it wouldn't make sense that someone would all of a sudden show up just because we've now read the note. Whoever wrote it must not know you've been snooping around all this week." He jabbed her shoulder with a finger. "It doesn't mean they won't find out, though."

His words made sense to Beth, but she still jumped every time a car pulled alongside them at a traffic light. "Please, drive around a few blocks and let's make sure no one follows. I don't want to put Meg and Paul in danger, too."

"Oh, okay, if it'll make you happy."

Arnie turned off onto a side street in order to cut through a couple of neighborhoods. Beth peered through the back window to see if they were being followed. She saw Clay and Janae zoom past the intersection, but no one turned to follow behind them.

"Good," Beth said, "At least we'll confuse anyone who might be following."

After they'd gone two blocks without seeing a car, she decided she was being silly. Unless—the bad guy could have followed Clay and Janae instead! At that moment, a dark red sedan appeared from a side street and turned in their direction.

"Arnie," Beth said, "the guy took a short cut and now he's in back of us! We've got to lose him!"

Before Arnie could react in any way, Beth craned her neck to peek back. She let only her eyes and the top of her head show above the seat back. Her suspect in the red car pulled into a driveway, and his garage door opened. Beth faced forward, and her heart returned to a near-normal rhythm. Her husband didn't say a thing, and when she turned her head to see if he was laughing at her, she caught him suppressing a grin.

The afternoon faded into evening. The dark, the gloom, and the chilly air reflected the mood of the little line of people who filed into Meg's house. Beth's cell phone buzzed—a missed call and a text message sent by Talia.

> Quinn and I are on our way home from
> Arkansas. Bringing items used by Caitlin, with her
> DNA. Quinn thinks the photo you sent is of Double
> M. Not sure. Tell you more tomorrow.

Maybe, like Arnie imagined, Myron Martin had changed in the seven years since Quinn had seen him. She hoped he'd be certain when he saw the picture she'd printed. Wait—she was letting the police do the investigating now, wasn't she?

Chapter 34

February—Kansas City, Missouri

Monday morning, start of a new work week—but not for Beth— she considered herself trapped at her sister's house, waiting. Meg and Paul went to work. Clay and Janae left for work and school, their belongings with them so they could check into campus housing that afternoon. Arnie appeared lost in contemplation in front of the lap-top he'd set up at the dining room table.

Beth found herself pacing. After cleaning up from breakfast, she tried to read a book but soon gave up. She used Meg's desktop computer to search for more information about Myron Martin but didn't find more than she'd seen before. Then she stood by the front window and scanned the street, sidewalk, and bushes outside for suspicious activity. She thought she might collapse into a million pieces if she couldn't control her jitters.

On her way back to the easy chair where she left her book, Beth stooped to run her hand over Psycho Cat's soft fur. The kitty seemed to be currently in his cute, curled-up sleep mode, looking as if he'd never caused trouble in his life. He'd spent part of the night yowling, another part pawing at the basement door, and the rest undertaking both annoying exploits at the same time. Meg had insisted he be kept in her basement, along with his litter box and food bowl, until he became accustomed to her house. For a cat used to having free access to Beth and Arnie's home, their bed, and their stuffed furniture, the unfamiliar basement probably felt like a dungeon. He was making up for his nighttime grumps by catnapping all day so far on a towel Beth slipped under him on Meg's sofa. If only she could sleep the day away. It'd be better than sitting there knowing nothing. When her phone rang, Psycho Cat twitched his ears and stretched a white paw over his eyes.

"According to Bernie," Talia reported from home, "not only was Essie in town after the murder, but also she and Bernie were arrested. They have police records. I assume they've had fingerprints taken and maybe DNA samples. If the body in the trunk is Essie, the police would know, I think."

Beth wished mere phone calls could be the cure for all depression and anxiety in the world. This one lifted her spirits like the sun dries a wet umbrella. It brought news! Now, they knew for sure that the victim was neither Bernie nor Essie.

"I guess you're right," Beth said. "The murderer could knock out teeth to make dental records useless, and decomposition might take away fingerprints, but as far as I know, DNA remains forever in bones. Did you learn any more about where Caitlin might be?"

"No. We took a hairbrush and a tube of lipstick from her bedroom, though. Can you take them to your CSI friend?"

Neither Beth nor Talia voiced the obvious. Beth's good mood diminished. The teenaged girl she never knew but about whom she cared, for Quinn's and Talia's sakes, might be the only logical identity for the victim. The murderer must be a monster to have killed a young girl like that.

When Beth told Talia about the threatening letter she received and that Arnie and she were staying in a safe place, Talia offered to take Caitlin's hairbrush and lipstick to Mark Overos. Beth thought it over.

"No, I don't want you involved any more than you are already. The last thing I want to do is put another person in danger. We don't know who left the letter or how serious it is, but if the person who wrote it knows what I've been doing and has threatened my family, then that person can learn about your involvement as well."

"Do you have any theory about who wrote that letter?"

"There are several possibilities. You've eliminated two of them. Bernie is in Arkansas, and Quinn took you down there to get a DNA sample. I think that leaves those two out as suspects."

"But there are Devon and Essie Wild."

"And maybe Double M."

"Unless someone we don't know about was killed by another unknown person and the body for some reason stuffed inside that trunk, I think those are the suspects," Talia said. "I hope these items will help clear it all up. How can we get it to the investigators?"

Beth asked Talia to drive by Meg's house and stash the bag of artifacts inside the storm door. Then Beth could retrieve the bag without being seen and then pass it along to Detective Rinquire. Her thoughts flipped to Mark Overos, to whom she'd given all of her previous bits of evidence. However, she promised Carl Rinquire and Arnie she'd rely on the detective to handle everything. She guessed the detective would have to take the items to the CSI for testing. Would someone, like Double M, perhaps, be able to stop the testing from being done?

Arnie appeared behind Beth while she stood in the middle of the living room holding her phone against her chest. After talking to Talia, she'd become lost in a terrible daydream, in which she contemplated visions of skeletal remains with remnants of mummified skin and rotted clothing, a short, dark, beady-eyed man, bloodied fireplace bricks, and a waif-like girl. Sensing Arnie's presence, she turned and took hold of his arm for support.

"Quinn and Talia brought back some of Quinn's little sister's things for forensic analysis," she said. "I told Talia she should bring it here for us to hand over to Detective Rinquire."

"Why here?"

"I don't know how our letter writer found out about my investigating, but I don't want Talia and Quinn to be threatened next because they're helping. Who knows who might see Talia take Caitlin's stuff into the police station?"

"Okay. Good thought."

Arnie and Beth took turns lifting slats a bit and peering through the blinds, like little kids sneaking peeks out the windows in anticipation of spying the arrival of Santa's sleigh. Talia didn't waste time. She parked by the curb, ran to the house, and placed a brown paper sack between the front doors.

Beth and Arnie waited a few minutes after the car disappeared before Arnie opened the door a crack, grabbed the sack, and then shut the door and clicked the lock. Arnie opened the bag while Beth stood close. Beth didn't know what she expected, a magical aura of some kind maybe, but inside she saw an ordinary dusty white hairbrush and a tired tube of cheap lipstick.

She let out a disappointed puff of air, and Arnie started to fold the top of the bag back down, when Psycho Cat jumped off the sofa and crept toward them in hunting-cat style with his ears drawn back and the pupils of his eyes large and staring. He stopped, sat on his haunches at Arnie's feet, and made a low moan deep in his throat.

"It'll be okay, Kitty," Beth said. "Nothing's going to hurt you."

Maybe there was an aura there she couldn't feel.

Detective Rinquire had interrogated Bernie Landoff earlier, according to Talia's tale. Therefore, when the detective came by the house for the evidence, Beth didn't say anything about Bernie, nor did she mention Talia Johnson. She handed over the bag of items containing Caitlin's DNA and told Detective Rinquire she hoped the lab people could match it with the DNA from the corpse.

Arnie had warned her to be brief—to let the police do the investigating. Beth thought about that, just before she kept right on talking.

"Detective Rinquire," she said, "It's as sad as can be. I don't know why or how, but I think the body in that trunk has to be that of Quinlin Turley's little sister, Caitlin. I believe the DNA from the brush and lipstick will match the body. And—and—I know it doesn't make sense, I can't imagine what motive he would have to kill a seventeen-year-old girl, but I think Myron Martin must have had something to do with her death. I know Devon and Essie Wild lived in that duplex, but Double M was a regular visitor. His scar looks exactly like the design on the fireplace mantel in the duplex next door where Caitlin lived for a short time before she disappeared. And...."

Detective Rinquire declined to comment on her speculations. He was closemouthed about his investigation. He only asked for a key to Side B of the duplex so he could send in the CSI to investigate the fireplace with the metal decoration that matched the scar on Double M's arm. Beth decided that part of her sleuthing appeared valuable to him, anyway.

It'd been less than a day, but she couldn't help asking, "How long do you think we'll need to stay away from our house and the duplex?"

"We'll let you know, Mrs. Stockwell," Rinquire said. "Please be patient."

Beth didn't think patience was part of *her* DNA. She started to ask another question, one about Essie Wild. But before she could get it out, the detective raised a hand, in farewell or perhaps to ward off her query, and left with the paper bag and her spare duplex key. After Beth closed the door, she remembered she hadn't asked if he had determined who left the threatening letter, but when she opened the door, Detective Rinquire had already backed his car into the street.

Chapter 35

August, Seven Years Earlier—Kansas City, Missouri

Part of the reason Caitlin had decided to go to California was that she couldn't find a job in Kansas City and hoped her Aunt Sharon could give her a home until she could land a job, save some money, and maybe start taking college classes. Mostly, though, she felt she needed to leave so Quinn could quit thinking he needed to take care of her and be tempted to help Bernie with his drug deals. But now Bernie, by stealing from Quinn, had set Quinn up to need that drug money with or without her presence. Caitlin was furious at Bernie, at Essie, at Double M, at the drug world, at her own frustrating situation, at her father, and with life in general.

Shortly after finishing his lunch, Quinn got ready and left for his band's afternoon rehearsal in preparation for the evening's performance. Caitlin hugged him since she wasn't sure she'd see him again soon, if she decided to leave for California early tomorrow morning before he awoke.

"I know your performance will be great," she said, "but please be careful when you talk to Bernie. The drugs make people crazy. You know that."

Quinn screwed up his face. "Don't worry about me. I won't be stupid about it. My plan is to confront that jerk when the band members are around. You just take care of yourself."

She was prepared to leave. Her bag and her few possessions were sitting by the door in her bedroom. The old car was full of gasoline. Quinn and she had packed his belongings into boxes gathered from the liquor store in preparation for help from a band buddy with a pick-up truck. Caitlin decided she might just be in the way when the guys started carrying things to the truck and into the small apartment tomorrow afternoon. That is, they would carry the stuff into the new apartment if Quinn could give the landlord six hundred dollars for advance rent and deposit.

After her brother left, Caitlin sat, as if in a trance, on the dilapidated sofa in the living room. The TV was unplugged and sitting with the boxes, lamps, and crates against the wall near the front door. During a workday, the neighborhood became quiet. Only the faint whoosh of a car going past and the airy sound through the partly open windows of a warm wind blowing flirtatiously through the leafy oaks broke the silence. Caitlin sat floundering with the indecision that left her powerless. She had to resolve what action to take. How could she leave Quinn in this situation? How could she stay and make him keep struggling?

Less than a thousand dollars remained in the small flowered cosmetics bag where Caitlin had stashed the money withdrawn from her account not even two months ago. Now she realized she'd been too liberal with her resources. She'd furnished the basement, bought groceries, helped with the utility bills, gave Quinn money to buy clothes for job interviews, and generally acted as if there was no end to the funds, until recently.

After some hesitation, Caitlin came to a decision about giving Quinn part of the money. Four hundred dollars—um, three hundred sixty-five, to be exact—would have to get her to California. She would set aside six hundred dollars in a note for Quinn and take off before he could argue about taking it. The band members would be paid tonight or tomorrow, and Quinn would have enough money to get by until the next performance. If Bernie coughed up the money he stole, then so much the better.

Thoughts about her departure swam through Caitlin's head. She considered taking the jar of peanut butter, what remained of a box of crackers, the lone apple in the crisper, and maybe part of the cheese and bread to get her by a couple of days without having to buy food on the road. She decided to take the pillow and one of the blankets from the bed upstairs so she could lock herself into the car at a rest stop to sleep, in order not to have to pay for a room. She didn't carefully calculate the amount of money her old gas-guzzling car's tank was going to require to keep it filled for all those miles through the mountainous terrain. With the optimism of youth, she imagined three hundred sixty-five dollars to be enough to get her there and provide a little food money.

With these decisions made, Caitlin directed her energy into preparation. She wrote a note explaining her early departure and apologizing for taking the food, enclosed the bills, and slipped it all under Quinn's pillow. He could find the money when he woke up tomorrow, and it would be too late to force her to take it back. The foodstuff she packed into a grocery sack and placed the sack beside her other belongings. Finally, she sat down again with the atlas, regretting she had neglected to ask to use Quinn's phone before he left. With all the consternation about the theft, she'd forgotten, but she consoled herself with the probability of being allowed to use the phone at a gas station or a convenience store along the way to call her aunt.

As she traced the possible routes again, Caitlin heard a car pulling into the driveway. Through the kitchen window she watched Double M park in front of Devon's and Essie's garage, get out of his car, and begin walking toward the door with a brown-paper-wrapped bundle in one hand. All of Caitlin's frustration returned in a flash of fury that didn't allow room for caution. She rushed out onto the back stoop.

"Mr. Martin," she called out in a high pleading voice. Even in anger, Caitlin displayed her ingrained manners. "I have to ask you to please leave my brother alone. He doesn't want to work for you. He doesn't need to be involved in your drug business. Please, please, you and Essie and Bernie just have to leave him be."

Double M kept advancing, but he changed his course slightly toward her back door rather than Essie's. His eyes snapped as dark and menacing as those of a wolf advancing on its prey. Meanwhile, Essie heard Caitlin's loud entreaty through her back screen door and stepped outside. She displayed enough alarm and anger to make Caitlin back away from her in fear.

Essie hissed at her through clenched teeth. "Back off of Double M, girl, if you know what's good for you. And don't go screaming about our business so the whole neighborhood can hear."

"Go back inside, Essie," Double M said in a calm voice, not taking his flashing eyes off of Caitlin, "and take this package with you. I'll take care of this."

He handed off his package, grabbed Caitlin's arm with one strong hand, and opened her screen door. He pushed the girl into the kitchen so hard she fell against the stove, wrenching her back on the oven handle. Nevertheless, she scrambled away, doubled with pain, and ran toward the front door while Double M slammed and locked the back door. The front door was locked, and her assailant easily caught up to Caitlin as she was trying to unlock and open it with shaky hands. He grabbed both of her arms and, in a business-like way, pulled her back into the room, in front of the fireplace.

"You know, I gave you a chance to help your brother and yourself. You threw it away. Now you yell about my business outside this building and tell me who to leave alone? That doesn't make sense to me, you little bitch, and I'm going to show you what that kind of behavior gets you." Double M savagely pulled Caitlin's summer capris down and her T-shirt up and punched her hard in the bare abdomen. "You think about telling the police or your precious brother about what you're getting, and that brother of yours won't live long enough to see you recover."

While Caitlin bent over, holding her stomach and catching her breath, Double M unbuckled his belt and started to open his pants. Although strong, the man was small and not used to doing his own bullying. Caitlin, almost as tall as him and furious enough to fight off a mad dog, recovered her breath before he finished. She reared forward and butted him in the chest with her head. The momentum took him off guard, and, as he tried to recover his footing, he fell sideways against the fireplace. With the force of his weight and the speed of the fall, he hit against a piece of sharp metal décor hard enough to cut deep into his arm.

Caitlin stood for several seconds, still bent over holding her stomach, and watched him push himself away and finger the blood issuing from his arm. Amazed at her own strength, she stood there frozen. When she came to her senses and made a move toward the door again, it was too late. Double M forgot about rape and came at her in a rage. He grabbed her and threw her against the fireplace. She hit her head and dropped. It wasn't enough for the hardened criminal, used to using and destroying people at his leisure. He took Caitlin's limp head and hit it again and again against the brick hearth until his energy abated.

The rest was calm and mechanical. A job needed to be done, and Myron Martin knew how to do it. He made sure the front door was locked and all the blinds were drawn, went through the back door to Essie's duplex where the shaky woman bandaged his wound and agreed, without question, to help him clean up the blood and get rid of the body.

Double M knew about the trunk in Essie's attic where she stored her narcotics. They rolled the body in a blanket and shoved it through the door in the closet ceiling. Double M swore a blue streak when he tore his pants and cut his leg on a nail at one side of the opening. While Essie used soap and water to clean up the blood around the fireplace, Double M drove to the local lawn and garden store and bought heavy white plastic and some quick lime, the kind he knew would speed the decomposition of the body. Before he doused the body with the lime, while Essie was still cleaning, he knocked out most of the teeth and stored them in a plastic sandwich bag to be disposed of later.

The explanation for the girl's disappearance was easy. Essie knew about Caitlin's plans to leave for California. The two conspirators searched through Caitlin's and Quinn's rooms, found the note she had written—the perfect set-up. They put everything she'd packed into her car, found her purse and keys, and drove the car to one of Double M's warehouses where it was thoroughly dismantled and trashed. By the time Devon came home from work, earlier than expected, Myron and Essie were rolling in the sheets of Devon's marriage bed.

Chapter 36

Beginning of March—Kansas City, Missouri

The club seemed to be packed with as many people as the gymnasium-sized room could hold. Talia sat at a table near the front, as close to the stage as she could get, with a few friends from work. She felt a smudge of guilt since Beth was still stuck at her sister's house, but she needed to hear Quinn play after what they'd discovered together. She arrived early to snag the good table, but now she paid only enough attention to her tablemates' chatter to be polite. Talia had eyes only for the band's lead singer and guitarist.

~~~

Quinn spotted Talia soon after the band tuned its instruments. He smiled broadly in her direction, causing her insides to flutter. He wanted to invite her to every performance, but he knew she started work at an ungodly early time in the mornings, and he didn't want to impose his late hours on her. Now, here she was, without being asked, and his good mood radiated all the way to the back of the room as he introduced the music, joked with the crowd, and played every note of the first set for Talia.

He didn't notice the platinum blond woman sitting between two muscle men at the bar near the back of the room. Not until the first break did the woman make her way to the table where Quinn and his bandmates greeted the crowd and sold their CDs. Quinn was about to excuse himself, in order to visit Talia's table, when he was pulled aside by the busty straw-haired woman. Her lined face was almost clownish, covered with makeup, and her bad teeth showed when she gave him a cloying smile. His first unsavory thought was that some junkie was flirting with him.

"You remember me, don't you, sweetie?" the woman asked, the practiced oiliness of her voice suggesting sexual favors, even in such an unlikely situation.

Quinn looked at her more closely, and then his courteous fan demeanor faded into a frown of disbelief and distaste. "Essie Wild?"

"Same woman, different name, different life," she said, her smile also fading. "Estelle Star, please. Listen, I need to talk to you in private. Can we do that?"

Essie's two muscle men stood a couple of paces behind her, but Quinn detected their steely eyes on him and told her he must stay in view of the crowd for the band's sake. Undeterred, Essie crooked a finger at the gangsters, who cornered him against the wall. Essie closed in so her face almost touched his. Her nicotine breath almost made Quinn turn his face away, but he managed to look her in the eye.

Her voice was low, almost like a sneer. "Okay honey, so I hear you've been talking to the cops about something that happened in the old duplex when we were such close neighbors. Let me just warn you if you tell them anything about me and Double M and our, uh, business there, my friends here will have to knock a little sense into you."

She nodded toward the burly guys who closed in behind Essie as if in protection, or, more accurately, to punctuate her threats. "Or, possibly they'll knock all the sense *out* of you," she said with a leer, apparently pleased with her turn of phrase. "You understand, don't you? I can tell by your face. You do."

At that, Essie gave Quinn a kiss on the mouth and backed away with her saccharine smile again in place. "That seals it. You go play your pretty music now, and don't forget the deal." Quinn recoiled, and Estelle Star didn't wait for his answer. Instead, she swaggered away, followed by the arrogant bullies.

Quinn stood in place and watched the little group file around the tables, through the crowd near the bar, and out the back door. He was too stunned to decide what to do next.

~~~

Talia had witnessed the entire episode happen as Quinn walked toward her table. She stood, shook her head in the direction of her friends who wanted to know what was wrong, and saw Quinn's stricken expression turn into an angry one. There was no reason for Talia to recognize the tottering floosy who'd just kissed Quinn. Seven years ago, the times Talia noticed Essie Wild at all, she thought the woman vaguely glamorous. But after the events of the last couple of weeks, it wasn't hard to guess the identity of the hussy who caused Quinn to stand with his fists balled tightly against his sides while he strived to control his breathing. Talia walked up to him and gently touched his arm.

"That was Essie Wild and a couple of Double M's strongmen, wasn't it?" she whispered.

"Talia," Quinn groaned, "I don't want to involve you in this anymore. It's getting dangerous. I lost a sister to these vipers. I won't lose you."

"Did they threaten you, too? Beth and her family, and now you? You—I mean, all of you—are important to me. I'm already involved. What are you going to do? I want to help."

Quinn took Talia's hands in his, frowned, and told her, "I'm going to the police. As soon as the band finishes tonight, I'll call. That may put me in more jeopardy, and I don't want you to share it."

"Quinn," Talia said with eyes wide, "if this is what you're going to do, you have to call Detective Carl Rinquire, specifically. Beth believes Double M, or Myron Martin, may have some of the police on his payroll. Will you do that—call Detective Rinquire?"

The sound of band instruments pulled Quinn's attention back to the stage, but he nodded to Talia and whispered a thank you in her ear before he squeezed her hands and turned toward the band. During the second set, Quinn's performance was competent but not infectious like all through the first set, and a few in the crowd left before the end. When Quinn rushed off stage after the final song, Talia said her goodbyes to her friends and followed him.

~~~

Two days later, Detective Rinquire called Beth and Arnie to let them know two suspects were in custody and they and Clay and Janae could return to their homes. Beth shouted the good news to Arnie before she peppered the detective with questions.

"Who are the suspects?" she asked. "Have you discovered the identity of the victim for sure? Do you have enough evidence to convict the suspects? How did you finally..."

"Hold on," Carl Rinquire said. "There is still an ongoing internal investigation. I can't tell you many details. But since the arrests are a matter of record, I can tell you that. Myron Martin and your old tenant, Essie Wild, now known as Estelle Star, are being held. Since the charge is murder, we hope to keep them incarcerated without bail."

"But does that make my family safe? Do you know who threatened us?"

"Ms. Star confessed she put the letter in your door. Her ex-husband, Devon Wild, let her know about your questioning by way of a mutual friend. You asked about his ex and made him suspicious that she may have left some drugs in the attic. He wanted to warn his friend to stay clear of her in the event she might be in trouble with the law again, and the friend let her know. She now knows you and your family aren't witnesses against her. I don't believe she or Mr. Martin have any reason to hurt you."

"That's a relief. What about the victim?"

"You've already guessed the victim. DNA from the two items you provided belonging to Caitlin Turley matched DNA from the body. That piece of evidence plus the DNA from the blood we found embedded in the fireplace bricks also helped us get a confession from Estelle Star, I'm happy to tell you."

"Oh!" Beth put her hand over her heart. "Then she must have pointed the finger at Double M. Did they murder the poor little girl together? Will Essie be a witness against Double M? How did you find out she was the one who helped him?" She had a sudden thought. "I bet her fingerprints were on the threatening letter she sent to me, weren't they?"

"I'm afraid I've told you all I can, Mrs. Stockwell," Detective Rinquire said with a tiny glint of humor beneath his noncommittal monotone. "Please go home, feel free to go back to your property management, and we'll get hold of you if we need more information. I'm sorry this ugly business disrupted your life."

Beth didn't have to wait to find out why Detective Rinquire picked up Essie. After telling all her family the good news, she called Talia. Talia was working at her office but took the time to talk to Beth and went into great detail about Quinn's experience two nights earlier during the band's performance. She described their visit with Detective Rinquire, and the detective's promise to arrest Essie and charge her with everything he could think of, including murder, to get her to talk.

"Quinn stayed at my condo the last two nights for safety. We found out this morning both Essie and Myron Martin had been arrested," Talia said. "It sounds as if Essie will testify against Double M in order to get a lesser charge—so she's the threat to him. I'm still scared for Quinn, because he turned Essie in, and the thugs and some bad cops are still out there. But Detective Rinquire believes it was Essie's idea alone to threaten you and Quinn, and since she turned state's evidence, she'll be the one to need protection, not Quinn. I would have told you sooner, but the detective told us to keep it quiet until they could make the arrests."

"I'm so sorry for Quinn to have to find out his sister is dead and that she died in such a despicable way."

"I am too." Talia sighed. "But I think he had already decided that skeleton was his sister. My job now, I think, is to help him realize he needs to blame the monster who killed her instead of faulting himself for not being there to stop it."

Epilogue
Frog Springs, Arkansas and Kansas City, Missouri

Solving the murder mystery was hardly the end, by any means. Every violent crime has consequences for the victims, the perpetrators, the families of the victims, and even for bystanders like Beth's family. Unfathomable violent death of an innocent person sometimes pulls people apart, and it sometimes draws people together. Some fall into despondency and depression after the brutal death of a loved one. Others work extra hard to be there for the surviving family and friends, make a special effort to improve themselves and make a difference in honor of the deceased, or even start campaigns or organizations to prevent further victims.

Clay, Janae, Arnie, and Beth all took the trip to Frog Springs for the burial and memorial service for Caitlin Turley. Talia had already spent several days in Arkansas with Quinn working on preparations to make the event a special celebration of the girl's life. Beth was happy to see Talia giving up her "work comes first" attitude. Watching Quinn mourn his sister was sad. But seeing the large number of family friends and relatives who showed up for the Saturday service and greeted Quinn so warmly made Beth glad she came. Quinn's father looked like the hard-living derelict she'd heard him to be, but he was cleaned up and, perhaps only temporarily, seemed to be sober for the occasion. In fact, he looked more shaken and saddened than she would have expected, from the story Talia told her about him.

~~~

Back at home, the events and news of the spring and summer tended toward the good as if circumstances tried to make up for the shock, pain, and fear of the previous weeks. First, Beth heard Quinn's father had forked over the entire amount of the trust put away for Quinn and Caitlin by their mother, meant to have gone to them when they turned twenty-one. Quinn announced he would use the money to attend conservatory classes, which is what his sister would have wanted. Beth believed Caitlin would've wished Quinn to fall for her caring friend Talia, too. In a way, Caitlin took care of her big brother, as she'd intended.

Janae sold a large piece of sculpture to the Kansas Farm Bureau, which Beth reasoned was indirectly related to the discovery of the skeleton in the attic. That event had caused her to move to the art district and get an adequate studio.

Quinn and Talia were invited to the opening reception, along with Beth and Arnie and Janae's parents, who came all the way from Minnesota. They all gazed in awe at the seven-foot-tall stylized metal shock of wheat that embellished the lobby of the new Farm Bureau administration building. Beth's spirits that evening could not have been higher, bolstered as they were by the recent rental of both sides of the duplex.

On the grittier side of the fall-out, it took months, but the internal investigation in the police department turned up a small group of law enforcement professionals who had been acting on behalf of Double M. At the top of the heap was the director of the CSI, Mr. Martin's politically motivated friend who caused that agency to be stymied in its investigations of any case related to Myron Martin's activities, including the murder of Caitlin Turley. By the time the trial of Myron Martin drew near, accompanied by the highly anticipated testimony of Estelle Star, the star witness, there were a number of related cases on the agenda.

A newspaper reporter called Beth for an interview when the former city councilman's upcoming trial created top news for the media. She downplayed any part she performed in the investigation. Instead, she gave all the credit to Detective Carl Rinquire and Crime Scene Investigation Supervisor Mark Overos. They did the real work.

Beth did tell the reporter how Psycho Cat led everyone to the mummified body in the attic trunk and directed them to evidence in the bathroom sink and on the fireplace bricks. That creative journalist set up a photo shoot for the big orange cat and wrote an extraordinary feature story about how Sylvester (Psycho Cat) brought down the underground organization of the most unscrupulous and dangerous drug lord in Kansas City. Psycho Cat became a sensation for a few weeks. He actually had fan mail pouring in. Beth was about ready to ask for a cat hero protection program, until the serious news about the conviction of the criminals became the front page news and uppermost on the public agenda.

It sounded melodramatic, even to her, but Beth told Arnie how good life seemed after they had been exposed to brutality and to a chink in the fabric of society and then, thank goodness, witnessed her beloved city being cleansed of that unsavory element.

Mark Overos and Arnie now played golf together, Clay and Janae considered Quinn and Talia best friends, and Beth had the time to take more ceramics classes—in Kansas City. Maybe the *following* year Arnie and she would be able to spend the winter somewhere warm.

###

A Word From the Author

Thank you for adding *FURtive Investigation* to your library. Readers depend on readers to recommend good books, and authors depend on readers to generate positive word-of-mouth for their books. If you liked this cozy mystery, I hope you'll leave a review on Amazon, Goodreads, or your favorite retailer even if it's only a few words. It will make a big difference. I and other readers will be thankful.

ABOUT THE AUTHOR

Joyce Ann Brown (http://joyceannbrown.com/) owns rental properties in Kansas City with her husband, but none of their tenants have so far found a skeleton in their attics. Her two cats, Moose and Chloe, are cuddly, not psycho. Besides being a landlady, Joyce has worked as a story teller, a library media specialist, a Realtor, and a freelance writer. Her writing has appeared in local and national publications and in the book *Cozy Food*. Her short stories have won numerous awards.

Preview the first book in the
"Psycho Cat and the Landlady Mysteries" series:

CATASTROPHIC CONNECTIONS

In the Nighttime

To the individual working in near darkness, the place felt like a basement at midnight, illuminated only by a dim light bulb at the top of the stairway. No. Better. It felt like a mortuary in the middle of the night, the perfectionist mortician preparing a corpse for a starring role at its own funeral. An undertaker is an artist, after all, who must exult in the unveiling of his handiwork—or her creative artwork—as gawkers pass by the open casket.

The lone figure's grin appeared as grotesque as the thoughts in its wearer's head, illuminated as it was by the dim glow from the flickering computer screen. The only other light in the room came from distant street lamps through the two small office windows. During workday hours this large room, which housed the construction company's accounting and human resources departments, suffered from harsh fluorescent lighting and the constant noise of clicking keyboards, telephone conversations, and inner-office communication. Not now. Now—stillness, dark shadows, the circumspect use of a muted flashlight, necessary upon arrival for finding the correct workspace.

Overtime work, even late into the evening hours, was not unusual here when a big project came toward a close. All essential employees knew the door codes. But at two o'clock in the morning, no one else was likely to be around the building to observe this covert operation. To make sure, the lone worker had parked on a residential street three blocks away among autos belonging to apartment dwellers. The car wouldn't be associated with anyone headed for Renfro Construction Company. Being discovered would require an explanation, and the prepared story might appear a little thin.

This task wouldn't take long. The transaction had been set up earlier on a computer in a different room. All that remained to be done was to make sure the last of the payments to Master Flooring duplicated to a bogus Masters Flooring account located in a Virgin Islands bank. It had to be routed before the company's annual audit began the next day.

A few final gloved keystrokes, a couple final minutes of frequenting this gloomy place during the wee hours, and all those pesky money problems would be solved. The collaborator would be set. The lady would be impressed. A few million dollars would bring not only security, but also respect.

Oh, there might be some old so-called friends sacrificed along the way. All for the greater good, of course. Besides, people who left, who lacked loyalty, who were more concerned about their own interests—those people deserved whatever happened to them. It was a dirty shame most of them would never know the details of the careful planning or of the brilliant execution of this scheme. Foolproof. The money had disappeared; the getaway was assured. By the time connections were uncovered, if ever, there would be too many miles to work across and too many scapegoats to investigate.

One last check, at a different desktop. One couldn't be too careful. Yes! The transaction would be recorded at the Kansas City bank early next morning and received in the Virgin Islands a little later in the day. Some people claimed accounting work and bookkeeping were slow and boring occupations. It might be true when dealing with someone else's money, when working for one company and doing the same work over and over. But this clandestine bookkeeping activity sent a thrill straight through the body. Now—now, all the uncertainties, all the disappointments, and all the humdrum days were about to end.

Banging and bumping sounds reverberated through the empty building. The edgy computer user logged out and shut down while peering back and forth into the darkness and listening for noises—sounds which could be heard beyond the individual's own thumping heartbeat. The wind. Damn. It had blown open the dumpster out back. That was all it was.

The computer screen faded like a shimmering dream interrupted by a harsh alarm clock. Its final pinpricks of gray light illuminated a deep frown, a focused squint, and a clenched jaw.

Chapter 1—Caterwauling Cat

"Cats are cats the world over! These intelligent, peace-loving, four-footed friends—who are without prejudice, without hate, without greed—may someday teach us something.
- James Mackintosh Qwilleran"
- Lilian Jackson Braun, *The Cat Who Saw Stars*

The low resonance of three low funereal organ notes reverberated throughout Beth's body. She shuddered, stopped with a gasp, and clutched her knees in the middle of the Trolley Track Trail where she power-walked several days a week. Beth shook her head of floppy curls to fend off her feeling of foreboding and straightened up when she heard, or rather felt, the unnerving tones again.

Then she rolled her eyes. Arnie had been switching her mobile phone ring tones again. This one was spooky. As she caught her breath and dug her cell phone out of the pocket of her windbreaker, she made a mental note to devise an evil plan to get him back. She held the phone to her ear.

"H—puff—hello?"

"Is this Mrs. Stockwell?" the caller said in a high-pitched and shaky voice.

"Yes, this is Beth Stockwell."

"This is Eva Standish. I live in the condo next door to your tenant Adrianna Knells. I got your number from the Condo Association."

"How can I help you, Eva?" Beth said. She bent over again to massage her left calf.

"You know about Adrianna's cat?" Eva asked.

"Sure."

"Well, it has been yowling for the last two days, maybe longer. Do you know where Adrianna is? I tried calling her but got no answer and no return call. Can you do something? The Condo folks told me to ask you to handle it first before they step in and require her to get rid of the cat. I'm not normally a complainer, but I can hardly hear my television set, let alone sleep, with that noise."

Beth looked skyward as if asking for help from beyond, although none was forthcoming, and resumed her walk on the trail at a pace more leisurely than before. The eerie phone tone was appropriate. A call from Eva definitely qualified as a creepy thing.

"Well, I'm sorry about the disturbance," Beth said. "I'll be right over to find out what's ailing the kitty. He's usually so quiet and good." She mentally crossed the fingers of both hands—since that last part could have been a little white lie. "Thank you for calling me about this. I wouldn't want Adrianna to lose the pet that she loves so much."

"I hope you make it soon. My nerves can't take this much longer."

"It'll only take me a few minutes to get there, dear. Thanks again for calling."

Beth remembered other run-ins she had with Eva Standish, the tiny seventy-five-year-old with the white fly-away hair who lived next door to the rental units Beth and her husband, Arnie, owned on the sixth floor of the funky West-Gate Condos, sided with salmon-colored panels, in the Brookside subdivision of Kansas City. The

Puce Goose, as locals called it, restricted its residents to people twenty-one and older but contained mostly senior citizens. Eva, a long-time resident of the condo building, wore a scowling expression that made her look like a grumpy leprechaun guarding a pot of gold every time Beth saw her.

Was Eva Standish a complainer? Sheesh. When Beth was renovating the condo unit Adrianna now rented, hadn't Eva Standish complained about the smell of paint and the noise of the power tools? When a nice computer guy lived there, didn't Eva grumble about the young man coming in late at night? Adrianna said Eva left her notes comprised of crazy predictions about how soon she would marry her boyfriend, when she might have a terrible bicycle accident, or even how a pretty girl like her might be kidnapped by some evil man she wouldn't suspect—notes Adrianna laughed about and threw away. Now Eva complained about the pet. Well, the best bet was to find out at once what was going on with the unpredictable Psycho Cat.

Erratic as a funnel cloud better described the feline. Adrianna Knells, Beth's tenant and also her step-niece, could set the whole family rolling on the floor at family gatherings with her stories about Sylvester, dubbed Psycho Cat early on. She told how he could be sweet and lovable to visitors one minute and then attack with his claws bared the next, sleep without moving for hours and then charge around the apartment knocking over lamps and vases for half an hour, jump into a bathtub full of water while his unsuspecting owner was in it, and undertake any variety of other crazy antics. Maybe the yowling was merely a result of one of the cat's moods.

Only a few blocks north of Brookside on her midtown walking trail, Beth turned and caught the toe of her running shoe on a crack. She almost fell, but only almost. She headed toward the condo building. On the way, she called Adrianna's cell phone but got no answer. After sending a text message that she was going to check on the cat, she followed the trail past the cafés and shops of Brookside. In ten minutes, Beth stood under the awning at the entrance to the ten-story building, becoming dizzy with the sweet aroma of the blooming red azaleas and violet lilacs which bordered each side. Before she could find her front door key, Chuck, the hunky security guard, opened the door for her, greeted her with familiarity, and recorded her visit.

"Hey, Chuck," said Beth. "I've got to take care of something up in my rental, but when I come back down I want to find out how your family is doing."

"No problem."

Beth wanted to linger long enough to have a little chat with Chuck as usual. This time, however, she felt obligated to get up there and find out about the cat. Without thinking, she took the stairs to the sixth floor—another way she jammed exercise into her daily routines. However, she sprinted up the stairs at such a rapid pace she stumbled and fell rounding the corner on the third landing.

"Ow! What a klutz." she said out loud. Why did she do this to herself—rush up here so fast she could have killed herself because of the convoluted whim of Adrianna's neighbor? She knew why. She always went out of her way to avoid conflict, to appease people. Beth continued up the steps at a slower pace, favoring her skinned knee.

The yowling became audible as soon as she stepped into the sixth floor hallway. She unlocked the condo door with her landlady key, peeked inside, and came to a dead stop. Her step-niece's usually clean neat apartment now smelled like a dirty litter box. Papers, pictures, and pillows littered the floor. Psycho Cat went bonkers when she entered, exploded toward her, hissed when she reached down to pet him, and then tried to climb her leg. She put her arms around the seventeen pound, yellow, tiger-striped kitty and hefted him to her shoulder in an attempt to pacify him. Beth's soothing had little effect, and he continued his plaintive meow.

When she put him down, Psycho Cat darted toward his food and water bowls in the kitchen. They were both quite empty. Beth filled the water bowl and then found the expensive cat food Adrianna preferred and poured a bunch of it into a hand-painted blue ceramic cat dish. Psycho Cat chowed down, lapped up some water, and finished by licking his chops and then his paws in prissy cat fashion. The litter box in the bathroom was foul, and it took a while to find clean-up supplies. After she scooped the box, added clean litter, and sprayed the condo with some air freshener, the atmosphere improved, as did Psycho Cat's manner. In fact, he rubbed around her legs and purred so loud she thought Eva Standish might start complaining again.

Finally, after giving the kitty what she hoped was a reassuring pat, Beth determined to give the condo a thorough inspection. As the landlady of several properties, she normally respected her tenants' privacy. If she, or she and her self-taught handy-man hubby, Arnie, had to go into one of the rental units to do some repair work or put a new air filter in the furnace, she would glance around and admire or disdain the decorating and housekeeping. The tidiness, especially, caught her eye because she knew how hard it was to clean a filthy apartment in order to rent it again after a tenant moved out.

In the case of this condo, however, Beth had been here several times for friendly visits, because Adrianna was her sister Meg's step-daughter. Since childhood, Adrianna had known her as Aunt Beth and her children as cousins. Adrianna kept her one-bedroom apartment clean and as well decorated as a 27-year-old single could afford.

Now why would she suddenly leave her cat alone so long that he would wreck the place? When she went on a vacation or a business trip, she always put her step-mom in charge of the kitty. Adrianna's step-mother, Beth's sister Meg Knells, had raised Adrianna and was more of a real mom than Adrianna's birth mother, who hadn't raised her daughter since Adrianna was about three years old.

It was 10:30 in the morning. Meg would be at school where she taught social studies to middle school students. Since Beth had received no reply to her text message to Adrianna, she called Meg's cell phone, knowing Meg checked her messages around noon when she had time. "Meg, call me on my cell phone, please. Nothing to worry about, but I need to ask you about Adrianna's cat." That wasn't much information, but she guessed it would be enough to get a return call.

Meanwhile, what would Beth do about Psycho Cat? She picked him up. He nuzzled her ear and started purring again. There was no doubt the kitty had been left alone for several days. Beth realized she would feel bad setting the appreciative kitty down, and she couldn't walk out and leave him there alone. Maybe she should carry him the short distance to her house. That might also avert another call from the irritated condo neighbor, Eva Standish. Beth could hand the cat over to her sister or maybe to Adrianna later this afternoon.

Eva Standish opened her door a crack while Beth was shuffling her load of cat and cat paraphernalia in order to lock up. Beth turned her head toward the opening and glimpsed Eva raise a shaggy eyebrow before she yanked the door closed with her shrunken apple hand.

Find CATastrophic Connections on Amazon.com/.